The Dorset Boy – Book 7: The

Credits

Thanks to Allison from Allison Leslie Editing & Coaching who edited this book, and to Dawn Spears the brilliant artist who created the cover artwork. My wife who is so supportive and believes in me. Last my dogs Blaez and Zeeva and cats Vaskr and Rosa who watch me act out the fight scenes and must wonder what the hell has gotten into their boss.

Illustration of the Basque Roads courtesy of
PHGCOM - Own work by uploader, background file File:Oleron SPOT 1251.jpg

The Dorset Boy – Book 7: The Trojan Horse

THANK YOU FOR READING!

I hope you enjoy reading this book as much as I enjoyed writing it. Reviews are so helpful to authors. I really appreciate all reviews, both positive and negative. If you want to leave one, you can do so on Amazon, through the website or Twitter.

About the Author

Christopher C Tubbs is a descendent of a long line of Dorset clay miners and has chased his family tree back to the 16th century in the Isle of Purbeck. He left school at sixteen to train as an Avionics Craftsman, has been a public speaker at conferences for most of his career in the Aerospace and Automotive industries and was one of the founders of a successful games company back in the 1990's. Now in his sixties, he finally got around to writing the story he had been dreaming about for years. Thanks to Inspiration from the great sea authors like Alexander Kent, Dewey Lambdin, Patrick O'Brian and Dudley Pope he was finally able to put digit to keyboard. He lives in the Netherlands with his wife, two Dutch Shepherds and two Norwegian Forest cats.

You can visit him on his website
www.thedorsetboy.com

The Dorset Boy, Facebook page.

Or tweet him @ChristopherCTu3

The Dorset Boy Series Timeline

1792 – 1795   Book 1: A Talent for Trouble
Marty joins the Navy as an Assistant Steward and ends up a midshipman.

1795 – 1798   Book 2: The Special Operations Flotilla
Marty is a founder member of the Special Operations Flotilla, learns to be a spy and passes as lieutenant.

1799 – 1802   Book 3: Agent Provocateur
Marty teams up with Linette to infiltrate Paris, marries Caroline, becomes a father and fights pirates in Madagascar.

1802 – 1804   Book 4: In Dangerous Company
Marty and Caroline are in India helping out Arthur Wellesley, combating French efforts to disrupt the East India Company and French sponsored pirates on Reunion. James Stockley born

1804 – 1805   Book 5: The Tempest
Piracy in the Caribbean, French interference, Spanish gold and the death of Nelson. Marty makes Captain.

1806 – 1807   Book 6: Vendetta
A favour carried out for a prince, a new ship, the S.O.F. move to Gibraltar, the battle of Maida, counter espionage in Malta and a Vendetta declared and closed.

1807 – 1809   Book 7: The Trojan Horse
Rescue of the Portuguese royal family, Battle of the Basque Roads with Thomas Cochrane, and back to the Indian Ocean and another conflict with the French Intelligence Service.

The Dorset Boy – Book 7: The Trojan Horse

Contents

The Dorset Boy – Book 7: The Trojan Horse

Chapter 1: Family time

Marty lay in bed, tracing the scar that ran across Caroline's ribs with his fingertip, and marvelling that she already started to recover her figure after the birth of the twins.

He shuddered at the memory of Shelby stitching up the wound, which was the result of a close encounter with a splinter in a Caribbean sea battle. An inch further and it would have killed her.

It was dawn on a wet November morning in Gibraltar and Marty was relishing the quiet. None of the children were awake yet, and Blaez slept peacefully in his place at the foot of their bed. The only sound, besides Blaez's gentle snoring, was the rain on the window.

The previous month, the French signed the Fontainebleau Accord, which committed them both to kicking the legitimate rulers of Portugal out and dividing up the country between them. Marty's friend, Rear Admiral Sir Sidney Smith, was given command of a task force by the Admiralty. He could either blockade the Portuguese port of Lisbon or destroy their fleet to prevent it falling into enemy hands. The Flotilla was being attached to the expedition in the hope that Marty could act as a moderating influence on the mercurial Smith.

But today was for his family. Marty promised to take the children to his ship for the morning. Beth and James were both excited and he knew that his followers, the Shadows, would spoil them rotten.

He leaned forward and kissed Caroline on the stomach. She opened her eyes and reached for him, a smile on her face that promised much. Just then, the door burst open and in rushed Beth and James like a tornado, which only settled as they climbed in bed. *Timing is impeccable,* he smiled ruefully and grabbed his daughter, tickling her and making her giggle.

The Formidiable was tied up at the dock and had a faint smell of sawdust, paint, and tar hanging over her as they just finished repairing the damage caused by their encounter with the Viala, a French seventy-four. Sir Sidney arrived just in time to win the battle after the Flotilla mercilessly harassed her to stop her running away.

Marty carried Beth and Caroline, James, while Mary had the twins in a pram. Wilson, a six-foot eight giant of a man and one of the Shadows, strode down the gang plank and walked over to Mary. The big man looked shy and quietly offered to help her get the pram onboard.

Caroline exchanged a knowing look with Marty. They knew Mary was seeing someone on her evenings off, but now they thought they knew who! Mary giggled at something he said, then he picked up the pram and carried it up the gangway.

"Uncle John!" Beth cried as she spotted Marty's quartermaster standing on the deck and struggled in his arms to get down. Marty laughed and put her down so she could run over to the laughing sailor brandishing her favourite toy, a wooden sword.

They spent a pleasant morning sitting under an awning out of the steady rain. Caroline took over caring for the twins so Mary could spend some time with

Wilson.   At the end of the morning, Wilson approached and asked permission to have a word with Marty.

"Well, what can I do for you?" Marty asked with a glint in his eye.

"Well, Captain, it's like this: I been walking out with Mary for a while now and I find I have a real care for her." He blushed and wrung his hands before he continued, "We have talked, and we would like to get married if that's alright with you, of course."

"You don't need my permission, Wilson, nor does Mary but I will give you my blessing. I think you will make a wonderful couple." He shook hands with the big man and clapped him on the back; he couldn't really reach his shoulder. The two joined the ladies, who were already hugging in celebration.

After the rain stopped, they started to walk the half mile to the house and were about halfway back when a man stepped out from behind a tree and confronted them. Marty saw the blunderbuss he was carrying swing in his direction, but there was nothing he could do as he was carrying James and couldn't get to his weapons!

Caroline was walking hand in hand with Beth and saw the man step forward. He was focused on Marty and was swinging the massive, brass, bell-mouthed gun towards him. Marty turned so his back was to the man, protecting James from harm.

The world slowed down.

Her vision zoomed in on the man's face as it contorted and he shouted something in French.

She let go of Beth, and her hand flew to the muff she wore suspended around her neck.

She knew it would take too long to pull the concealed gun out and cock it, so she just pushed it through the cloth tube and drew back the hammer with her left hand as it cleared the material.

The pistol, one of a pair that were a gift from Marty, was a fifty calibre, rifled, four-inch barrelled Manton that was the preferred weapon for ladies as it was easily concealed. It packed a punch and she was an expert shot even hampered by the muff.

The pistol fired, and the bullet smashed into the man's chest, dead centre through his sternum. The force of the impact knocked him backwards as he pulled the trigger of his weapon, which was held at waist level, jerking the barrel upwards.

The enormous spread of deer shot flew high, missing Marty's dipping back by scant inches. However, because he ducked, he exposed Mary, who was walking behind him pushing the pram with the twins in it. A single piece of shot on the edge of the spread sliced through her scalp above her right eye. She dropped to her knees blood pouring from the wound.

Caroline stepped over to Marty and reached under his coat. She pulled out his fighting knife and turned to the prone man who lay groaning on the floor. She stepped over to him, knelt, and placed the knife on his throat.

"Who are you?" she asked.

The man looked up into the coldest grey eyes he had ever seen. There was no mercy, just cold beauty.

"A patriot," he replied as blood dribbled out the side of his mouth.

"Why?" she asked, her head cocked slightly to one side.

"He killed my love," he gasped as the life started to fade from his eyes.

"Claudette?"

"Yes," he sighed with his last breath.

She turned back and saw Marty kneeling over Mary, who sat on the floor going into shock. He was holding what looked like a spare nappy to her head, which was soaked in blood. Beth was crying, and James stood, looking at Mary, not understanding what happened.

The dead man was forgotten as Caroline went to care for her family.

"That was a bloody good shot, all things considered," Marty told her as they sat together in the drawing room that evening. Shelby, the physician from the Formidiable, examined Mary and pronounced that it was just a flesh wound. A deer shot parted the skin on her scalp, which bled profusely, but hadn't done any more damage than that.

"I have been practicing," Caroline replied offhandedly. Her eyes narrowed in thought. "Did you leave any more of Claudette's lovers behind you?"

"This one slipped through the net; we didn't identify him during the investigation," Marty replied thoughtfully. "I can't honestly say if there are any more out there. She was pretty prolific."

"If they can't get to you, they may try and get to you through us," Caroline stated, causing him to frown in thought.

"Maybe you should take the children back to England," he suggested.

"That's not happening," she replied determinedly. "Can you spare some marines for a security team? Just until we are sure?"

"Of course, I will talk to Paul," he assured her, knowing it was useless to argue.

Marty was summoned to a meeting with Collingwood and Smith and, after arranging a security detail of marines with Paul for his family, reported aboard the Flagship with all due ceremony. He was ushered into the main cabin, and after formally greeting Sir Sydney and Admiral Collingwood, settled into a comfortable chair for the conference.

"First of all, Captain Stockley, we would like to congratulate you on making post," Collingwood opened, and Marty realised it was three years ago he was made; the time flew!

Both admirals congratulated him, and the steward served port for them to toast his elevation to the vaunted rank. He would have to get his tailor to add an extra epaulette to all his uniforms.

"As you are well aware, the French and Spanish are preparing to invade Portugal, oust the legitimate rulers, the Bragança family, and carve up the country between them. Sir Sidney has been tasked to lead an expedition to blockade Lisbon, and if all is lost, to destroy the Portuguese fleet," Collingwood stated by way of introduction. "Captain Stockley, your Flotilla is assigned to the expedition as scouts and pathfinders.

The French, under Junot, started entering Spain in mid-October before the treaty of Fontainbleau was signed, and as far as we know, number some twenty-five thousand troops and cavalry. They are already marching on Portugal backed up by another twenty-five thousand Spanish troops. We do not expect the Portuguese to put up any kind of resistance."

"The Portuguese Queen mother is insane," Sir Sidney contributed, "the Regent, Prince John, is a spineless ninny as is his government. They declared war on us at the end of October to try and appease Napoleon and a fat lot of good that did."

Collingwood coughed to hide a smile at this rather blunt assessment and said,

"The Prince is inexperienced and is more interested in trade than martial activities. He refused to close his ports to the British and to obey Napoleon's edict that no one in Europe trade with us. Napoleon is using that as an excuse to invade."

Marty smiled at the different views and contributed his own,

"Napoleon also gets a large standing army on to the peninsula without firing a shot. I will put fifty guineas on his taking over Spain next."

"Exactly!" agreed Collingwood. "There is an added complication that there is a Russian squadron in Lisbon. They are now allied with France under the Treaties of Tilsit and could cause a problem."

"So, what do you want us to do? We can't stop Napoleon with a hundred marines."

"We need to eliminate French interference with the Royal family and get them to at least mobilize their forces to defend against the invasion. Once Portugal falls, which it will, we want you and that fellow Ridgely to help the Portuguese loyalists organize a counter revolution," Collingwood replied. "I won't tell you how to do that as you are the experts in that type of game," he continued with a look of distaste.

You might not like the taste, but you will eat the fruit if it suits you, Marty thought, *don't want to dirty your hands with it though.*

"I understand, Sir. I will take care of it, quietly of course," he stated with a slight bow.

"We sail in two days; I trust you can be ready by then?" Sir Sidney enquired.

"We are always ready to sail with one day's notice," Marty answered, "I will have my Marines polish up their uniforms; we will need them to liberate the British merchants held in port."

"Excellent. Then we are ready to go. Now I would be delighted to entertain you both for lunch," Collingwood said in closing.

Chapter 2: From Russia with . . .

They sailed on the morning of the 19th of November with the intention of arriving at Lisbon sometime on the 21st or 22nd ahead of the fleet. They had over four-hundred and eighty sea miles to cover and the cumbersome fleet led by Sir Sidney would only average six knots beating against the wind. If the weather turned against them, it could take longer.

As it turned out, the conditions were fair for the season. They made good progress, and the Flotilla arrived off Lisbon on the morning of the 21st. They hove to in the mouth of the Tagus near to the decommissioned fort of São Sebastião de Caparica bypassing the fort of São Julião da Barra that was situated on the Northern entrance to the estuary.

Even though the Portuguese had declared war on Britain, not a shot was fired, nor challenge made, so Marty took the Formidiable and Hornfleur further up into the natural harbour and anchored. He examined the forts he could see on the North shore and came to the conclusion they were either abandoned or more likely just used as residences.

"Set a lookout to watch those Russian ships. I want to know if they prepare to sail," he instructed his first lieutenant, Wolfgang Ackermann, indicating the half dozen Russian warships anchored together near the town. "I think we can ignore those fortifications as the Portuguese don't seem to have bothered arming them."

He climbed to the topsail yard and scanned the whole of the natural harbour. He could see that there were shipyards on the North shore with extensive dry-docks and slips where there were a couple of hulls under construction that looked as if they could be frigate size.

Scanning along the shore, he could see there was an extended dock front where merchant ships were loaded and unloaded, consistent with Lisbon being a major trading centre. There were a number of merchant ships tied up, all flying the Portuguese flag.

He looked for the Portuguese fleet and spotted them moored in front of what looked like a military installation by the town of Almada on the southern shore.

Now, where were the impounded British merchantmen? He looked to the South and East and couldn't see any. Then he swung his glass to the Northeast and spotted a union flag flying from the mainmast of a ship moored where the Lisbon shore swung around to the North.

He returned to the deck and was marking the location of all the different elements on a chart when Midshipman Hart reported,

"Sir, the lookout has reported that there is a boat approaching from the direction of the Russian ships."

Marty stepped over to the rail and lifted his telescope to his eye. It was a new one the children gave him for his birthday that year. It had beautifully clear lenses and a ten times magnification.

"Looks like we have a delegation approaching," he informed the quarterdeck as he saw a pair of ornately uniformed officers in the stern of the cutter heading straight at them. "Prepare a side party to greet an Admiral."

Marty went down to his cabin where his steward, Adam Cooper, already had his dress uniform with his honours sash laid out on his cot. He quickly changed; thankful he had shaved that morning. Blaez woke up and looked on with interest. He had learned that when Marty changed clothes during the day, something interesting would happen.

"You behave yourself and don't bite the nice Russian gentlemen," Marty told him as he adjusted his dress sword.

He heard the hail from the side party as the boat approached and went up on deck, Blaez at his side. Thankfully, it was not raining, and the sun was forcing itself out between the clouds.

Two officers came up the side and doffed their hats to the quarterdeck. Marty recognized one as an admiral and the other, a captain.

"Good morning, gentlemen. May I present Captain Sir Martin Stockley," Ackermann greeted them and introduced Marty.

Both men bowed, and the captain introduced them,

"Good morning. May I introduce, Admiral Senyavin of the Russian Imperial Navy and myself Captain Boycov."

Marty shook their hands and invited them to join him in his cabin.

"Now gentlemen, to what do I owe the pleasure of your company?" Marty asked once they were all seated.

The Admiral accepted a cup of coffee from Cooper and eyed Blaez,

"That is an impressive dog, Sir Martin. I am not familiar with the breed. Tell me, where is he from?" The admiral enquired in almost perfect English.

"He is a Dutch Herding dog, an extremely loyal and protective breed," Marty replied, patting Blaez on the head.

The admiral nodded then looked Marty in the eye.

"How is my friend Admiral Collingwood?" he asked.

"He was well the last time I saw him. May I ask; where do you know him from?" Marty replied.

"We met in the Aegean during the joint action against the Turks. I saw him last in August."

Marty nodded and waited for the admiral to get to the point of his visit.

"I find myself in an awkward position," he stated. "My country has signed a peace treaty with France, which I do not agree with, and I believe you are the vanguard of British fleet to blockade the Tagus, which politically puts me in the position that I should fight you."

"But that is not what you want to do?" Marty surmised.

"Exactly. For one thing, I think such an action would just result in the destruction of my ships and achieve nothing. For another, I don't want to fight those I see as my natural ally."

"I assume you have a proposal?" Marty asked.

"Yes. I understand that as an enemy of the British by treaty, we will not be allowed to leave the Tagus. Therefore, I will declare my ships and men as neutral in the conflict between the British and the members of

Napoleon's coalition over Portugal. We will stay at our anchorage and not interfere or aid either side."

Interesting, Marty thought, *If you stay where you are, we won't be able to burn your ships without risking the magazines going up and destroying half of Lisbon.*

"I will inform Admiral Smith of your intent and send a message to Admiral Collingwood to inform him as well. I am sure Admiral Collingwood will be happy to hear from an old friend," Marty replied, knowing he couldn't do more.

"Now, may I offer you something stronger to drink so we may toast our ongoing friendship?"

The Russians left the ship after a good lunch specially prepared by Rolland. Marty could see why Collingwood and Senyavin were friends. The man was intelligent, entertaining, and charming.

Now he needed to get things done.

He called Phillip Trenchard, "Take a boat and visit the British Merchantmen to ascertain the conditions under which they were being held."

Then he called for his Captain of marines, "Paul please dispatch a number of scouts to find out where the French and Spanish are and when they will arrive. Delay them if possible and set up a signal chain to get the warning back with all possible haste, but don't get into an open fight," he ordered.

Marty settled at his desk to write letters and reports. Sam came in, opened his weapons chest and started to service the contents. Sam was the only person he trusted to do that besides himself and Tom, his former cox who had retired now. His presence, and efficiency in performing the task, settled him.

He braced himself and got his head down. He wrote in a fine copperplate script that would be the envy of many clerks and didn't need to be rewritten to make fine copies. He would have them copied for the record, of course, but the originals would be the ones that were sent. After his clerk returned them, he called for Midshipmen Williams and Hart, who arrived as he finished sealing them into waxed paper packets.

"Mr. Williams, I would be obliged if you would deliver these to Commander Thompson on the Eagle. Please give him my compliments and tell him the letter for Admiral Smith is to be delivered as soon as the Fleet arrives. He is to sail to Gibraltar to deliver the other to Admiral Collingwood." Williams took the packets and touched his forelock before exiting.

"Mr. Hart, I have a riskier enterprise for you."

Hart's face lit up in anticipation as any mission Marty classified as risky was bound to be fun.

"You are to sail over to Lisbon under a flag of truce and deliver this dispatch to Prince John himself. Do not allow anyone else to see it, especially the French. Am I clear?"

"Aye, aye, Sir!"

"Take Antton, Matai, and two marines as escorts. Conduct yourself as an ambassador and do not let palace officials divert you in your mission."

Marty handed him the letter, which was closed with both the Navy fouled anchor and his personal seal.

"Remember to use my full title, which is?"

"Captain Sir Martin Stockley, Baron Candor."

Marty frowned as he considered this then suggested,

"Make that, Captain Martin Stockley, Knight of the Bath and Baron of Candor. Sounds more impressive. He is a prince and will be sensitive of status."

Hart nodded, memorizing the title and getting himself into the persona of an emissary of a Lord. He stood a little taller, and his face assumed a slightly haughty expression.

Marty looked him up and down. He was in his best uniform, which was brand new and never been worn before.

"You look ready, so get to it younger," he dismissed him and settled down to catch up on the ship's paperwork.

Stanley Hart sat in the centre of the cutter as he was pulled to a point on the docks close to the building they observed flying the Portuguese royal flag. They flew a white flag on the mast.

Antton was cox and Matai was bow man; both were dressed in their best matching uniforms. Two enormous marines, resplendent in full uniform, made up the other element of his escort.

He had taken a leaf out of Marty's book and had two concealed knives hidden under his uniform to supplement his midshipman's dirk. He was now fifteen years old and had already killed men in close combat. He was trained in hand-to-hand fighting as well as fencing and knife fighting by Marty, la Pierre, and the Shadows. He was a better than average shot with pistol and musket and could stand with the best of them.

The boat bumped up to the steps on the dock. Matai stepped ashore to tie the bow line off to a mooring ring, then he held the boat so the Marines and Antton could step off followed by Stanley.

An official looking man with a squad of soldiers was waiting for him at the top. He said something in Portuguese, and Stanley just looked at him. The man stepped forward and Matai put his hand on his chest and said something in Spanish then repeated in English.

"Mr. Hart is an emissary from the Baron of Candor to His Highness Prince John. Please escort us to His Highness immediately."

The marines looked at the soldiers belligerently, and they glared back in turn. Stanley stood impassively as though it was all beneath him.

The official looked from the Marines to the white flag still flying from the mast and decided this was above his competence level; he would pass it on to the next in the chain.

They were escorted down the docks to a building facing the waterfront. Inside, they were greeted by an official who spoke English.

"I understand you have a message for Prince John. Give it to me, and I will take it to him," he offered pompously.

Stanley looked down his nose at him and replied,

"My orders are to speak directly to the Prince and the Prince alone. I must insist that you take me to him immediately."

"That is impossible. We are at war with England and you are in no position to insist on anything," he replied angrily.

"What is your name?" Stanley asked.

"Why do you want to know that?" the official answered belligerently.

"So I can tell His Highness who delayed the communication of Baron Candor's message."

The man blustered and looked even more stubborn when the door opened, and a richly dressed man walked in. He wore a fancy hat adorned with feathers and carried a gold topped cane. His coat was decorated with gold thread and his shirt with lace.

"That will do. I will take this from here," he said in English with a distinct Oxford accent. He turned to Stanley.

"I am Don Nuno Caetano Álvares Pereira de Melo, Duke of Cadeval. How may I be of assistance?"

Stanley bowed deeply, making a leg and replied,

"My Lord, I have a message from Captain Martin Stockley, Knight of the Bath and Baron of Candor for his Highness Prince John, which I am instructed to deliver to his hand alone."

"Do you now?" the Don replied thoughtfully, "then you had better come with me."

The official stood red faced with embarrassment and anger at being so abruptly overruled, and the Don looked at him and said,

"Put you ruffled feathers away, Avila. This is way above you, no matter how ambitious you are," and to Stanley,

"Shall we?" as he led them out of the door.

He brought him to a carriage,

"I am sorry there is no room for your men, but I will guarantee your safety if you would leave them here."

Stanley knew this would be a matter of honour for the Don, so he agreed and instructed the men to stay with the boat.

"May I ask where you learned your English, Sir?" Stanley asked as the carriage rumbled along.

"I was educated at Wadham college in Oxford. That was where the famous architect Christopher Wren was educated. I am a supporter of our historical ties with Britain and against the foolishness with the French. I knew the former Baron Candor, who I remember as an elderly man with a beautiful young wife and no children."

"Captain Stockley married Lady Candor after the old Baron died and the King allowed them to keep the title."

"Interesting and unusual. He must be an exceptional man," Don Nuno observed. "I would like to meet him myself." He kept up a running commentary of the buildings they passed, probably to stop Stanley asking questions.

They pulled up in front of the Ajuda palace, a grand baroque-Rococo building in the neoclassical style. What struck Stanley was the lack of a military presence. There were a few soldiers wandering around but nothing to suggest there was a French invasion force approaching.

Don Nuno noticed him looking.

"You are looking for our army? I am afraid both the government and our Monarchy are in a state of panic and confusion at the prospect of a French invasion and do not know what to do. The army has not been mobilized nor will it be, I fear."

They entered through the columned entrance and walked down a cool corridor to a room with a cupola held up by plain columns with Corinthian capitols and a parquet floor.

"If you will wait here, I will announce you and arrange for you to meet the Prince in private," instructed the Don.

Stanley waited and kept from worrying by examining the artwork around the room. After around twenty minutes, the door opened, and Don Nuno entered followed by another man. He was quite portly and richly dressed in a red coat with numerous honours pinned to it, a multicoloured sash, and a ribbon around his neck with a silver and gold pendant hanging from it. His face was round, lips a little over full, and he wore a tight white wig.

"Your highness, may I introduce Midshipman Hart, the personal emissary of Captain Stockley, Knight of the bath and Baron of Candor."

The Prince nodded to him said,

"I apologize for meeting you here in this ante room, but Don Nuno insists we have our meeting out of sight and sound of the many French 'diplomats' present in the palace."

"Your Highness," Stanley bowed deeply in reply and held out the letter from Marty.

The Prince looked at the seals then broke open the envelope. He read it and showed it to Don Nuno.

"Do you know the content of this letter?" asked the Prince.

"No, your Highness," Stanley replied.

"Please tell your captain I understand and appreciate his warning, but I believe the French will treat my family honourably."

With that, he turned and left the room.

Don Nuno came upright from his bow and sighed with a shake of his head.

"He still believes the French are honourable, my God he is deluded."

"Sir, my captain asked me to find out if there were any particular French that were influencing the Prince," Stanley asked.

"Did he, now? Well, the ambassador, of course, but there is another who has the Prince's ear. His name is Eric Bouchon and I believe he is a member of French Intelligence and a spy. He is very persuasive and whispers in the Prince's ear constantly. Now the other part of your captain's request was an invitation to dine with him on his ship. That will not be possible, but I can arrange for him to attend a ball here in the palace. Now I will escort you back to your boat."

Marty took Stanley's report and thanked him. He'd achieved what he wanted and that was to find out who the French had influencing matters in the Portuguese court. His letter contained a warning to the Prince that the French sought his and his family's lives and that they had commenced their march on his country. The invitation to dinner also reaped rewards because if he attended the ball, the chances were the French would too and he could put some faces to names.

Lieutenant Trenchard was announced and entered.

"I have my report on the British merchantmen, Sir," he said.

"Excellent," Marty commented and indicated he should proceed.

"There are seven being detained, all are moored in the quarantine area and have a contingent of Portuguese soldiers on board. As far as I could see, there are around five guards per ship plus a pair of guard boats circling them. I was only allowed to board one of the ships, the Arabella out of Newcastle, and according to her captain, Masters, the Portuguese are treating them decently, but they are restricted to their ships. He wanted to know what the Navy was going to do about it."

"Interesting; and what is the general condition of the ships?"

"All look to be in fair condition and able to sail at short notice. Here is a list of the ships and the names of their captains I got from Masters. The list of ships is correct as I checked the names when I rowed around them."

"How did the guard boats react to you?"

"Largely ignored us as long as we didn't get too close to the merchantmen. We were waved away once when we got within 20 yards of one."

"Thank you, Philip. That is all useful information," Marty concluded and dismissed him.

There was not much Marty could do now until he received an invitation to the ball or Smith arrived with his fleet and rather than worry, he decided to hone his weapons skills.

Normally, he wanted to test all the new men himself or have at least one of the shadows do it, and that afternoon he was feeling in need of exercise. He went up on deck dressed in an old set of clothes and his weapons harness.

He chose his first opponent from the new men, Billy Thatcher, a Bristol man who escaped the gallows by joining the Navy. The charge? Stealing a side of beef and battering a sheriff's man half to death when they caught him. He told the judge he stole the beef to feed the many poor people around the docks as the butcher wouldn't even donate his offcuts. He was sentenced to deportation or the Navy.

They faced off with wooden practice swords and soon, the two were working up a sweat. Billy had some skill, but Marty pulled a couple of sneaky tricks from his repertoire and soon had him on his backside. He pulled him to his feet and passed him to Garai to teach him some close quarters fighting techniques.

Another of the other new recruits Ryan brought back from London on their last recruitment drive was a China man. He was short, stocky and had proven to be a lot stronger than he looked. His head was mostly shaved except a long cue that hung down in a plat from the middle of his cranium. He spoke English with an accent that was a combination of Chinese and Bristol, had a dry sense of humour and a keen sense of observation.

Marty beckoned him over and the man, who called himself Chin Lee, stepped forward.

"What is your preferred weapon?" Marty asked, indicating the selection of practice weapons.

Chin Lee looked them over, then at Marty, and picked up a pair of three-foot-long staves normally used to teach novices how to use a sword. Marty picked up a matching pair, and the two stepped out into the centre of the deck.

Marty adopted his usual knife fighter's stance. Chin Lee watched him carefully, frowned, and dropped into a stance with one foot forward knee bent, the other extended behind him. He held his right-hand stave horizontally in front of him and the other high above his head at around a forty-five-degree angle.

Marty twirled his right-hand stave to distract him and launched an attack with his left followed by a rapid series of strikes from high and low. Chin Lee blocked or deflected all of them and when Marty slightly overextended, he launched a counterattack at almost blinding speed. Marty was stretched to block, avoid, or deflect every strike.

Unfamiliar with the deck, Chin Lee's foot hit a ring bolt and he momentarily lost his balance enough to cause his attack to falter. Marty immediately launched into a counter, throwing feints, double strikes, thrusts, and every combination he could think of. Now it was Chin Lee's turn to retreat and defend. Both men were sweating, the pace of the combat was unbelievable, and all the other matchups stopped to watch.

By mutual consent, they stepped back and took a breather. Both men scored minor hits but nothing that could be deemed decisive.

"You are very good, Captain, but your footwork needs improvement. You could have won at least three times if your balance had been better," Chin Lee said.

Marty eyed him curiously. "There is more to you than meets the eye," he said, "I think you have military training."

Chin Lee lowered his weapons.

"Can we talk privately?"

Marty looked at him for a moment, head cocked to one side, then nodded. He tossed his staves back on to the stack and walked up to the quarterdeck.

"Get back to work you lubbers, the show is over!" he called to the men still watching.

Once on the quarterdeck, he cleared it with a look and stood by the stern rail waiting. Chin Lee caught up with him and bowed.

"Well, what is it you want to tell me?" Marty asked, more than a little curious.

"I was a member of the Imperial Guard at the palace in Beijing and I was under command of one of the Emperor's nephews. He was a man of little honour, and I clashed with him a number of times. Unfortunately, I was a much better swordsman than he, and one day I caught him stealing some jewels from the Royal apartments. He drew his sword and attacked me. "

"You killed him?"

"That was my mistake; I just wounded him, and he accused me of being the thief. Somehow, he got one of his followers to plant some of the jewels in my room."

"And you had to run for your life?"

"Yes. I signed up on an American ship that was leaving for Boston and from there, worked my way to London where your officer found me."

"Lucky us," Marty said without a flicker of a smile.

"No, lucky me. I have been looking for a man I can serve who has honour and can fight as well as I can."

Marty waited.

Chin Lee bowed and said,

"Captain Stockley, will you accept me as your humble servant?"

Marty smiled and replied,

"Not as a servant but as a follower and a member of the Shadows, my personal team."

Chin Lee looked surprised then gave him a beaming smile.

"I will not let you down, Sir."

"I am sure you won't," Marty replied, "Now I would be obliged if you would go down there and teach my crew how to stay alive in a fight."

Chin Lee bowed and walked down the steps to the deck where he was greeted by the other Shadows who had guessed what was going on. Like all the rest of them he was a humble but highly skilled man and would fit in really well if Marty was any judge.

With the addition of Chin Lee, weapons and combat training took on another dimension. Not only was he a superb swordsman but expert in close combat as well. He had the men doing what he called open handed fighting, which built upon the street fighting training that Marty had introduced. He kept it simple, showing how to use the elbow and edge of the hand to incapacitate an opponent with blows to the sternum, throat, and face.

He asked Marty's permission to get the Tool Shed to prototype a number of new weapons for him and showed Marty some sketches. Marty was intrigued and agreed; any new weapons that gave them an edge were welcome!

The Alouette's barge appeared and a message was passed by Archie Davidson that Smith had arrived. He had sealed up the mouth of the Tagus and Marty was to expect a visit in the next couple of days. It was the 10th of November 1807. To complicate matters, he received an invitation to a ball held by Prince John the following evening. The lateness of the invitation made him think Don Nuno had done some hard talking to get him invited.

Sir Sidney didn't visit the next day, so Marty had plenty of time to prepare for the ball. He dressed in his finest and wore gold buckled shoes instead of his everyday boots. His number one dress uniform was closely tailored to his muscular frame, which meant he had to go without his usual armoury of weapons. In fact, he felt almost naked going into enemy territory so lightly armed, he only had a garrotte wire under the ribbon of his cue with a couple of lock picks and his dress sword. He dared not offend his host by carrying more than that.

He was rowed to the dock in his barge with its uniformly dressed rowers in their white trousers, blue striped shirts, and black tarred hats. Samuel was his cox, of course, resplendent in his white trousers and blue jacket with its silver buttons. Blaez had to stay at home.

He was met at the dock by an open landau carriage and driven to the palace of Ajuda. He was escorted through the entrance and led up an enclosed staircase with carvings on the ceiling that zigzagged to an upper landing. This was decorated with rounded stained glass and the royal coat of arms. From there, he was led down a corridor to the ballroom, and as he entered, noted that there was an upper gallery where the musicians variously tooted and scraped their instruments opposite the entrance. The walls were covered in red silk and the ceiling had a number of panels from which hung three huge chandeliers.

Marty was announced and made a leg to the room, which was returned by many of the guests. Two relatively plainly dressed men, who were near the Prince, stood out. *French, if I am not mistaken, he thought.* He was intercepted by Don Nuno, who escorted him through the crowd to be presented.

"Your Highness, may I present Captain Sir Martin Stockley, Knight of the Bath and Baron of Candor," he introduced him. Marty noticed that the two men beat a hasty retreat and now stood a safe distance away.

"Your Highness," Marty greeted him and bowed elegantly as Caroline taught him.

"Baron, welcome!" the Prince replied with a smile and then looked at him closely. "You are much younger than I imagined the man that terrifies the French would be."

"Me? Terrify the French?" Marty laughed incredulously.

The Prince laughed along and clarified,

"Well, you have certainly frightened those two," he said, indicating the two plainly dressed men. "They have been warning me that you are an assassin and a spy."

Marty laughed that off and changed the subject,

"Prince George bade me send you his greetings and felicitations."

"You know Georgie?" the Prince asked in surprise.

"I have the pleasure of being his acquaintance and sometime confidant," Marty elaborated, only polishing the lily a little.

The conversation was curtailed as the Prince had to receive more people as a queue was building up.

"We must talk again at more leisure," he said in parting.

"Can you introduce me?" Marty asked Don Nuno nodding to the French.

"I can, but they do not speak English," he informed him.

"That's not a problem. I speak French well enough," Marty replied.

They moved over to the two Frenchmen and Nuno made the introduction. Marty smiled his wolf smile as he was introduced to Alexander du Font and Eric Bouchon. Du Font was the ambassador and that left Bouchon to be the spy.

"I knew the Ambassador in Madrid, you know," Marty told them conversationally, *"Such a shame he had such nasty accident. Shot by his own gamekeeper!"*

The Ambassador visibly paled and stuttered a reply then Marty turned to Bouchon.

"It was a shame about Messier as well. He had such a beautiful villa in Naples; it was a pity it burned down. Did he send a report before he died?"

Bouchon blanched then went red with anger and hissed,

"he was my friend and you will pay for his death, you bastard."

Marty's smile got even more feral, and he leaned close to the fuming man and said quietly,

"If you want to avenge him, we can duel, if you have the balls, but you must know I never leave a live enemy behind me."

With that, he bowed politely and walked away, leading the startled Don by the arm as if nothing had happened.

"So, it's true! They really are afraid of you. You know, they told us you were an assassin," the Don said.

Marty stopped and turned to him,

"I am a Captain in His Majesties Royal Navy and it is my duty to cause confusion and destruction to his enemies. It just happens that I get to do it in, let's say, less conventional ways than my brother officers."

The Don smiled at that and let the subject drop.

Marty made a point of being in the eyeline of the French all evening, and every time he made eye contact with either of them, he gave them a wolf smile. Towards the end of the evening, he deliberately bumped into Bouchon, spilling red wine on his shirt. That was too much for the already angry man, who spun and swore at Marty, calling him a pig and the son of a whore.

There were gasps from the revellers in the vicinity that spoke French and translations were quickly supplied to those who didn't. Marty assumed a shocked expression, which turned to one of amusement,

"Monsieur, that was quite accidental, I assure you, but as you have now insulted me and my mother, god rest her soul, I must demand satisfaction. My seconds will call on you in the morning," and to set it in stone, he slapped the man hard enough across the face to leave a red mark.

"He chose pistols and will meet you in the grounds of the Castle of Saint George tomorrow at dawn," Phillip Trenchard announced on his return from meeting with

Bouchon's seconds. "He insists on supplying the pistols as well as he thinks you would cheat somehow."

"Then we must suspect him of cheating as well. Be very thorough when you inspect them. I wouldn't put it past them to try and slip in a trick gun that fires backwards," Marty concluded grimly. "I also want a sweep of the area immediately before the duel as well. Let's be sure he doesn't have a sharpshooter anywhere within range either."

He looked over to the Shadows that were gathered in his cabin.

"You have located the Ambassador's residence?"

"Yes, he lives in an apartment on the third floor of the Torre de Menagem on the edge of the same garden that the duel is in," Garai reported.

"Within line of sight?" Marty asked.

"Not from his apartment but certainly from the rampart," Garai replied.

Marty looked at him and said,

"Be up there in the morning with Chin, and if the Ambassador shows up, give him a flying lesson. Make sure you are not seen."

Adam Cooper came in with a letter on a tray.

"This has just been delivered by a midshipman from the Pompée,"

Marty opened and read it.

"Admiral Smith will visit tomorrow afternoon."

It was a cool and slightly misty morning at sea level when Marty and his seconds left for the shore. The Shadows had left the ship in the middle of the night to set up around the site of the duel to ensure there would be no interference. Garai and Chin Lee went to the tower the minister's apartment was in.

Marty's seconds were Phillip Trenchard and Sergeant Bright of the Marines. He chose the sergeant because of his expertise with weapons.

There was a carriage waiting for them when the boat pulled up at the dock steps, courtesy of Don Nuno, and they arrived in the castle grounds on time. Marty dressed for the occasion in a silk shirt open to the waist despite the morning chill, tight riding trousers, and hessian boots.

Bouchon and his entourage were already there, along with a number of spectators from the court and a table was set up with the pistols on it. Sergeant Bright inspected both very closely, which elicited an outraged complaint from the French seconds.

Ignoring them, he finished his inspection and pronounced them fit for purpose in a parade ground voice, making Marty smile. He then proceeded to meticulously load them, making sure the French could see his every move.

Marty chose twenty paces separation. That is, each combatant would walk ten paces before turning and firing. It was the longer option as many duels were fought at just ten paces, which Marty thought took the skill factor out of the equation.

The master of ceremonies, an official from the court appointed by the Prince to ensure fair play, called them to order and asked Marty if he would withdraw the challenge. He refused, and they were stood back to back.

"On my command, you will walk forward to my count. After you have taken the tenth pace, you can turn

and fire. If you turn early, I will shoot you myself. Do you understand?

Both men acknowledged that they did.

"Ready! One, two, three, four . . ." he counted and the men stepped out.

"nine, ten!"

Both turned and fired almost simultaneously.

Marty felt a sharp pain across the front of his ribs and stepped backwards.

He looked down.

The bullet had cut a gash across his chest above his heart. Bouchon missed by scant inches.

He looked toward his opponent, who stood with a fixed expression on his face, a rose of blood welling from his right side and with a sigh, folded to the ground.

Chapter 3: Lisbon End Game

"You killed him then," Sir Sidney stated as they sipped a glass of madeira before having lunch.

Marty just nodded.

"And the Ambassador?"

"Turned up on the roof of his residence with a hunting rifle, then discovered he couldn't fly."

Smith grinned as he didn't see this as an assassination, more as a preservation of honour.

"When they find the body, they will assume he slipped on the roof while trying to influence the duel," Marty concluded.

"Excellent, we remove their influence and discredit the French in one fell swoop," Sidney crowed happily. "And at no cost to us!"

"I wouldn't go that far," Marty replied, wincing as he shifted position, the bandage was constricting.

"You will heal, you have had worse," Sidney laughed.

"What next?" Marty asked, scowling.

"We have the port blockaded and the Russians committed to staying neutral. So, the only concern is the Portuguese fleet. How many ships are here?" Sidney asked.

"Fourteen Ships of the line, eleven Frigates, and seven smaller vessels that can be classified as warships and a baker's dozen of merchantmen," Marty replied.

"You say the majority of the aristocracy are here in Lisbon at the moment?" Sidney reflected.

Marty didn't respond as he could see that Sidney was thinking.

"What would hurt the French most?" Sidney finally asked. "Or rather, what are they hoping to get from the invasion that we could deny them?"

Marty considered that then put his own thoughts into words. "The treasury and the personal wealth of the aristocrats Napoleon's coffers are empty."

"Exactly what I was thinking," Sidney agreed. "Now, how do we deny them that!"

The next morning, Marty was summoned to attend the Prince. This time in the throne room.

"Baron Candor," the Prince greeted him, looking stern.

"You have denied me of the company of not only Monsieur Bouchon but the Ambassador as well!"

Marty feigned surprise,

"The Ambassador?"

"Apparently, according to my head of security, he fell from the parapet of the tower where he had an apartment yesterday morning. Would you know anything about that?"

"Your Highness, how could I? I was engaged with Monsieur Bouchon yesterday morning," Marty pleaded innocently.

"Hmm, yes, that is what everybody said. The perfect alibi." The Prince sounded sceptical. "He was found with a hunting rifle next to his body, a very good one with a rifled barrel and calibrated sights."

"At the time of my duel?" Marty gasped.

"It would appear so; the conclusion is he slipped while trying to effect the outcome." The prince sighed,

"I had assumed he was a man of honour; it would appear I was mistaken."

He looked at Marty then indicated he should sit.

"They both painted you as some kind of spy and assassin, told me you had murdered the ambassador in Madrid and several people in Naples."

"Your Highness, I have never killed anyone but in the line of duty," Marty stated emphatically, looking him straight in the eyes.

The prince considered him for a moment then glanced down at his chest.

"I hear you were wounded."

"A flesh wound. Just another scar to add to the collection." Marty smiled, dismissing it as trivial though it stung like blazes at the moment.

The conversation turned to domestic matters, the Prince enquiring about his family, children and his estates in England. *He is trying to get to know* me, Marty thought, as they chatted about Prince George and the twins. Eventually he asked.

"Sir Sidney Smith, is he an honourable man? I have heard a lot about him."

"He is, your Highness, a gentleman," Marty assured him.

"Good, I have taken enough of your time today. We must speak again." The Prince rose to leave, dismissing Marty in the process.

Marty rose and bowed as he backed away before turning to the door.

Reports came in on the 25th of November from his Scouts that the French invasion force had crossed the border at Abrantes and were camped just seventy-five miles from Lisbon. He sent the information to the Prince.

He got a message back from Don Nuno saying the Prince had sent an emissary to Junot offering to, as he described, 'roll over and offer our arses up to the French.'

Junot's response was to set out for Lisbon with four battalions with the obvious intent to capture the city.

Sir Sydney met Marty at the dock on the morning of the 27th. Marty had forewarned Nuno, and a carriage was waiting to carry them to the Prince.

"Your Highness, the French mean to have your head," Smith told him and showed him a copy of Le Moniteur from the 13th October that declared the house of Briganza deposed.

"My God! The arrogance!" The Prince cried when he read it. "What am I to do?"

Smith nodded to Marty to make the suggestion that they had come up with.

"You Highness, if I may suggest a possible solution?" Marty offered.

The Prince indicated he should continue.

"If the French capture your family here in Lisbon, they will not only remove you from the throne and possibly send you to the guillotine, they will confiscate all your goods, leaving you with nothing even if they let you live.

However, you have probably four days. I have men in position to slow Junot down by destroying bridges and setting ambushes. I will delay them as long as I can." He paused to let that sink in then continued,

"You have a fleet here, which if the French take over Lisbon, we will be forced to destroy to keep out of their hands. Now, if you were to take that fleet and all the personal wealth that you can carry and sail to Brazil, that would satisfy our remit and deny the French both the ships and the benefit of your money."

The Prince pondered Marty's remarks then sighed and said,

"I don't seem to have much choice, do I?" and started giving orders.

He isn't slow to make a decision when his arse is on the line. Marty smiled to himself.

Two days later, there were lines of wagons loaded with gold, silver, works of art, dinner services and all manner of treasures along the shoreline, waiting to be loaded on ships of the line and merchantmen that moored up to the dock in turn. In the end, fifteen warships and twenty transports (some of them frigates en flute) were loaded when Marty's marines appeared on the docks saying that the French were almost at the gates.

The Prince waited no longer, and the refugees set sail for Brazil on the 29th November. Sir Sidney provided three ships as escorts, and the rest of his Fleet stayed on blockade duty. Marty watched the last of them go and looked along the dock to the fourteen wagons that were left unloaded and the few small warships that were left behind.

He joined the British fleet at the mouth of the Tagus the next morning, the eastern skyline grey with the smoke of burning ships and empty wagons. He had taken onboard any British citizens he could find that were left in Lisbon and escorted the British merchantmen out of the estuary.

The Formidiable sat a little lower than normal in the water and had an armed cutter in attendance that Marty had spared from being burnt. He would give that to Collingwood as a gift when he returned to Gibraltar.

Junot entered Lisbon at the head of a ragged, rabble of an army. They had taken the fastest but hardest route from Spain into Portugal along the Tagus Valley as ordered by Napoleon. The going was not so much hard as almost impossible as there was almost no food that could be foraged along its entire length. He lost almost all his horse and cannon and was only able to enter Portugal with four pieces of horse artillery he requisitioned from the Spanish. The main body of his force would not join him for another ten days.

"We could have stopped them with our hundred marines," Marty said afterwards, "but they walked in without firing a shot."

Junot had been relying on capturing the wealth of Lisbon to re-equip and pay his troops, but he found that the royal family and the rest of the refugees had taken it all with them. Around half the specie (available coin) in the country had been taken. His men had to resort to looting to feed themselves and replace their shredded uniforms, which didn't endear them to the locals at all.

Chapter 4: A different Bonaparte

Back in Gibraltar, the Formidiable's cargo was unloaded and securely stored in a locked and guarded cellar. Marty decided it should be used to fund resistance activities in Portugal and anything that was left would be returned to the Royal Family on their return. The Admiralty might have disagreed, but he didn't ask them. The cutter was presented to Collingwood who expressed his gratitude and would use it for message carrying.

During December, news trickled back from Portugal that Napoleon was extremely angry that the majority of the country's wealth was gone, and he levied a punitive fine of one-hundred million Francs on the nation. He also ordered Junot to confiscate the property of the refugees. Consequently, the population rose and rioted.

In January, reinforcements arrived and Junot was back up to his full strength of twenty-five thousand troops. In February, he disbanded the governing council and sent the Portuguese Army to France.

During this time, the Flotilla prowled up the West coast of Portugal to the Bay of Biscay, taking any French or Spanish merchantmen. They made a nuisance of themselves and mapped places where they could land and pickup agents.

Marty enjoyed being based out of Gibraltar as he got to see his family more often. No more attempts had been made on his or their lives, but he kept the standing security detail of marines in place all the same. Caroline had practiced with pistol and sword, and Marty found

Senior Dominguez, a Spanish armorer, on the peninsula to have a custom-made sword forged for her.

On one of his stop overs between sweeps, he visited the armourer and specified what he wanted.

"The blade should be around thirty inches, like a French small sword, sharp on both sides and finely balanced. The hilt should be narrow enough for her hand," he had one of her gloves to show the size, "wrapped in shagreen, and a basket guard."

"Si, Señor, I can make that. Have you seen a sword being made before?"

"Can't say that I have," Marty replied.

"Would you like to assist me?" Dominguez offered.

Marty's face lit up like a kid in a sweetshop.

He expected that they would just take a bar of steel and hammer a sword out of it, but he was wrong. Dominguez had other ideas. He took two different pieces of steel, that he explained were of different hardness, and proceeded to start forging them together. What followed was a long and intricate process that involved heating, hammering, and cooling the steel. The timing, he was told, had to be exact and Dominguez would recite psalms and prayers to make sure it was.

The process was long, and Marty returned to the forge many times between sailing trips to monitor progress. He showed Dominguez his fighting knife, and the smith admired the steel and workmanship, telling him that it was forged using a different method. What he was making was Toledo steel and the knife was made of Damascus. The processes were similar, he thought, but the secret of making Damascus was only known to a few

Muslim smiths, whereas the process for Toledo steel was only know to a handful of Spanish smiths.

The blade was finally finished, thirty inches long, was razor sharp on both sides, and tapered to a point just as specified. The balance point was perfectly placed four inches in front of the cross guard, the hilt wrapped in shark skin (Shagreen), and it had a deceptively delicate basket hilt that had gold intertwined through the elements and jewels set in the base of the cross guard. The hilt hid a surprise, a catch, concealed near the cross guard - it would release a six-inch sprung blade from the pommel. Something that would give an opponent a nasty surprise.

Their family arms were etched at the balance point and the Latin moto Mortiferum et Pulcherrima (Deadly and Beautiful), etched along the blade, which applied to both the sword and Caroline. Dominguez had a leatherworker friend of his make a beautiful scabbard.

Marty was stunned at its beauty. He paid Dominguez the three hundred pounds without a second's hesitation.

Meanwhile, at the end of March in Spain, the French under Murat had occupied Madrid with forty thousand troops. Prior to that, the Spanish kicked King Charles off the throne and installed his son Ferdinand in his place. Napoleon demanded Ferdinand take his family to France and took them hostage. It was the beginning of the French domination of Spain.

Ridgely found a number of Portuguese speaking agents, which the Flotilla infiltrated into Lisbon, Alhão, and Porto. The Hornfleur was used to deliver and recover the agents either by using its whalers where the rendezvous point was a beach or the fishing boat Marty had acquired the year before. While they were at it, they started smuggling port and Dao wine back to Gibraltar as a cover. Which was then was shipped back to England by one of his personal fleet and distributed by Caroline's network.

Marty continued to support the Spanish in Grenada with advisors and regularly visited to maintain his personal relationship with the council. The Formidiable, under a Spanish flag, was the perfect ship for this.

Unexpectedly in mid-April, he received orders to report back to London for a meeting with Hood. He duly sailed back, with a shopping list Caroline had given him, and reported to the Admiralty as soon as he could. Fletcher was given the list.

Marty kicked his heels for an hour in the waiting room and chatted to some of the other officers waiting there. Many were looking for ships and many, who had read of him in the Gazette, offered themselves if he had vacancies. He was a 'lucky' captain who was known to be well connected. He was eventually summoned, made his way down the familiar corridors to Hood's office, and was surprised to see a soberly dressed man with a bald pate and bushy sideburns there as well.

"Martin! How are you?" Hood greeted him in his familiar way. He was looking well for his advanced years.

"I am well Sir; I must say you are looking in particularly good health!" Marty responded.

"Quite so, I am blessed. May I introduce Mr George Canning, Foreign Secretary of his Majesty's Government and William's successor," Hood introduced the second man.

"Pleased to meet you Captain Stockley, I have heard and read much about you," Canning welcomed him.

"Mr Canning has a mission for you Martin," Hood interjected, it seemed he wanted to move things along.

Canning threw Hood a look that said, 'I know when I'm being shepherded,' and continued as he wanted.

"That was a very satisfactory outcome to the Portuguese Royal family affair. Whose idea was it to repatriate them and their wealth to Brazil?"

"Sir Sidney and I came up with the plan together, Sir," Marty replied modestly. "We concluded that the real reason for Napoleon to invade Portugal was to get his hands on its wealth and to get a standing army onto the peninsula. Getting the Royal family and their treasures out of the country seemed the best way to cause him some discomfort. We hadn't banked on the general exodus of the wealthy citizens that it triggered as well."

"How many left in the end?" Hood asked, trying to regain some control.

"Around sixteen thousand, they took everything they could cram onto the ships. I understand that around half the available coin went with them."

"You burnt the remaining ships?" Canning enquired.

"Yes Sir, every one that could carry a gun."

"What are you doing now?"

"Supporting the rebels in Granada, infiltrating spies into Portugal where they can agitate and encourage rebellion against the French, and raiding up and down the coast to prevent the French from resupplying their troops by sea. In Italy, we are also infiltrating agents as required."

"What about Malta?" Canning asked with an arch of the eyebrows.

"You mean the clean up?" Marty asked.

Canning nodded.

"A messy affair, but we managed to sweep up all the elements of the French network back to their controller in Naples," Marty summarized.

"A huge understatement if ever I heard one," Canning smiled, "considering that you also managed to wipe out most of the French ships in the region as well."

"Ships can be replaced, Sir; it didn't take the French long to send more."

"Be that as it may, it was still a considerable achievement," Canning concluded. "Now I need you to perform a more diplomatic mission."

Diplomatic? He's got the wrong man! Marty thought.

"Napoleon appointed his brother Louis, the King of Holland in 1806. It would appear that Louis has since gone native, adopted the name of Lodwijk, speaks only Dutch and resists Napoleon's demands for troops. Napoleon has consequently blockaded the country economically, and that is causing extensive damage to their economy."

Marty was surprised at the news; his experience of Holland went back many years to the time when they kicked out their king and founded the Batavian republic. He was out of date on developments since then. He wondered what it was they wanted him to do.

The secretary brought in coffee at that point, and the conversation stopped. Marty helped himself to a cup, strong and black as he liked it.

"What we want you to do is to visit King Lodwijk in Amsterdam and make him an offer," Canning continued.

Marty almost choked on his coffee.

"Why me, Sir, and not a diplomat?" he asked.

"Because we think we have a leak in the Foreign Office, and this is something we don't want getting back to Paris," Canning admitted ruefully. "That is something I may ask your help with at a later date, if we can't find it ourselves, but for now we want you to take care of this."

He went on to brief Marty on an offer of economic assistance for the Kingdom of Holland, as it was now called, including trade and financial support in return for them staying as neutral as they could.

This is as hair-brained a scheme as I've ever heard, Marty thought once he heard it all, but he had no choice but to give it his best shot.

"I will sail as soon as we have replenished," Marty assured him.

"Good, we have forewarned the Dutch you are coming, so they will be expecting you," Canning said as he rose, shook his hand, and excused himself as he had another meeting he had to attend.

As soon as he left, Hood indicated Marty should join him in the comfortable chairs by the fire. He gazed into the flames then sighed,

"be careful, Marty. This is, at best, a shot in the dark. Remember, it is Napoleon's brother we are dealing with here and even if he has gone native, I don't believe he will knowingly betray his brother. Defy him, yes, but betray him, no."

"Is that the real reason they won't risk a diplomat?" Marty asked.

"No, they really do have a leak, and we may well be asked to find and plug it given your track record in Malta," Hood confirmed. "Now, give me the full details of your recent escapades in Portugal."

Marty returned to the Formidiable the next morning, Hood having kept him busy until after it was too late to get back to the ship that was moored at Admiralty dock. He stayed the night in his London home, much to the surprise of the staff. It also gave the men the night in town as before he left the Admiralty, he sent a message granting shore leave until six o'clock the next morning to all those who wanted it.

It was a rather surprised and damp Marty, the weather had turned particularly foul, who arrived at the Formidiable to find it not only fully manned at 6 AM but almost fully provisioned. When asked, his first lieutenant replied,

"I thought if they recalled us from Gibraltar, it was probably for something urgent, so I started re-provisioning as soon as you left. Fletcher went into town to see to Lady Caroline's shopping but came back in a couple of hours. Apparently he asked one of his old contacts to do it so he could get on with sourcing the ship's needs." He looked pleased and continued,

"we acquired a couple of new main spars for the Alouette to replace those short ones the yard in Gibraltar fitted when she was repaired and a number of replacements that are suitable for all our ships."

"Excellent, when will we be ready to sail?" Marty asked, looking at the pennant and seeing a nice South-westerly breeze blowing.

Ackermann looked down the dock and saw a pair of hackney carriage approaching with a large number of boxes tied to their roofs.

"If I'm not mistaken, that is Lady Caroline's shopping and the water hoys are just pulling up alongside, so we should be ready for the next high tide."

They set sail as the tide started to ebb and apart from dodging the usual Thames barges, they had an uneventful trip down river. Caroline's shopping list had been fulfilled admirably for just a small commission and they stocked up on all the ship's spares that were hard to get in Gibraltar.

Once clear of the estuary, they turned North-by-Northeast and headed up the Channel.

"Mr. Grey," Marty approached the Master, "we need to enter the port of Amsterdam. Do you know how to do that?"

"I have done it in the past," Grey replied, "you have to enter from the North past the island of Texel, then travel down the Texel Stroom into the Zuyderzee, but that route is surrounded by sandbanks that move year on year. I'm afraid it would be a slow trip down with men in the chains all the way."

Marty frowned and asked,

"Well, how do we do it then?"

"We will need to get a pilot; they wait on the island for ships and guide them in," Grey answered.

Marty had one thing he wanted to do before he got to Amsterdam, and they hove to off the beach at Noordwijk where he, Matai and Blaez went ashore.

He made his way to the farm where he first met Blaez and knocked on the door. The old lady, Mrs. Jongeline, answered the door and when she saw Marty and Blaez, she grabbed him and gave him the three kisses he knew were traditional. Blaez got a thorough petting and told he was a 'mooie jongen.'

Once inside and settled with a coffee and a piece of cake, Marty recited a sentence he'd memorized for some time now in the hope he would be able to use it.

"I want to find a mate for Blaez, he needs to make some puppies before he gets too old."

Mrs. Jongeline's face lit up and started to speak in rapid fire Dutch. When Marty looked at her blankly, she waved at him to stay where he was and disappeared out of the back door.

She came back thirty minutes later with a middle-aged man in tow.

"Hello, I am Kees Jongbloed. Mevrouw Jongeline says you want to find a mate for your dog," he said in heavily accented English. He looked at Blaez then knelt beside him. He offered his hand to the dog to smell then ran his hands over his body. He got him to stand and checked his testicles, causing Blaez to give Marty a 'what the hell?' look, then went over his teeth and eyes.

"He is a fine dog. I know his background and bloodline. I have a bitch coming into season that would be a good match and would be happy to have him as the father of her next nest."

"I want one of the puppies, a male like him," Marty said.

"It is tradition that the owner of the dog gets first choice of the puppies. Can you leave him with me?"

"I can leave him if Matai here stays with him. If one of us doesn't stay, he won't either," Marty replied.

"My bitch is almost ready, but he should stay here a week," Kees told them.

Marty did some sums in his head, "The earliest we can return is in six days. After that, it won't be for another week."

"Do not worry; we will look after your friend and dog until you get back. They will stay with Mevrouw Jongeline until you can collect them both. The puppies will be ready for you to choose one at twelve weeks and to collect sixteen weeks after the mating."

They arrived off Texel at dawn the next day and hove to at the entrance to Heldar. They flew British colours and waited for a pilot.

After a couple of hours, a boat approached and pulled alongside. Marty had the side ropes already mounted and a red faced, jolly looking man appeared at the entry port. He stomped over to Marty, who was in full uniform, and thrust out his hand, "Guus van Meppel, Captain. I am to show you the way into Amsterdam." He looked around at the Formidiable. "Spanish built with English rigging. She was a prize, no? Draws about 4 meters."

He didn't wait for an answer but went straight up onto the quarter deck and stood next to the helm. Marty exchanged an amused look with Ackermann and followed him up.

"Right, Captain, we need to head due West from here and take it slowly, no more than five knots please."

Van Meppel navigated them into the Zuyderzee and South down the navigable channel. Mr. Grey was taking bearings from landmarks and marking them on his charts, which made van Meppel laugh.

"Mark away, my friend, the next storm will make that chart useless when all the sandbars shift," he boomed in a voice that could probably be heard on shore.

They entered the port of Amsterdam and Marty was surprised at how busy it was.

"You should have seen it in the old days when the Dutch East India Company was at its height!" van Meppel told them, "you could walk from one side to the other, there were so many ships."

A mixture of mismanagement, corruption, and changing world dynamics all contributed to the fall of the company, which was now a shadow of its former self.

They dropped anchor where they were directed, and Ackermann went about making sure she was shipshape and Navy fashion. He wasn't going to give any Dutchman an excuse to criticize his ship.

Marty went to call his barge around but van Meppel stopped him.

"Sorry, Captain, but you must wait until they send over a boat for you. You do not have permission to debark yet, and none of your crew may go ashore."

A boat came and collected the pilot, and he waved as he was rowed ashore. Marty scowled after him and wondered how long they would keep him waiting.

He knew they would be watching and wouldn't give them the satisfaction of seeing him pace the deck, so he went to his cabin. His paperwork was, for once, up to date, so he settled down to read the latest edition of the Times he bought while in London.

An article caught his eye. It was about a chap called Trevithick, who was a Cornishman that had built a high-pressure steam engine. That was fairly revolutionary in itself, but he made it small enough to power a land carriage! Apparently, the development and refinement of the means to bore an accurate gun barrel enabled him to create an accurate enough cylinder and piston to take steam at one-hundred and fifty pounds per square inch.

Marty had read about the beam engines of Bolton and Watt used to pump water, but they were static and only used around twenty-five pounds of pressure. This was a major development!

The article continued with a rather sarcastic account of how the inventor and friends had driven the land carriage along a public road and were so pleased with the performance of the engine that they had stopped at a pub for lunch. Unfortunately, they neglected the engine, which ran dry and caught fire. He had now built another engine that ran on rails, but it was too heavy for the wooden rails at the mine and they crowed about another of Trevithick's follies.

But if that could power a land carriage, surely it could power a boat or even a ship! Marty thought but before he could take the idea any further, there was a knock at the door.

"Midshipman Hart, Sir," announced the sentry.

"Enter!" Marty called.

"Please, Sir, Mr. Ackermann's complements, but there is a boat with some kind of official heading this way."

"Have him brought down to my cabin when he boards, please," Marty instructed and called his steward to help him dress in his best uniform and honours.

There was another knock, and the sentry announced,

"Mr. Trenchard and a Dutch gentleman, Sir!"

"Enter!" Marty called and his second lieutenant and a tall, well dressed gentleman with a sash of office entered his cabin.

"Captain, may I present Mr. van Rijen, who is the secretary to the Foreign Minister of the Dutch Government. Mr. van Rijen, Captain Sir Martin Stockley."

"Welcome, please take a seat and kindly mind you don't bang your head." Marty smiled at him as the man had to stoop to avoid the deck beams.

Once they were both seated and Marty had ordered coffee for them both, van Rijen opened the conversation.

"I have seen your name before, Captain. I remember seeing it on the bottom of a treaty with the islands of Curaçao and Bonaire, to stop their trading with privateers in return for the British leaving them alone and not attacking Dutch ships."

Marty smiled and inclined his head in acknowledgement.

"That was me," Marty admitted, still proud of what he had achieved. "Did the Burgermeister of Bonaire get over the disappointment?"

"Alas, no. He still writes complaining about the loss of revenue and that a British Frigate will turn up unannounced to make sure they are honouring it."

Marty grinned at that, and van Rijen continued,

"he made a formal complaint about you blowing him across his boat."

"He should have moved faster. I told him what we were going to do," Marty replied then continued, "but we are not here to revisit old treaties are we."

"Indeed not, we understand that you have an offer from your government."

"Which I would like to make to the King and his ministers in person," Marty interrupted.

Van Rijen looked down his nose at him in what Marty thought was typical civil servant fashion, so he sat back in his chair and waited.

"I need to know what the offer is to be able to persuade the Minister to take this to the King," van Rijen stated after the silence had lasted a minute or two.

"The fact that it comes from my King and his government should be enough to get me a meeting," Marty replied.

Van Rijen looked at him and saw no sign of his giving an inch, and irritated, stood to take his leave, cracking his head on the deck beam directly above him.

Marty winced for him as he saw the pain on his face. He stood and took him by the arm to guide him to the door.

"You are too tall for a ship, my friend," he consoled him, "and oak is harder than heads. Let's hope the next time we meet its somewhere the ceilings are higher."

They heard nothing for the rest of the day, and Marty ordered a double watch set that night as being in an enemy harbour with so many ships in it made him nervous.

The next day around midmorning, another boat approached, this time with a uniformed man next to van Rijen who was introduced as Flag Captain Maurice Den Helder.

"Captain, we are here to escort you to a meeting with the Foreign Minister and Minister of War," van Rijen announced.

"Will the King attend?" Marty asked.

"Captain, your reputation precedes you and we are not about to give you access to our King, who also happens to be Napoleons brother!"

"You think I would try and kill him?" Marty asked bluntly.

"Frankly yes, we believe you capable of that," Captain Den Helder replied.

"I may be an enemy of the French, but I have never done the Dutch any harm. In fact, I believe you to be natural allies to the British." He looked them both in the eye and stood very straight. "I give you my word as an officer and a gentleman that I mean your King no harm and am only here to convey the offer from my Government."

Den Helder took van Rijen by the elbow and led him several steps away for a whispered conversation. When they returned he asked,

"If we grant you access, will you submit to being searched for weapons?"

Marty bristled and was about to say something about them doubting his word, but he swallowed his anger.

"If that is what it takes, then I will, but take note, this is an offence to my honour!"

"We apologize for that but when faced with someone who we have been warned directly about by Paris, then we have to take all precautions."

Back in his cabin, Marty changed into his dress uniform and made sure he had all his honours, including the Tiger from India on display. He removed all his weapons, except a dress sword, and left them on his desk. He didn't even wear his special boots and instead wore shoes with gold buckles.

He returned to the deck and followed the two officials into their boat. They rowed across to the town and from there to a large ornate brick building, which den Helder told him used to be the Staadhuis but was now the palace.

Once inside, they were joined by two soldiers with swords held at the port, who fell into step behind Marty. *They're serious about not taking any chances,* he thought as he glimpsed them in a mirror.

They came to a large ornate door guarded by another two soldiers armed with halberds. However, van Rijen led them to a smaller door to one side which led into an anteroom.

"I am afraid I must ask you to surrender your sword and allow yourself to be searched," he said in a voice meant to brook no argument.

Marty gave him a hard look and removed his sword belt, placing it on a table to the side. He also removed his coat and hung it on the back of a chair, held out his arms, and allowed den Helder to search him. He wasn't as thorough as Sam but was good enough.

He was allowed a moment to replace his coat, which was also patted down, straighten his clothes, then was led through another door into a large expensively decorated room with a large table as the centre piece.

At the head of the table sat a man who could only be King Lodwijk. Another six men sat at the table, three to a side. *Must be the ministers,* Marty concluded.

"Sir Martin Stockley, Baron of Candor and emissary for the British Government," van Rijen announced.

"I understand you have an offer for me," the King stated bluntly.

He looks like his brother, Marty thought and said,

"indeed, I do, your Majesty, and I would like to say it is made with the best will towards the Dutch people and their government."

"But not to me, I imagine, being brother to the hated Napoleon," the King replied.

"Aux contraire!" Marty replied, "We have been told that you have the best interests of the Dutch at heart as well."

Lodwijk half smiled at that and motioned him to continue.

"My government is aware that the trade blockade that Napoleon has imposed on the Dutch is causing great hardship to its economy and people and would like to make an offer of economic assistance, a trade agreement, and financial support in return for staying as neutral as you can."

He took another deep breath.

"Dutch ships would be able to trade with England and her allies under the protection of the Royal Navy. Essential goods would be sent to alleviate the suffering of the people and ongoing financial assistance to help rebuild the economy given on very favourable terms."

The six ministers looked at first surprised, then interested, then expectant as they looked to their King.

"And how does the British government mean to protect us when my brother takes steps to prevent this and punish the Dutch for contemplating such an - - agreement?"

He stood and paced around the table until he was face to face with Marty.

"I will tell you. Nothing. Napoleon will walk in here with an army like he has with Portugal and Spain and just take over, and the British will be powerless to prevent it."

He was angry now.

"The Dutch, who have suffered enough, will be caught in the middle and squeezed until they are bled dry! The answer is NO!"

Marty wasn't surprised and kept a straight face throughout. What did surprise him was what came next.

"You, my dear Captain, are wanted for the murder of both an ambassador and a minister, the burning of at least one embassy, and many acts of piracy against the French State!"

"Your ship will be released to carry our refusal back to England, but you will remain here under arrest and be sent to my brother as a gesture of good will."

Marty was taken aback! This went in the face of any diplomatic protocol he had ever read about, but he didn't have time to protest as he was seized and dragged away through the large door by the two soldiers with swords.

Behind him, he heard the ministers protesting to the King, their voices fading as he was dragged down the corridor to a small room and pushed inside.

The room was only ten feet to a side and had a small window high up on one wall. Like all the rooms he had seen the ceiling was high and it was furnished with a chair, a cot, a washstand with a jug and bowl and a chamber pot. The door had no lock but bolts on the outside at the top, middle, and bottom.

He sat on the cot and waited to see what would happen next. He didn't have to wait long when there was the sound of the bolts being drawn and the door opened.

Den Helder stepped in with a guard behind him, armed with a pistol. Two more guards were visible outside.

"I want you to know this is not the doing of the ministers or the rest of us. It is purely the action of the King. Is there a message you want given to your ship?"

He paused, looking embarrassed.

"Please tell them to sail immediately, not to try a rescue here and not to forget to look after my dog and his puppies," Marty asked of him.

Den Helder assured him he would, and the door closed behind him.

On the Formidiable, they received the message with anger, but Ackermann read something into it that the others missed. He smiled as they set sail and the pilot started guiding them out. A Dutch frigate fell into line behind them, they were taking no chances.

Chapter 5: Escape and Evade

Marty unpinned the gold tiger and fiddled with the pin. A sliver of steel came loose with a click and fell into the palm of his hand. He then took off his star of the Order of the Garter, and another slightly wider sliver with a ninety-degree bend at one end came loose. Last, he undid the ribbon that tied his hair back in a navy cue, unwrapped a thin wire from around it, then dug into the cue with his fingers and removed a two-inch-long section of razor that had resin along the sharp edge to protect it. All of which were stowed about his person where they could be reached at a moment's notice. He expected someone to steal his honours at some time but now he was armed and equipped with the means to escape.

A week passed during which he was treated well enough, but now the door opened, and the blue uniforms of French soldiers could be seen outside. One entered the room and put a pair of manacles on his wrists, locking them with a key, which he handed to a cavalry officer.

They marched him outside into bright sunlight, which dazzled him after the gloom of his room. A carriage was waiting, and he was pushed inside, the officer entering behind him.

The coach set off and Marty could hear that there were at least four horses behind them. The officer sat comfortably across from him with a pistol cocked and pointing straight at him.

"You don't look like your reputation," he observed.

"And what am I supposed to look like?" Marty asked.

"Some sort of superman, if I were to believe the Department, an ogre who eats children and assassinates ministers and ambassadors."

"That would be the Department for Internal Affairs," Marty stated with a sneer, *"They have always been prone to exaggeration. Little grey men with little grey matter."*

The lieutenant laughed and relaxed a little.

"They mean to guillotine you in front of Notre Damme," he taunted.

"Well, it's a picturesque spot. There are worse places to lose your head," Marty quipped then snuggled down to get some sleep.

They stopped at a hotel in Vianen just South of Utrecht where they left Marty shackled to a bedpost in a third-floor room with the youngest of his escort as guard. He had gotten the short straw and had to stay in the room as his companions ate and drank in the bar all evening.

At two in the morning, Marty's eyes opened, he stayed still and listened for several minutes. The guards breathing was steady and deep from the chair he sat in near the fire that had burnt down to embers. Marty fiddled with his cuffs and after a few seconds, they were placed on the carpet without a clink.

The guard died, his jugular expertly severed, and any noise stifled by a pillow held over his face. Marty assumed there would be at least one more guard outside the door, so he ignored that.

The window was unlocked, and he climbed out and down onto the stable roof, finding finger and toe holds between the bricks where the mortar had crumbled. He crept along to the far end of the stables where there was a hoist sticking out with a rope attached that he used to slip into the hay loft.

He checked the horses and decided against them, it would be too conspicuous to be seen riding a horse with French tack. However, he needed to delay the pursuit, so he went through their tack cutting girth straps and reins. He removed the stirrups and bits, dropping them down the well in the yard as he passed it on his way out.

A good night for a walk, he thought and headed Northwest steering by the stars towards, he hoped, the coast and the Hague. After just a mile, he came upon a river, *rivers flow to the sea,* he thought and followed its banks.

At dawn, he found a large weeping willow whose branches hung down to the water and settled down under it to rest. He had plenty of water and the remnants of the supper they had served him the night before to eat.

He removed his coat and looked regretfully at the pinholes where his honours were taken by the French lieutenant, who also took his gold buttons and buckles from his shoes. He would settle accounts with him if they ever met again.

Fed and relatively comfortable, he settled down for the day. He had lived on meagre rations before, so the prospect of going short didn't bother him. What would have been better was a fire. As it was, he just wrapped himself in his coat and slept.

He was awoken by the sound of voices. He could just see the sun through the leaves of the willow surrounding him, and he guessed it was mid-afternoon. He crawled carefully forward.

There coming down the bank, were the French, and they were searching every nook and cranny. He had to move and find a better hiding place. He slipped out from the cover of the tree, being careful to keep it between him and the soldiers. He scurried across the field and down into a deep drainage ditch that ran perpendicular to the river. There was a network of these ditches crisscrossing the fields, which made good, if muddy, cover.

He followed the ditch and could hear the French calling to each other.

They were getting closer.

He continued along the ditch, trying hard not to make unnecessary noise or leave footprints that could give him away until he came upon a culvert. These occurred wherever the farmers needed to bridge the drainage ditch from one field to the next and rather go to the expense of building a bridge they built a low tunnel out of brick and filled in above it with earth to create a crossing point.

He decided he had no choice and crawled in, it was tight he only just fit, luckily the water was only a couple of inches deep.

He could hear hoofbeats coming closer, a soldier was following the ditch.

He held his breath.

The hoofbeats crossed above him and stopped.

He waited, his pistol would be useless, the priming and charge would be sodden. If the soldier stepped down, he would be done.

There was a scrabbling noise as the Frenchman slid down the steep bank of the ditch and a splash as he hit the water.

"Shit! Fucking Dutch and their fucking ditches!" he shouted. There was a laugh from further away.

"My boots are full of water!"

Marty kept his face lowered and winced as a spear tip narrowly missed impaling his arm as the soldier shoved it into the culvert. The spear was withdrawn, and Marty braced himself for another thrust but with more swearing and shouts at his horse to back up, the Frenchman climbed out of the ditch.

Marty waited for another hour, getting colder and colder. His limbs would hardly move when he decided it was safe to come out. He tried to go forward but discovered that the culvert got narrower, he had to go out backwards.

He had gotten his legs clear when someone grabbed his ankles and roughly dragged him out. He was exhausted but tried to turn himself to defend against the attack he was sure was coming.

As he rolled on his back, he looked up into the smiling face of a Dutch farmer and the curious face of a Dutch Shepherd dog.

"U verbergt zich van die Franse Bastards. Nou, ze zijn verdwenen en je ziet eruit alsof je wat hulp nodig hebt," the man said.

Marty caught, 'French bastards,' and, 'hulp.' He smiled up at the man and sat.

"Yes, I am running from the French bastards. I am English."

"Oh, ho ho. Kom met me mee, we zullen je droog en gevoed krijgen."

Marty heard 'droog,' which he knew meant dry, so he took the hand that was held out and let himself be pulled to his feet.

The farmer, who introduced himself as Joss, helped him up the bank and out of the ditch. Marty noticed he wore wooden shoes with thick socks that squelched now they were waterlogged. They walked across the fields to a farmhouse, where they were greeted by the farmer's wife, Thea, who fussed over him as the farmer told her how he had found him.

"Guus must have heard him in the culvert and stood there with his ears up and his front leg raised like when he sees something he isn't sure of," he told Thea. *"Then these legs appeared, and I pulled our fugitive out of the pipe."*

"He is the one the French have been looking for?" she asked as she handed Marty a blanket and a bucket of warm water to wash with.

"Neem al je kleren uit!" she instructed him and signed he should take all his clothes off.

"He must be. He is English and looks like a sailor," he replied then stopped and looked in surprise at the small pile of metal implements Marty piled on the table with the useless pistol and knife.

Marty stepped outside, stripped, and washed himself all over, even undoing his cue to rinse his hair. Clean, he wrapped himself in the blanket and went back into the kitchen.

There was a bowl of rabbit stew with dumplings steaming on the table and a loaf of fresh bread. Joss pointed to it and said, "Eten!" He poured a liquor from a stone bottle, and Marty immediately identified it as Corenwijn the lethal Dutch drink that was cross between gin and whiskey.

He sipped it and said, "Corenwijn. It's good!"

Joss laughed and reached forward to slap him on the shoulder.

"See, he knows some Dutch!"

Thea disappeared to the room, where Marty knew from Mrs. Jongeline's house, they slept. She returned with a pair of trousers, a shirt, socks, and wooden shoes, which Marty put on once he finished his meal.

He sat by the fire, warming himself and sipping his drink.

"I must get to den Hague," he told them, "I have friends there who can help me."

"He wants to go where?" Thea asked and made a sign that said she didn't understand.

Marty thought he heard Mrs. Jongeline call it something else. His memory coughed it up.

"Grawenhage!"

The two of them smiled as they understood.

"I will go and talk to Hogenboom in the morning and see what he suggests," Joss told his wife.

Marty stayed the night and made moves to leave first thing in the morning, but Thea made him understand he had to stay. Joss left before dawn and when he returned told her,

"Gerard has a cart leaving for Gouda with a cargo of cheese, he can take him as far as there. He has a little English from trading with them as well."

He took Marty to the farm of Peter Hogenboom. It was a walk of around a mile and a half and Marty was surprised at how comfortable the wooden shoes were. He learned they were called klompen.

Peter was a small man and ran a dairy farm of the typical red and tan cows the Dutch preferred. He made cheese with the milk and sold it in the cheese market in Gouda. He looked Marty over and judged that with his hair loose and the clothes from Joss and Thea, he could pass for a farmhand, as long as he kept his mouth shut.

Marty was grateful for any help he could get; the alternative being trying to stay away from the French and a visit with madam guillotine.

They set off; Marty sat beside Hogenboom on the driver's seat. After an hour, the taciturn man handed Marty the reins and let him drive while he nodded off to sleep.

The horse plodded along and seemed to know where it was going, so Marty let it set its own pace. Around mid-morning, it stopped and no matter what Marty did, it wouldn't move. He was just getting cross with it when he heard a chuckle from beside him.

Hogenboom reached under the seat and pulled out a sack with bread, cheese, and sausage. He divided it up and passed a portion over to Marty. It was lunchtime. The horse got a nose bag of oats and was happy.

They entered Gouda in the middle of the afternoon, and Marty helped unload the cheeses onto a strange sled-like contraption. He was surprised when two men dressed in some kind of uniform and straw hats picked up the sled by looping the straps that were attached to either end over their shoulders and slinging it between them.

In that fashion, the entire cargo was unloaded quickly and efficiently. Hogenboom talked to some other farmers and eventually came back to Marty with another man.

"This is Mijneer van Stavast. He will take you to Grawenhage. Can you find your own way from there?"

"Yes, I know where to go once I get to the edge of town," Marty assured him.

"You English must beat the French; Napoleon and his Empire must go. Whatever our so-called King says, the Dutch people would be pleased to help!" he told Marty in parting and shook his hand.

The next leg of his trip was uneventful. There was no sign of the French and Marty doubted they would recognize him if they did encounter them.

He left his ride on the edge of the town, skirted around to the North, and headed to Mrs. Jongeline's home.

He approached it cautiously from the back of the house across the fields. There was smoke coming from the chimney and all seemed peaceful.

He climbed the wall surrounding the orchard behind the house and his feet had just hit the ground when a brown and black brindled blur shot out of the house and headed straight for him.

Blaez hit him in the chest with his front paws at a dead run, knocking him on his back. His face was washed by a long-wet tongue as the big dog pinned him to the ground, absolutely ecstatic he was back.

He finally got Blaez to let him sit up and looked around to see all the Shadows standing around him, grinning.

"I think he's gorn native," John Smith observed, "he's even wearin' them wooden shoes!"

"Suits him though," Wilson chipped in, "He always said he came from humble stock.

More comments followed; Marty knew it was just an expression of their relief that he was back with them.

Matai finally brought the banter to a halt when he said, "Mrs. Jongeline was told by a friend of hers that there is a squad of French cavalry out looking for someone and is patrolling up and down the coast. They are getting help from local Dutch army units."

Marty frowned, "I'm not surprised they guessed I would head for the sea. We need to deal with them; their lieutenant has some things that are very dear to me."

They'd brought a spare set of clothes for Marty, including his weapons harness and calf-length lace up boots.

Blaez, Marty decided, had developed a cocky strut to his walk. He stood taller, chest out, and had a 'I'm the man!' attitude about him. He mentioned it to Matai.

"Yes, he thinks he's the top dog since he mated with that bitch a couple of weeks ago. He's even more aggressive to other male dogs and struts around the place like he owns it."

"Was it successful?" Marty asked hopefully.

"So I was told. They did it four or five times, and they locked together every time. It was really funny watching him try and walk after he got loose with all his bits in the wrong place. Now she is behaving differently and won't let him near her."

"Sounds good then." Marty grinned happily.

"Oh, by the way, we heard the French have put a reward on your head," Matai chipped in.

"Really?" Marty exclaimed in surprise, "how much?"

"Ten thousand Louis," Matai grinned.

"Phew!" Marty breathed.

They left Mrs. Jongeline with a promise to return for the puppy in around fourteen weeks and made their way towards Scheveningen. The French had guessed that the fishing port or a part of the coast near it would be an ideal place for Marty to try and leave Holland. They enlisted the help of some local mounted troops and there were patrols running along the coast day and night.

The boys told Marty that the Hornfleur and Eagle were patrolling along the coast from Scheveningen to Noordwijk ready to pick them up. They'd designated pickup points and times and all they needed to do was be in the right place at the right time and they were home free.

Marty, however, wanted the French lieutenant, and even more, he wanted his stuff back. So, they hatched a plan to turn the hunters into the hunted using Marty as bait.

They let it be known, through their local contacts, that Marty made it to the coast and was seen heading for the beach North of Scheveningen at Wassenaar. That was close enough to attract the French but not so close as to make it easy.

They wanted to isolate the French troops, so they let it be known to the troops patrolling further North that Marty was heading for Zandvoort. The reward did the rest.

Two nights later, a lonely figure exited the dunes from the direction of Wassenaar and waved a lantern back and forth, which could be seen for miles along the beach as well as out to sea.

The French saw it and raced along the beach to intercept Marty before he could be picked up. He let them get to about half a mile and ran for the dunes, getting there just before they did.

Marty dodged down between two dunes, the drum of the horse's hooves loud in his ears, at the end, he turned almost ninety degrees left and carried on running. His breathing was getting laboured and his muscles were burning as he threw himself over a discoloured patch of sand in front of him. The French whooped as they saw him on the ground and spurred forward.

A shout went up and two poles were hauled up from where they lay across the path, pulling up a fishing net between them and Marty. The horses skidded to a stop, confronted with what looked like an impenetrable barrier.

The riders, knowing it was a trap, spun their mounts and spurred them back the way they came only to find that blocked as well. Shots rang out, and men fell, panicked horses reared and crashed into each other, spilling their riders and trampling them under their hooves.

In the end, one man was left standing, holding his sabre as the barriers dropped, allowing the horses to get away.

Marty faced the French lieutenant, who looked around at the remnants of his command, who were bleeding out into the sand.

"I believe you have some things that belong to me," he said as he walked forward sword in one hand and a pistol in the other.

The Lieutenant looked at him and sneered in the absolute conviction that no sailor could match a chasseur with a sword, *"Why don't you came and take them, sailor boy."*

Marty gave him his wolf grin,

"Off your dead body or alive- makes no difference to me."

"For the record, my name is Francis du Bastille, and I am going to claim the ten thousand by presenting your severed head to Napoleon himself."

"You talk too much!" said Marty and shot him right through the heart.

Matai returned with the lieutenant's horse. They were well trained and stopped running once they got to a quieter place. The reins were knotted, and the saddle had no stirrups, a quick search recovered Marty's things from the saddlebags.

They were waiting at the designated pickup point

"I was tired, alright!" Marty snapped in exasperation at yet another joke about his shooting the lieutenant.

"Typical French, though," said John Smith, "Only one of them would bring a sword to a gunfight."

Marty bit his lip and resisted the temptation to say anything more.

Chapter 6: I am a mole and I live in . . .

"It was a complete setup," Marty swore as he paced angrily back and forth across Hood's office. "The offer was never going to be accepted and I was sent to put me in the hands of the French."

"Are you accusing George Canning?" Hood asked, looking shocked.

"No, not him, but someone close to him. He suspected there was a leak, didn't he?" Marty replied after a pause.

"Yes, he was worried the French would hear that you were going to make the offer."

Marty paced and thought, his face a mask of concentration.

"We need to know who came up with the idea and if he put it to Canning himself or got someone else to," Marty concluded and plopped himself down into one of the chairs.

"Then we need to ......"

As far as the Foreign Office were concerned, Marty and his ship were on their way back to Gibraltar. The Formidiable was indeed on her way back but with Ackermann in charge, Marty and the Shadows stayed in London.

Marty launched an investigation without informing Canning, with Hood's blessing, as they concluded that whoever the mole was, he had to be close to him. They had identified several people who could be in a position to leak information to the French but only three of them were privy to the Dutch mission, so they concentrated on them.

Antton and Chin Lee were following their target as he walked down Drury Lane towards a notorious, high-class brothel. He was a well-dressed man, in fact, a little foppish, dressed fashionably and carrying a silver topped cane that Antton suspected concealed a blade.

Chin followed from behind, dressed as a Chinese laundry worker and scuttled along carrying a bundle of clothes. Antton was ahead, carrying out the more difficult forward tail.

They had followed him for a week now and learned enough that they stopped following their other suspects to concentrate on him.

The person being followed was Sir Henry Bloomfield, a junior secretary in the foreign office with direct access to Canning. They discovered that he had exotic tastes and a lifestyle that was more lavish than his income should be able to support.

He was a regular visitor to the brothel where he preferred young boys as his companions. The Shadows had marked him for that as they detested people who preyed on children.

Bloomfield entered the establishment and was greeted by the doorman by name. Antton was about to follow him, approaching from the opposite direction, when he spotted another man who looked suspicious. He waited.

The man, dressed in black trousers and tailed jacket, wore a hat that reminded Antton of those worn by men in Paris. Curious, he held back to let him enter first.

Once inside, Antton went straight through to the back and into a lounge that was reserved for the Madam and her close associates. There he found Marty drinking tea and chatting to a buxom blond dressed in a fine dress that was just a little too low cut and blousy.

Marty looked up and asked,

"Is he here?"

"Yes, and I think there may be someone here to see him."

Marty raised an eyebrow and looked at the madam,

"Rose, can we look into his room?"

"Yes, of course you can, all our rooms have spy holes. I hope you remember that I'm only doing this for my sister!" Rose replied sulkily.

"Of course!" Marty replied. He recognized the family resemblance between Rose and Delphia Truelove, the mistress of Admiral Duckworth in Jamaica. She had made the mistake of having a loose mouth about Marty that almost got him killed and he used that leverage to persuade Rose to cooperate.

Rose led them through a dark corridor, lit only by a lamp she carried, which had regularly spaced teardrop shaped covers that could be pivoted to uncover spy holes. She got to the one they were interested in, waved at Marty to help himself then shuttered the lamp plunging them into darkness.

He gently pulled the cover to one side and put his eye to the hole. Bloomfield sat on the bed and had his arm around a half-naked boy of around fifteen years, but he was talking to someone else. Marty tried to see who it was, but he was just out of his field of view. He could, however, hear what they were saying.

"The trap in Holland failed. We caught him but the incompetent idiots they sent to escort him back to France

let him escape and then got themselves slaughtered," reported the unknown man in Parisian French.

"I did my part and set it up, it's not my fault your people screwed up. I still want my money," Bloomfield replied, stroking the boy's hair.

"You will get it. Where is Stockley now?"

"On his way back to Gibraltar. They left a week ago. Is there really a ten thousand Louis reward on his head?"

"Yes,"

"I have an idea your people may be interested in."

"For the reward?" the unknown man sneered.

"For a fee, and if you catch him, the reward," Bloomfield smiled.

"If the idea is workable."

"His family is in Gibraltar; we get him sent on a mission that takes him away on a fool's errand and kidnap them while he is away."

"You can do that? Doesn't Canning need to approve it?"

"Oh yes he should, but I can send a mission request to Ridgley, the local man, that looks like it came from Canning and he will pass it on. Canning need never know it was sent."

Marty had to hold on to his temper as he heard that, his fists clenched, and veins popped up on his forehead.

"We can get a team into Gibraltar from Algeciras disguised as workers," the mystery man stated. *"I assume once we have them, we force him to give himself up to us?"*

"That would be the plan, but I don't care if you let them go or slaughter the bitch and her brats once you have him," Bloomfield spat.

"What have you got against her?"

"My half-brother Rufus was her lover, and she spurned him. The bastard Stockley killed him in a duel."

Marty's eyebrows shot up and he almost said something in surprise. That was when he was seventeen and met Caroline for the very first time!"

"Rufus Arbuthnot was your half-brother?"

"My mother was widowed and married again; I was born to her second husband. I swore to avenge his death and when Canning replaced Wickham, I saw my chance. He was Wickham's protégé as much as he is Hood's and I couldn't get to him then, but Canning is new to this and easily led as are his inner circle."

Marty sat in Hood's office with the Admiral and Canning.

"You started a bloody investigation without consulting me?" Canning swore in anger and embarrassment at Marty's frank report that they had been investigating his department for over a month. "You presume too much!"

"Calm down, George," Hood barked in his Admiral's voice, causing a look of surprise on the offended man's face, "We couldn't be sure who or where in your office the traitor was. As it is, he sits just outside your inner circle."

Canning's look of surprise at Hood's tone and the news that they knew who the traitor was, turned him thoughtful.

"Does he now! And his contacts?"

"We have a watch on the man he met at the brothel and intend to identify any people he works with, whether he has more contacts, or a network of informants. We can either sweep them all up and dump them in the Thames or you can use the informants to feed false information to the French. In which case, we will simply identify them and leave the rest to you."

"Now, that is an interesting idea; I have just the man to run something like that," Canning thought out loud, "Why don't we proceed on that basis for now. We can always 'sweep them up' as you say later. Now, what about this planned move against your family?"

Marty looked thoughtful. He was thinking what Caroline would want him to do. He knew that as much as he disliked the idea, she would not want him to stop it for her sake.

"We let it go ahead," he stated flatly. "If we stop it now, we would blow the whole operation. In any case, we can use this to see how they get over the border and if we let one get away, follow him back to their base in Algeciras."

"Not to mention, we will eliminate a whole group of their agents in the process," Hood chipped in.

Marty borrowed the Bethany to get the team back to Gibraltar via Scheveningen to pick up the new puppy. A robust, feisty little fellow he named Troy. Blaez took to him immediately, and the two played happily together. Marty was amazed at how gentle Blaez was, even when Troy nipped his ears with needle sharp milk teeth.

They sailed in to Rosia bay having made good time to see the Formidiable at anchor. Marty first called in at the barracks to see what was afoot. Old Will, the mess steward, informed him that the Eagle and Alouette were out delivering an agent into Northeast Spain and making a nuisance of themselves respectively. Will also informed him that the Hornfleur was in Malaga picking up the marine instructors.

There were around thirty marines still in the base commanded by Sergeant Bright, including the Tool Shed. He picked up his correspondence from his desk and walked to the family home with Blaez and Troy in close attendance.

It was all quiet as he walked in, and he paused. It was unnaturally quiet. His stomach tensed, and he quietly put the letters on the table in the hall and drew his left-hand pistol.

He stepped quietly forward. Blaez picked up on his tension and went on to alert, slinking forward with his belly close to the ground, senses high. The puppy sat and watched with his head tilted. He moved up to the door to the drawing room and listened.

He looked at Blaez, who was watching the door with his head to one side, hackles slightly raised. He reached out, wrapped his hand around the doorknob, and slowly turned it. The latch came free, he gently opened the door a crack, and looked through. He couldn't see anybody, so he eased it open a little more and stepped into the room.

He smelled something; he wasn't sure what it was, but it was vaguely familiar. The room was empty.

Caroline's latest needlepoint project on the table looked abandoned.

He took a deep breath to steady himself and crossed the room to the door to the parlour. It was slightly ajar, and he could hear someone moving around quietly.

Blaez was sniffing something in a basket on the other side of the room. Marty looked at him, distracted for a second, and the door opened.

Tabetha stepped through, threw up her hands, and screamed as she saw a man with a pistol standing in front of her. She then realized it was Marty and cajoled him in her rich Jamaican accent,

"What you doin', Massa?! Creapin' around wid date gun? You scared me half to death!!" She looked across at Troy, who was pulling a cloth from the basket watched by Blaez.

"And you get away from those dirty nappies, you disgustin' dogs!"

Caroline appeared making shushing noises, but it was too late. The twins woke up and burst into full-voiced howls.

Marty looked into the parlour and saw a harassed Marie picking up Constance, Amara held Edwin.

"We just got them off to sleep!" Caroline scolded him, then saw Troy, "You got the puppy!"

Marty grinned and put his pistol back inside his jacket, and knowing he just ducked a scolding, walked over and took Edwin from Tabetha. The baby immediately quieted, gave Marty a big smile, gurgled, and went to sleep.

"Well really!" Caroline huffed, and picked up the puppy to get to know it.

Later, when family equilibrium had been restored, Marty sat with Caroline in the drawing room.

"I was going to let them use us as bait to trap the French, but I will write to Hood and tell him I have changed my mind," Marty concluded after he explained to Caroline the plan.

"Why?" she asked in surprise.

"When I got home and it was so quiet, I was suddenly terrified you had all been taken," he confessed.

"Love, we know they are coming and where from. We can move the children to James' house and secure them there," she suggested.

"That won't work. They will watch the house before they move. Better we make a secure room the children can be moved into when the attack comes. But I think it's still too big a risk," he responded.

"Well, I don't!" she told him firmly, "as long as the children are protected the risk to me is manageable. Every member of this household can defend themselves and we have extra marines on guard. We make the house a fortress and too risky for them to try and me an easier target."

Marty looked at her in wonder. She was beautiful, brave, strong, and determined. He was such a lucky man!

"Alright, we will stick with the plan," he agreed, then shuddered as a chill ran down his back.

Chapter 7: The best laid plans

No warning came for the next month and Marty was beginning to think the French had given up on the idea. Then he got orders to sail.

"They want us to take the Flotilla up to the French/Spanish border at Cerbère and try to intercept a shipment of arms the French are supposed to be sending to Barcelona. This would conveniently empty the base of almost all the marines and remove me and the Shadows from the peninsula," Marty told the assembled officers and Ridgley. "We can assume that they will be watching for us to leave, so we will make a show of preparing and embarking."

"Where will we drop you and the team off?" Wolfgang Ackermann asked.

"As soon as we get around the other side of the peninsula, we will return by Sandy Bay," Marty answered.

He was reassured that his men felt the same as him, that this was a ruse to get them out of Gibraltar and that he was making the right call. The marine contingent on guard at the house were on the alert and all the staff armed. They were as ready as they could be.

"We sail on the next tide."

The weather made getting the Flotilla out of Rosia bay and around Europa Point a lot slower than usual. But every cloud brings a silver lining, and the lousy weather effectively concealed the boat that brought Marty and the Shadows ashore.

They had just left the beach when a figure appeared and ran towards them. It was Tom, he almost fell as he rushed up to them and cried out,

"They got Caroline and Josee!"

"What? How the fuck did that happen?" Marty shouted in shock.

Tom stopped in front of them and caught his breath.

"They ambushed them about halfway between the base and the house, killed the escort, and grabbed the women. Caroline got off a shot, which alerted us. But by the time we got there, they were gone."

Marty realized they had been duped. The French never planned to attack the house and his children were never the target. It had been Caroline all the time. It was like India all over again but this time he was up against determined professionals, not a bunch of amateurs.

"Matai, Antton, Garai - get over the border and see if you can find where they have been taken. They either left Gibraltar through the border or by boat to Algeciras, so you should be able to pick up their trail."

The rest of them headed back to base where Marty found Billy Hooper, who had taken to hanging around old Will's kitchen where he could scrounge food and keep warm.

"Go and get Frances Ridgley and tell him its urgent," Marty told him and flipped him a shilling.

When Francis arrived, he told him what happened and that they should expect a message to be sent by some means or another. Then he started making preparations for all the contingencies he could imagine. One thing he was certain of, he would get the girls back and the

French would pay. Oh, and when he got his hands on Bloomfield. . .

A note was found by a guard, pinned to the doors of the base two days later addressed to Captain Stockley. It was left in the dead of night and the sentries saw nothing.

'If you want your women to be freed, you are to come by boat to the Torre de l'Almirante at midday on the 15th of the month where you will surrender yourself to us in exchange for your wife and her companion. The boat must only have a minimum crew sufficient to row it.'

"Short and to the point, the 15th is in two days," Francis observed.

"This was written by an Englishman; can we assume that our bird in Canning's office has flown?" Marty pondered and then determinedly, "We can assume that whoever is behind this has thought out their plan carefully. The rendezvous is an old fortified tower on a deserted beach with sight lines in all directions. It will be almost impossible for a team to get close enough to affect a rescue without being seen."

"We only have two days; what do you want to do?" Francis asked, concern in his eyes.

Marty looked at him and Francis was surprised to see he had a confident look.

"Get my wife and Josee back," Marty replied grimly.

It was a five-mile row across the Bay from Rosia to the Torre and the six-man crew of the barge was silent.

Marty was left to his thoughts as he steered, and he wondered at the mind behind the trap that was set.

The beach approached, and Marty got ready. He was wearing his working uniform, hair clubbed at the nape of his neck. He carried his dress sword but was otherwise unarmed. He decided on wearing shoes rather than his lace-up boots as he didn't know whether Bloomfield knew about their secrets. He wasn't taking any risks with Caroline or Josee's lives.

He could see the Torre behind the beach, which sloped up from the shore to a range of dunes. A glint of sunlight on a lens told him someone was watching from the top of the tower. There were eight blue uniformed soldiers stationed on top of the dunes nearest the beach in a large arc effectively isolating it.

A reception committee stood in a group above the high-water mark consisting of three civilians flanked by two Army officers and behind them a squad of six soldiers surrounding Caroline and Josee.

Marty's analytical mind quickly assessed the situation: *The two end soldiers on the dunes are too far away for an accurate shot with the French musket. That leaves the six in between, of which the centre four are the biggest threat. The six on the beach around the girls are all carrying muskets with bayonets fitted – not good. The two officers have swords, no pistols visible. The civilians look unarmed, but I must assume that at least one is carrying a pistol.*

The boat ground up onto the sand, and the bow men jumped out to steady it. Marty moved to the bow and jumped onto the sand without getting his feet wet. He took a moment and looked around at the landscape; the dunes were studded with scrubby clumps of Lyme grass, which presented very little cover if any. The beach was empty in both directions.

He looked up the beach to where Caroline and Josee stood surrounded by their escort. He smiled and nodded to them as he walked up toward the high-water mark.

"Stop there, Captain," Sir Henry Bloomfield commanded and when he complied, one of the officers stepped forward and searched him.

Not very thorough, Marty thought. They even left him his sword. Bloomfield stepped forward as the officer stepped back, a pistol appeared in his hand, which he held competently.

"If it were up to me, I would blow your brains out here and now then cut your bitch of a wife's throat, however, my French friends want to spend some time questioning you. I suspect their methods will be somewhat brutal, so I will have to satisfy myself watching you suffer," he gloated.

"When did you know we identified you as the traitor?" Marty asked, ignoring the tirade.

"You fools thought we were totally unaware of your men. We knew who and what you were from the time you arrived in England. You can flatter yourself that the whole operation was just to get you here. The French really want to get their hands on you."

That was a surprise! They had played Canning and Hood just to get their hands-on him and sacrificed a well embedded agent.

"The Dutch trap?"

"Not my idea; it was doomed to failure and I knew I would be exposed. My plan is fool proof. I know there is nothing you won't do to protect your wife."

He gestured with the gun. "Now, if you will step forward, we will exchange you for the women."

Marty's shoulders slumped and his head bowed a little as he stepped forward. The squad of soldiers pushed the women down the beach towards him, two split off and escorted them at bayonet point past Marty towards the boat. Caroline held out a hand, her face anguished as her man was surrounded by the other four and marched up the sand.

Caroline was surprised as she reached the boat. She didn't recognize any of the men manning it. Not a single one. One of the bow men stepped forward and scooped her up in his arms to lift her and as he did, said in an educated accent,

"Please be ready to drop into the bottom of the boat, Lady Caroline."

She looked closely at his face and realized it was York, Collingwood's flag lieutenant dressed as a common sailor. He winked at her as he passed her to a sailor waiting on board.

Josee followed and the two women moved to the centre of the boat.

She looked towards the shore and a movement caught her eye up in the dunes. The middle four soldiers who had been standing guard crumpled as what looked like clumps of grass rose up and enveloped them. At the same time, two dark figures rose up out of the sand behind the group on the beach, swords held in both hands, which whirled in dazzling arcs as they dispatched the two officers. The four outer soldiers on the dunes raised their rifles but only the outside two got a shot off as the inner two fell forward with broad headed spears in their backs.

Marty seemed to stumble, causing the two soldiers behind him to close up and the two in front to be a step ahead. His hands went to his hair, then flicked forward. The two leading men cried out as pencil-like darts embedded themselves in the nape of their necks. They stiffened and collapsed to the floor, quite immobile. The darts were tipped with a poison that Shelby told him was called Curare and paralyzed the victim in seconds.

Caroline felt something being pressed into her hand and realized it was one of her Manton pistols. She didn't hesitate; she cocked it as she lifted it into firing position and shot one of her former escorts, who was trying to bring his musket to bear. The other flew backwards as he took three pistol balls in the chest fired by York and two of the other 'sailors.'

Marty spun to face the soldiers behind him. There was a shot closely followed by another. A red rose bloomed in the centre of one's chest and the face of the other exploded as a ball took him directly on the nose.

Chin Lee and Antton stood with their swords at the throats of the French agent and Bloomfield. Marty looked for the two remaining soldiers on the dunes. They were gone, whether they were dead or had run, he didn't care.

They were met by the Flagship's pinnace a half mile offshore, which was a relief as the barge was overcrowded and overloaded by the addition of Marty, the Shadows, and four of Sam's African brothers. It was 'lucky' there were only six rowers rather than the usual eight in the first place. Bloomfield and the Frenchman were laid out in the bottom of the boat under the girl's feet.

Once the men redistributed themselves between the two boats, the trip back to Gibraltar was faster than the trip across as all eight oars were manned in the barge.

York, who sat on a thwart holding a pistol over the prisoners, answered Caroline's question on how he came to be there.

"Oh, that's quite simple. When Captain Stockley informed the Admiral that you were taken, I jumped at the chance to have a bit of action rather than being the Admiral's messenger boy. In fact, all the crew are officers from the Flagship." He looked at his hands. "Didn't bank on having to row though. This is a damn heavy boat for just six oars. It will take a week for the blisters to heal."

One of the prisoners moved, and York immediately pointed his pistol at him.

"Stay still. Captain Stockley has instructed me to shoot you in the gut if you try anything."

"I'm lying in four inches of water," complained Bloomfield.

Caroline stamped on his leg. "You are lucky it's not four inches of blood."

Bloomfield groaned in pain and shut up.

Back at Rosia bay, they were met by Ridgley, Admiral Smith, and Admiral Collingwood, who brought a marine escort for the prisoners.

Smith, who'd just arrived and heard the news was full of questions. Marty put him off until everyone was safely on shore and they had returned to the house.

Drinks were served with a buffet dinner in the drawing room for all the officers. The ladies were reunited with the children and took long relaxing baths.

"So, fill me in! What happened?" Sir Sidney demanded around a tongue sandwich.

"Well, we snuck the Shadows and a few other useful men off the Formidiable before we heard the ladies were taken," Marty explained. "Once we got the note, Antton and Chin Lee went over the border and scouted out the area around the Torre then came back and picked up the rest of the team. They had a plan and I just let them go with it.

From what they told me, they got into position before dawn. One of the marines used to be a gamekeeper in Scotland, they call them ghillies up there apparently, and he showed them how to use some hessian cotton sacks to make camouflage. The Africans were completely at home as they grew up sneaking up on enemies and animals back in Africa."

"So, they set up an ambush twelve hours before the exchange?" Smith said in astonishment. "Extraordinary! They were in place under the sand for all that time?"

"Yes, and they are all suffering from sand fly bites all over their bodies," Marty confirmed then continued, "The barge was manned by officers from the flagship. I was amazed they could collectively pull an oar, but they got it together after five minutes or so."

"We've all got blisters," chipped in York with a happy grin. He held out his hands, revealing the torn and blistered palms. "Worth it, though. Dashed exciting!"

Sidney shook his head. "It seems I am destined to be just too late for one of your adventures. One day, I will be there swinging a sword by your side."

Ridgley took charge of Bloomfield and the French agent, who they established was Louis Rufin. What was left of them would be transported back to England in chains after they had been interrogated in his soundproof room.

Chapter 8: Convoy

Marty received orders on the 14th of August to take the Flotilla along with a number of troop ships to Gothenburg. They were to collect nine thousand Spanish troops of the Northern Division that had secretly rebelled against Napoleon and deliver them to Santander. He was disappointed to have to leave as his friend Arthur Wellesley was due to arrive at any time to take command of a joint British and Portuguese force under the overall command of General Sir Hew Dalrymple. He had the feeling he would be missing something rather historic.

The puppy grew like a weed and was showing it could be just as aggressive as Blaez in defence of its pack, having bitten a delivery man who tried to pat young James on the head. Marty gave the man a guinea for his pain as the dog left several holes in his forearm.

However, he had his orders and set off for the Downs where they would rendezvous with the thirty-seven-ship convoy. He was surprised they got the job but when he thought about it, this was just the kind of thing the Flotilla had been formed for. Doing jobs nobody else wanted.

They left the Hornfleur behind as she was needed to support the growing rebellions in Granada and Northern Spain. Marty's marine advisors were in great demand and actively involved in a number of covert operations against the French.

The voyage North was uneventful, and he settled back into life at sea in a day or so. The weather was fine, the winds steady, light and out of the Northwest, meaning they only made about two hundred miles a day. It would take at least seven days sailing to get to the Downs and another four days to Gothenburg.

The troop ships were all lined up waiting for them when they arrived at the Downs midday on the 18th. They were a mix of older Navy third or fourth rates that were degraded to transports and custom-built civilian craft that were hired in.

Never one to miss the opportunity to take on some fresh supplies, Marty sent his boats into Deal then called a captains meeting.

There were too many captains for his cabin, so he held the meeting on the deck. Most of the Navy types were midshipmen or lieutenants with undistinguished careers and little imagination but were good enough to command a transport. The most senior, Lieutenant Rochester of the Signet, was forty years old, had a perpetual sneer and a bad attitude, and clearly resented being told what to do by a boy captain, who probably got his promotion through interest.

Marty had done his homework; the list of commanders and captains were passed to him with his orders and had a fair idea of each of their records.

"Gentlemen, welcome to the Formidiable. I will keep this short. Our destination is Gothenburg, Sweden, where we will collect some nine thousand Spanish troops of Napoleon's Northern Division who have rebelled. We will deliver them to Santander.

We set sail tomorrow at first light when the tide will be right. I intend us to make an average of ten knots day and night. You will sail in three columns as described in my written orders"

There was a snort from the direction of Rochester. Marty zeroed in on him,

"You have something to say, Commander?" he asked, deliberately not using the title of captain.

Rochester bristled and replied,

"to keep formation all night, we will need to be showing lights and we are very close to the French coast, Sir." He made the "sir" sound like an afterthought.

Marty didn't bite. He expected minor challenges like this.

"Yes, I am aware of that and in my written orders, you will see that you are required to burn navigation lamps. The Formidiable will lead the formation and will burn a stern lamp; the Eagle and Alouette will not. We do not want a raider to know where the escorts are." Marty's look was very direct, as he continued, "If you are worried about being cut out by a French privateer, we can put you in the middle of the formation, but I was hoping with your excellent navigational skills, you would take the forward position of the centre column."

Rochester flushed as this was aimed at a comment in his file that, although he was a more than adequate navigator and had sailed the route around the North of Denmark before, he was considered shy when it came to combat or taking risks.

"No Sir, I will take my place at the head of the line," he replied with a scowl.

"Excellent!" Marty exclaimed as if this was the best news he heard all week. "Now, if we do encounter any privateers at night, there are a set of signals which give the escorts a steer to where they are. I expect you to have learned those by heart by the time we sail. My ships are faster and heavier armed than you would probably expect, and we are used to fighting at night." James and Ryan, who stood to either side and behind him grinned wolfishly at the room. There were several nods and speculative looks as many had noted the unusual ships in the Flotilla and their armament.

A grizzled civilian raised his hand. Marty nodded to him.

"Captain Harvey of the Belle," he introduced himself.

"Just want to be clear that you intend running the same sail by night as by day?"

Marty had expected this as well. Merchantmen were notorious for reducing sail at night.

"We need to be in Gothenburg by the 23rd at the latest and to do that, we need to do the run from here in four days. I don't need to tell you that means we have to average ten knots and with only three escorts for your transports, we need to keep a tight formation."

"Sir, aren't the Spanish allied with the French?" Simon Allbright of the Angela asked.

Marty realized they probably weren't up to date with the latest situation on the peninsula.

"The latest development in the war with Napoleon has seen Spain occupied by the French, their King removed and replaced with one of Napoleon's brothers, Joseph. All of that has annoyed the Spanish people, who started a rebellion on the 2nd May. The Northern Division have rebelled, and our new allies will join the rebellion of other Spanish troops under General Joaquin Blake near Santander."

There was a rumble of muttered comments at this news and several smiles as they realized they would be making a difference.

They set sail as planned the next morning, and the transports shuffled into order reasonably quickly. He had placed the civilian ships in the centre, hoping the more disciplined Navy ships around them would keep them in formation.

It started out well, each of the ships a cable apart in their columns and each column two cables apart. Marty opted for a three-column formation with the Alouette positioned as the last ship in the centre column as rear guard. That would enable her to run up between the columns to support any ship that was attacked or round up any stragglers as required.

The Eagle would sail out to windward and range up and down the convoy, able to jump on any threats independently or in support of the Alouette.

Marty, in the Formidiable, was out in front providing the lead and setting the pace. If he thought Rochester could be relied upon, he would have let him lead but right now he didn't have confidence in the man.

Around four bells in the afternoon watch, a sail was spotted to the East. It came close enough to have a good look at the convoy then slid back out of sight. Marty signalled the Eagle and Alouette in their private code to be alert. The signal was passed down the line without the transports knowing what it said.

After dark, Marty looked back at the convoy and was pleased to see three lines of more or less evenly spaced lights. It was a clear night with some wispy clouds, which glowed in the three-quarter moon, blowing across from the Northwest. The stars were bright, and the milky way could be clearly seen spreading across the sky. It was the kind of night Caroline loved when she was at sea.

"Sail Ho!" called down the mainmast lookout who was significantly higher than any other lookout in the convoy.

Marty grabbed a night glass, slung it over his shoulder by its leather strap and headed up the mainmast. When he got up next to the lookout, Matthew, one of his African crewmen, pointed to where he saw the fleck of sail out the corner of his eye.

The view through the glass was upside down and back to front but Marty was used to that and compensated automatically. The sail appeared on his second sweep and it had the look of a sloop or corvette. It was running up close to the wind then tacked to run almost due West to cross behind them.

"He's trying to get the wind gauge," Marty observed.

Matthew assumed he was being talked to, so asked,

"he will pass close to the Alouette, won't he, Cap'ain?"

"Yes, and if I know James, he will give him a big surprise if he gets in range."

Marty watched as the strange sail closed on the rear of the convoy. He saw a flutter of sail from the end of the centre column then the Alouette dropped back, her mainsail in disarray as if she had a lubberly crew and they messed it up.

The stranger didn't bite and continued to head West. It was Ryan's problem now as James recovered control of his mainsail and resumed his position at the end of the central column.

"Keep a careful watch to the East," Marty admonished Matthew, fearing a trap.

"Aye, aye, Cap'ain," came the reply as he resumed his scan. Marty couldn't see the Eagle; it was somewhere out to the West. He wondered if they had seen him, but all he could do was wait.

He tracked the stranger with the night glass and saw the shape of his sails change as he swung to parallel them. He had to admire the audacity of a captain that would take on a convoy on as moonlit a night as this.

The sail shape changed again. He was starting a run in toward the Western column. Marty started as he thought he saw a shape coming up behind the stranger. He scanned again but he could see nothing and wondered if he had imagined it.

Then there was a flare of light as a rocket shot into the air followed closely by another from a point the other side of the strange ship. The sky lit up as the rockets burned bright white, illuminating both the stranger and the Eagle, which was a couple cables off his larboard beam.

"What the hell? Where did he get black sails from?" Marty exclaimed in surprise. He glanced at Matthew, who was diligently shading his eyes from the light of the flares and keeping his attention to the Eastern horizon.

The side of the Eagle lit up as they fired a full broadside into what Marty could see now was a corvette-style ship. The flash of the guns was so bright through the night glass that he was temporarily blinded in that eye and had to switch to the unaffected eye to follow the action.

More rockets shot into the air and burst into life and he could see that the stranger had suffered, her sails lost their definition and she looked to have damaged rigging. They opened up on the Eagle and when the sound reached him, he guessed they had nine-pound longs. The Eagle's side lit up again and now when the sound reached him, he heard a difference. They were firing cannister or grape? Then he heard the pop of swivels.

Dammit, are they boarding?

Dawn saw them somewhere to the North of Texel. The convoy was closing up into formation having drifted apart a little over night. The Eagle was stationed off the larboard column in line with the Formidiable, her prize following docilely behind. Marty watched as her black sails were changed one by one for regulation white ones without losing any speed.

That day and the following night, Marty noticed the convoy maintained a much better shape than before. Marty had the Formidiable drop back beside the Signet to hailing range and called across to Rochester.

"Captain, I would be obliged if you would take over the navigation from here to Gothenburg and lead us in. I will move the Formidiable out to the East."

Rochester shouted his understanding through a speaking trumpet and knew that Marty wanted to get earlier warning if they were approached from that side.

Marty put up a general signal of "HOLD STATION" then swung out beyond the Eastern column by around a mile.

The next three days passed without further contacts except for the odd merchant ship, which stayed well clear of the convoy, and they pulled into Gothenburg on time. The Baltic fleet were in port, and they saluted the flag, which ran up a signal with their number and 'Captain report on board.'

Admiral Keats received Marty in his cabin and introduced Don Pedro Caro y Soreda, Marquis de la Romana and Commander of the Spanish forces, and James Robinson, the British agent who organised the rebellion.

"I was sent by Mr. Canning, on the recommendation of Arthur Wellesley, to contact Don Pedro and arrange for his men to be picked up. Wellesley also recommended that you be put in charge of the convoy to take them to Spain."

"Did he, bedamned!" Marty exclaimed.

"Yes, he holds you in some esteem it seems," Robinson continued.

Admiral Keats hurumphed and interjected,

"we brought all nine-thousand off of Langeland by warship, but we need you to take them down to Santander. They made a mess of my ships just getting here."

Marty smiled sympathetically,

"Yes, I can imagine. I was at the evacuation of Toulon and it took weeks to get the ships straight after we dropped off the refugees."

He then turned to Don Pedro and said in Spanish,

"I am Captain Sir Martin Stockley, Baron of Candor, and am very pleased to meet you. I would like to offer you the comfort of my ship for the journey to Santander."

The Admiral and Robinson looked surprised and Robinson whispered a quick translation in his ear.

"Thank you, Sir Martin, I would be most grateful," the Don replied and bowed.

Marty bowed in reply then turned to Robinson.

"Will you be travelling down with us or will you stay here?"

"I will come with you; I was planning to be your interpreter, but I see that isn't required."

"An extra Spanish speaker is always welcome. It will be a slow journey down and something is bound to come up."

"We will embark the Spanish troops as soon as possible. Are all the ships provisioned?" Keats asked.

"Yes sir, they provisioned in England as they couldn't be sure there would be sufficient available here in Sweden," Marty confirmed then asked, "Can I ask if there are any cavalry?"

"There are but they've left their horses behind, thankfully," Keats replied.

Marty was more sympathetic; he knew the relationship that developed between a cavalryman and his horses and knew it must have been hard for them to leave them behind.

"Don Pedro, we will start embarking your men immediately, if you would accompany me to my ship, we can coordinate the operation from there."

They took their leave of a relieved Admiral Keats and returned to the Formidiable.

"She is Spanish built?" Don Pedro asked as the barge approached.

"Yes, she was captured in the Caribbean during the war," Marty replied, keeping a straight face.

Robinson looked concerned as he knew the story of how the Formidiable was captured - he was in England when it was announced in the Gazette. But Marty just carried on chatting to the Don and the subject soon passed.

Once aboard, the Don asked that messengers be sent to his officer cadre to summon them to a conference on the Formidiable. Midshipman Williams was summoned and put at the Don's disposal as liaison. He had a fair hand and wrote, as well as spoke, Spanish.

Three hours later, Marty's dining room had turned into a command centre and was the hub of the organisation for the transfer of the Spanish force. His boats were kept busy ferrying officers back and forth to the warships of the Baltic fleet, where many of the troops were still being accommodated, and in turn, their boats were employed to transfer the troops to the waiting transports.

It was a logistical nightmare in Marty's eyes and in his opinion, the Spanish could have made it easier, but in the end, all nine thousand were accommodated and they were ready to sail. Keats called Marty aboard the flagship one last time.

"I would like to congratulate you, Captain, on a job well done!" He toasted Marty over a glass of port, "The

Spanish were driving me insane; I have to admit. They are damn difficult and touchy to deal with."

Marty smiled sympathetically,

"I have a secret weapon," he confided, "a midshipman with a Spanish mother who took over the role of liaison officer. He smoothed over almost all the wrinkles and what he couldn't deal with, I did."

"And your title helped no end, what!" guffawed the highly amused Admiral.

Marty let that pass, the Admiral would think what he thought, and nothing he said would change it.

"You are a might under strength for an escort of such a big convoy. I will send the Thalia along with you, she's a thirty-six, captained by Arnold St. James. He's a fellow Dorset man, so you should get on famously."

They set sail on the next tide and slipped out of the Baltic back into the North Sea. Contrary to Admiral Keats expectation, Marty found St. James a cold fish. He was a few months junior to him on the list and came from a wealthy Bridport family. He had him to dinner one evening, and the conversation was stilted, strained, and boring.

The trip back was slower as they reduced sail every night to let the troops rest. So it was that they finally disembarked the troops on the eleventh of October, said goodbye to the transports and the Thalia and headed back to Gibraltar.

Chapter 9. Mongat

Marty got home in good time to organise the celebration of Caroline's birthday. He organised a ball with the cooperation of the new Governor, James Drummond, who saw the opportunity to lighten the mood as the war in the peninsula wasn't going that well for the allies.

Drummond replaced Dalrymple, who was recalled to England after the disastrous Convention of Cintra that allowed Juno to leave Portugal with all his troops on ships provided by the British. The Dowager, as he was being called, had not impressed the British and Portuguese governments and certainly not Arthur Wellesley, who he had overruled to sign the treaty. Napoleon was now heading into Spain with two hundred thousand seasoned veterans and would be hard to displace.

The Ball was held at the Governor's mansion and all the Flotilla's officers and senior warrants were invited. The tailors on the peninsula did a good trade in new suits and uniforms and the suppliers of food and wine profited enormously.

Security was tight and supplied by la Pierre's marines, two of the biggest of which acted as doormen and checked that everyone who entered had a genuine invitation. A wealthy merchant who left his invitation at home tried in vain to gain entry only to have to return to his home and find it before he was allowed in.

It was, to all accounts, a comical encounter as the marine was around six feet, four inches tall and went by the nickname of Lofty while the merchant was five feet, one and had the unfortunate surname of Smallbone. The merchant had resorted to shouting at Lofty, who stood at parade rest, looking down his nose at the unfortunate man as immovable as the rock he stood on.

Marty presented Caroline with her sword before the ball and she was stunned, overjoyed, and speechless. She made her appreciation clear when they finally got to bed, where he got to practice his own 'swordsmanship' extensively!

The winter passed quietly. The Flotilla kept busy using hit and run tactics along the coast of Spain and Southern France. Ridgley informed Marty that a group of rebel guerrillas in the Catalonia region sent word that there was a fortification near the coastal town of Mongat, which could cut the road from Girona to Barcelona, and thereby, hold up any French attempt at moving an army into the region.

Marty immediately sent the Eagle to find the leader of the guerrillas and set up a meeting. He followed as soon as possible with the Formidiable and Hornfleur. The weather gods smiled on them and they had reasonable winds all the way, making the trip in just under four days.

They rendezvoused just North of Barcelona and the Eagle's boat rowed over to the Formidiable. The man who accompanied Ryan up the side was not at all what Marty expected.

He was sharp-faced with close-cropped hair which exposed on old scar that ran across the top of his head from front to back. A second scar ran from the left side of his hooked nose to the corner of his jaw. He had gold rings in his ears and brown eyes that were so dark they looked almost black. He was dressed in a loose shirt with a bandana tied around his throat, tight trousers, a sash around his waist and knee-length boots.   There were a pair of pistols pushed into the waist sash and a rapier on his left hip. As he stepped on the deck, Marty noticed a knife in the top of one of his boots. He posed rather than stood while Ryan made the introductions,

"General Junqueras, may I present Captain Stockley. Captain, it is my pleasure to present General Juan Junqueras, leader of the local guerrilla force."

Marty took note that he called himself General as he looked more like a brigand and from the pose, wanted to be noticed and probably admired.

"General, it is a pleasure to meet you," Marty gave him his best wolf smile and held out his hand.

Junqueras had to shake hands or risk offending the officer in front of him. He looked carefully at the surprisingly young man and noted the well-made uniform that was functional rather than flashy, the way the jacket hung and the glimpse of a pistol butt inside it, the short sword with a well-worn hilt, and the callouses and scars on his hands that were from handling weapons not hauling on ropes. Junqueras decided this young man was to be respected and would watch him very carefully.

Junqueras led his men because he was the meanest son-of-a-bitch in the band and no one would challenge him. He knew as he looked at the Captain, he might have met his match.

The Captain led him down into a spacious cabin and he was invited to sit in a comfortable chair. A servant served him a glass of brandy. A big black man came in with a large dog and stood near the door, the dog lay in front of him and just watched. He recognised another fighter in the black man and decided he wouldn't want to face the dog either.

The Captain took off his jacket and tossed it onto an open chest full of weapons- long guns strapped to the lid, pistols and blades laid out in compartments in the body- all of which looked well cared for. He looked back at the Captain and could see he had not one, but two double-barrelled pistols clipped to a leather harness around his upper body as well as a sword on his left hip with a large knife balancing it on the right. He removed the pistols and sword, placing them on the desk before sitting in the other comfortable chair.

"General," Marty started the meeting after Captain la Pierre joined them, *"Our intelligence officer has informed us that you have identified a way to hold up the advance of the French towards Barcelona."*

Junqueras straightened a little at the use of the title,

"Yes Captain, there is a fortification that commands the road from Girona to Barcelona which the French have to pass to move into this part of Catalonia."

Ryan stepped over and handed Marty a map he had made after a short reconnaissance. It showed the fortification was about half a mile inshore and commanded the road. Notes, made by Ryan on the map, told him the terrain was very hilly and it would be difficult, if not impossible, to flank the position.

"Who holds this now?" Marty asked.

"Regular Spanish militia loyal to the Government," Ryan informed him.

"Traitors to Spain and toadies to the French," spat Junqueras. *"They will pay the price!"*

Marty knew how brutal the guerrillas could be when making their enemies 'pay the price' and knew that to keep the rebels on side, he would probably have to ignore whatever happened. He didn't like it, but necessity was a hard mistress.

"How many?" la Pierre asked, keeping the conversation on track.

"A reinforced platoon. They have a pair of small field pieces as well," Ryan replied and translated for the General.

"Does it have its own water source?" Marty asked, wondering whether a siege would work.

"I am told they have a well"

"Then we have to take it by assault," Marty concluded.

They moved to the dining table, where they could all see the map, and discussed the plan.

"Can't you just use your guns and blow them out of there?" asked Junqueras.

"We could, but that wouldn't leave you much of a fortification to defend," Marty answered with a smile.

"I think we can take this another way, what do you think Paul?"

The next morning about two hours before dawn, the Hornfleur's four whale boats slid up onto the beach with barely a sound. Marines scrambled over the side, dressed in dark clothes and faces blacked. Pathfinders set off while the rest formed up in squads and started inland.

Marty and the Shadows were landed around an hour before and in position just outside the perimeter wall of the fort. It was a half-moon, and by its light, they were watching the sentries walking the wall. The faintest of scuffs alerted them that the marines had arrived.

Marty persuaded Junqueras to leave the initial night assault to his men, once the wall had been taken the guerrillas could move in.

A shadow approached the wall and resolved into the shape of two men. One stood with his back against the wall while the other stepped into the cup then onto his shoulders. The climber waited until there was a low whistle, then reaching up and grabbing the top of the wall, silently pulled himself up and rolled over the top onto the shadowy walkway on the inside. Further down the wall, another figure slid over the top into the shadow under the parapet.

The sentries turned and walked back toward each other, their eyes on the ground outside the wall. Neither saw the dark shapes rise up behind them, garrottes in hand. They died silently.

The first two lowered ropes, and the rest of the Shadows shimmied up. Next were the marines and right behind them, the guerrillas. The combined force spread out. The first up were already dealing with the sentries further around the perimeter wall.

A militiaman left the barracks for a late-night piss and came face to face with a young guerrilla, which was unfortunate as unlike a marine, the guerrilla hesitated.

"ALARM, ALARM, INTRUDERS," the militiaman screamed, which turned into a wet gurgle as a broad-bladed spear emerged from the centre of his chest. Sam placed his foot on the dead man's back and pulled the spear free as he looked at the immobile, young Spaniard. He shook his head. The Spaniard was only a kid. Sam turned away leaving the boy looking down at the dead man.

All hell broke loose as the militia woke and grabbed their weapons. What should have been a relatively simple operation dissolved into a messy hand-to-hand fight. Marty swore and turned toward the door of the barracks, pistols in hand as men came boiling out.

He fired both barrels of his guns then switched to his blades. Blaez was suddenly beside him. Marty had no time to wonder where the hell he came from as they both threw themselves in to the fight.

Junqueras stood back and watched as Marty, Sam, and Blaez took the fight, at the head of a wave of marines, directly to the barracks. *Yes, my friend, I am right to be wary of you,* he thought then ran through a wounded militiaman, who staggered toward him, hands over a gaping wound in his stomach.

The sun came up over a fortress strewn with bodies. Fortunately, none of them British, but the guerrillas lost several men and all the militia were slaughtered.

Sam walked amongst the bodies and came to the young guerrilla. He had been bayonetted in the stomach and lay in a pool of his own blood. Sam went to a knee beside him. He was still alive and conscious. The boy tried to say something and raise his head. Sam propped him up against his knee and bent his head to listen to him. Junqueras appeared beside them and looked down on the dying boy dispassionately.

"Mi madre dijo que nunca sería un luchador," the boy whispered. Sam looked at Junqueras for a translation, but he just shrugged and walked away.

"He said, 'my mother said I would never be a fighter,'" translated midshipman Williams, who had come up unseen behind Sam.

Sam looked back down at the boy to tell him he had fought well, but his eyes were vacant and staring at the sky.

The guerrillas disposed of the bodies of the dead by throwing them in a cave and collapsing the entrance. They looted everything that was reusable or of value, leaving the corpses mostly naked.

Marty focused his men on improving the defences.

"We will need to close the road with something," Paul suggested to Marty, "a barricade that we can put some men behind preferably."

They looked at the layout of the fortress. There was a tower and curtain wall on one side of the road and a fortified building on the other. The Spanish militia had only manned the tower side, but they would man both as they had more men.

"What if we were to build a drystone wall, leaving a gap in the middle that can be blocked with a cart full of stone?" Sergeant Bright suggested.

"If we make the wall angled to form a funnel, we can rain fire down on them for longer and with more guns," George Fairbrother suggested.

Paul grinned at his lieutenant in pride, *the boy is coming good!*

Work teams were organised, and soon the walls were growing, narrowing the road to just over a cart width. A four-wheeled cart was found by the marines and filled with the stone that wasn't any good for the walls. A few of the Spaniards started to help, but many just sat and watched, causing a few of the marines to question why they were bothering to help the idle bastards.

Paul ignored the comments when he heard them and made sure the men doing the heavy work were spelled regularly and given ample water. When they finished, they were served up an extra rum ration, which soothed any hard feelings.

Back in Gibraltar, Caroline found herself a fencing master. The good ladies of the peninsula would have been mortified if they saw her in training. She wore a loose silk shirt open low enough to show some cleavage. Over that, she wore the leather corset she had made in Jamaica. It was supple enough to allow her free movement but supported and constrained her breasts to stop them 'bouncing around and getting in the way.' Tight riding breeches and calf-length boots completed the ensemble.

The master, a Spaniard named Don Aldo Elvares de la Cinquenta, agreed to teach her once she demonstrated what she already learned from Tom, which was more ship-style brawling than fencing. He decided that if the lady was determined to fight with a sword, she could at least do it with some style.

Caroline had a strong wrist and surprised Don Aldo with her speed. She lacked finesse but that could be taught, and he was soon immersed in their training sessions. Her daughter often came and watched, and he saw her imitating her mother's moves with her wooden sword.

Junqueras sent men up the road towards Girona on horses they found in the fortress. They wanted as much notice as possible when the French were approaching. Marty left the command of the fortress to the marines and returned to his ship. He wanted to see if their batteries could be used against the French as the road was well within range.

A short cruise up the coast showed that the road stayed on the coastal plain all the way up to Mataro when it wound through the hills inland to Girona. The closest it got to the coast was at Mongat at around five hundred yards, which was close enough for the carronades. After that, it moved out to one and a half miles, which was only reachable with round shot from the eighteen-pounders.

Marty and Ackermann stood over a chart discussing the situation and what they should do in support of the land operation.

"What do you think Wolfgang? We get a clear view of the road about two miles up the coast from the fort. That's a range of around a mile. If we catch the French there, we can target their baggage train while Paul and his boys chew their troops up at the fort.

They have mounted swivels all along the walls and moved one of their twelve pounders out of the Hornfleur and positioned it on the road so it can be fired through the gap."

"Charged with cannister, that will be devastating to troops charging down the road, but they will only be able to get a couple of rounds off before the French are on top of them." Wolfgang replied. He looked at the chart and ran his finger along the road, checking the depth of the water along the coast opposite it. He then took of a pair of dividers and measured the distance from the twenty-foot mark to the road.

"We can close the range to fifteen hundred yards without putting the ship in danger. If we position ourselves here," he pointed to a point on the chart, "we will give our gunners their best chance."

They cruised up and down the coast for a week. When they stopped off to check on the fort, a rider came to warn that the French were on the move, almost killing his horse in the process. Marty questioned the somewhat overexcited young Spaniard to establish the size and composition of the force. It looked like they were up against a full army of invasion with artillery and cavalry.

The Formidiable cruised slowly up the coast.

"Smoke or dust off the larboard bow about a mile and a 'alf inland," reported the mainmast lookout.

Thirty minutes later, Marty could see it with the naked eye. The dust cloud was huge and stretched back for a couple of miles.

The Formidiable continued up the coast, watching as the huge column passed then reversed course to come up on the pre-planned bombardment position.

They hove to, Marty didn't want to anchor, the French had artillery and he wanted to be able to move if they deployed it against him.

The last of the infantry and cavalry passed then came the horse drawn artillery pieces and limbers followed by the baggage train. They had about three hours until dark when Marty gave the order to open fire.

Because of the range, only the eighteen-pound longs were used, and they were effective! The first salvo landed a little short, but the balls ricocheted off the hard ground and ploughed through the column upending canon, smashing limbers and decimating horses and men. More broadsides followed as Ackerman skilfully managed the sails to creep them forward to present new targets.

It didn't take the French long to get themselves organised to respond. First one then three or four cannons fired in response. They neutralised the first battery, which had been set up in a hurry in the open, but then a battery of howitzers started sending some uncomfortably accurate return fire from behind a rise.

They managed to smash a seventy-five-yard-long section of the baggage train before the fire from the howitzers got accurate enough to force them to sail out of range.

Marty was disappointed, he hoped to do more.

Paul la Pierre watched the French marching down the road towards him. They were six abreast and seemed unaware that they were walking into a trap. He knew they would probably get one chance to kill as many as they could.

Junqueras was reinforced by men who came down from the mountains. These tough, independent individuals were there to fight for their independence and waited with grim determination.

A mounted officer noticed something was wrong at the fort and galloped ahead of the column to have a look. They left him alone, but he saw the cart blocking the road and galloped back to order the lead troops to halt and prepare their weapons.

Paul knew the word would be travelling back down the column to the general in command and sure enough, a group of mounted officers came to the fore and looked at the fort with telescopes. They were discussing things amongst themselves when there was the roar of the Formidiable's broadside from behind them.

"That will spur them on!" Angus Fraser commented to his Captain, and when the most flamboyantly dressed officer of the French group waved his arm impatiently, laughed expectantly.

The French formed up with their muskets at the ready, bayonets glinting in the sun. Someone shouted a command, and they advanced with a shout.

Paul la Pierre ran to where the twelve-pounder lay hidden behind the cart. It was loaded with a double charge of cannister, which made it a huge shotgun. He signalled the men holding ropes to haul the cart aside to get ready.

The French advanced and every ten paces or so, they roared a battle cry. Paul looked up and saw Junqueras looking down at him making 'get on with it' signs. His eyes wide, he held his hand up and watched the French.

He let them get to about thirty yards and signalled the cart team, who hauled as hard as they could, pulling the cart to the side. As soon as the barrel was clear, he pulled the lanyard. The cannon roared belching smoke and fire at point blank range. The marines on the swivels rose up and prepared their guns.

Paul's instructions were specific. "Wait and see what's left after the cannon has fired and kill anything that's left standing."

The light sea breeze blew the smoke away and revealed a scene from hell. The first four ranks had literally been blown away, shredded by the hail of shot. The ranks behind were winnowed of many of their men by shot that passed through the first four.

The swivels opened up, killing even more. Then the men manning the tower and walls poured musket fire into the stunned troops that were left. They broke and ran back up the road, many taking shots in the back on the way.

The cannon was reloaded but had nothing to shoot at. The French retreated out of range and were pausing to evaluate the situation, so the cart was replaced.

General Guillaume Philibert Duhesme was fuming. Not only was his progress to Barcelona blocked, but there was a British ship patrolling off the coast which was destroying a significant part of his baggage train.

He took a deep breath and addressed his officers,

"What is the situation with this fortification that is blocking the road?"

A Captain of the Grenadiers stepped forward and laid out a map.

"The fortress is here at a point that commands this pass, which is the only way through to Barcelona. To get the army through we have to take the fortification. As far as we can tell, there are Spanish guerrillas and British soldiers holding it. We think the British are from the ship anchored just offshore as they seem to have swivel guns and the canon is on a naval carriage."

"The ship that attacked our baggage train could be connected to them as well?" asked a Major of Artillery.

"Probably," Duhesme frowned and looked around at the terrain, "have the men make camp as far inland as we can away from the guns of that frigate. I want a battery set up to keep him away. Set up a second battery here," he pointed to a hill marked on the map that overlooked the fortification. "I want a bombardment started by tomorrow morning even if the men have to work all night. If we have to, we will reduce the fortification to a pile of rubble."

The battery set up by the French drove the Formidiable and the Hornfleur out beyond their range. The French were firing howitzers that had good range while being positioned on the blind side of hills. Their spotters were excellent and enabled the gunners to zero in on a target quickly.

The siege artillery went to work and soon, the casualties in the fortifications were mounting and moral dropping. It was no fun being on the end of a constant bombardment.

Marty continued to patrol up the coast and had some luck in blasting re-supply convoys that were trying to replenish the French with powder and shot. One such raid caused a powder wagon to explode, blocking the road for several days before they could fill in the crater.

He also looked to disrupt the French signalling system and identified an isolated semaphore station that would be easy to take. They surprised the garrison with a dawn attack and captured the signal and code books intact. Lieutenant Trenchard came up with the excellent idea to copy them and leave the originals in place as if the British hadn't found them. The French fell for it. They could now read the signals all along the coast and if they wanted intercept, modify, and send on fake information.

The siege lasted a month before the defences were so weakened that Paul decided they wouldn't be able to withstand a concerted French assault. He fired the rockets, telling Angus Frasier they were ready to evacuate.

Junqueras agreed with the timing, and the fortifications were quietly abandoned, the twelve-pounder spiked, and booby traps set before the marines retreated to the beach where the whale boats were waiting for them.

The marines lost five men, and eight Spaniards died. The French lost over fifty infantry, two officers and tons of stores, powder and supplies. More crucially, they had been held up for a month.

Chapter 10: The Battle of the Basque Roads

They returned to Gibraltar in March and received orders to head up to La Rochelle in the Bay of Biscay in support of Admiral Gambier. The orders didn't tell him why, just that he had to be there at his earliest convenience with the entire Flotilla, which, translated to normal speech, meant right away.

They re-provisioned as quickly as possible and, knowing that Gambler's command was on blockade duty, made sure they had enough for a couple of months.

They arrived four days after setting out from Gibraltar and as soon as they arrived, Marty was summoned to the flagship. He was shown to the Admiral's cabin and immediately felt tension in the room.

Admiral Gambier sat behind a desk, on top of which stood a large bible. Beside that was a chart with a number of ships marked on it. Across the room, looking both annoyed and ill at the same time, sat a post captain.

"Captain Stockley, reporting as ordered, my Lord," he announced as protocol demanded.

Gambier looked at him; he had the air of a man who just took a bite out of a plum and found it was a lemon.

"I am told that your Flotilla," and he made that sound like a swearword, "are specialists in infiltration and acquiring things from the French."

"Amongst other things, sir," Marty confirmed.

Gambier looked at him with obvious distaste, and his right hand moved to rest on the bible as if it could protect him from the evil standing before him.

"This is Captain Cochrane. He has orders from the Admiralty," there was that look again, "to attack the French fleet we have blockaded in the estuary and I am told you can be of service to him."

Cochrane stood and shook Marty's hand then looked at Gambier, who had opened the bible and was reading it.

"My Lord," he said and bowed slightly towards the Admiral, who waved a hand in dismissal.

Cochrane took Marty by the arm and led him out.

"Is your boat still here?" he asked, voice tight with controlled anger.

"Yes, they are stood off a ways, but waiting," Marty replied.

Cochrane ordered a mid to call the Formidiable's boat.

"We will go to my ship where we can talk openly."

If Sam was surprised that two captains came down the steps and boarded the barge, he didn't show it and when he was ordered to Imperious, he swung the rudder over with just a raised eyebrow to Marty at the cheek of the man giving orders in his boat.

The Imperious looked like an older version of the Formidiable with similar lines and a definite Spanish cast to the hull.

"Is she Spanish built?" Marty asked as they approached.

Cochrane looked surprised that Marty would notice, then remembered that Marty's ship was the Formidiable and was also Spanish built.

"Yes, similar lines to your Formidiable, built in 1797 in Ferrol. The Formidiable is newer I believe."

"Yes, Spanish built to a French hull design in 1802 as far as we know. Sails like a witch," Marty confirmed.

They arrived and Marty was pleased that his men brought the barge neatly and smartly to the side with hardly a bump. Being senior, Cochrane went up first.

Once they were in his cabin, Cochrane tossed his coat onto the seat that ran around the transom and invited Marty to make himself comfortable. Following his lead, Marty took off his coat and laid it on the transom seat as well.

"My word, I had no idea!" Cochrane exclaimed as he saw the pistols hooked to Marty's weapons harness.

"Never leave home without them," Marty quipped. "Nor this." He pulled his knife from behind his back and placed it on the arm of the chair.

Cochrane's eyebrows raised,

"I bumped into Hood when I was at the Admiralty, and he told me to ask you to help me. Said you were resourceful, dangerous, and had a team that could get into places nobody else could. I now see what he meant by dangerous," he smiled.

"Did he?" Marty smiled back.

Cochrane sighed.

"That fool Gambier is in a snit because the Admiralty has overruled him and ordered me to lead a fireship attack on the French fleet we have bottled up in the estuary."

Marty could understand that. His first impression of Gambier was one of a holier than thou type full of his own concept of what was right and honourable and his own superiority.

"He won't do a damn thing to help and would rather the French walked out of here than admit he was wrong."

"Will he actively hinder you?" Marty asked.

"Probably not, but he will follow his orders to the letter and not take a single step beyond them. Be careful of him. He has some very powerful friends," Cochrane warned.

"What do you want from me?" Marty asked, cutting to the chase.

"Fire ships, but more than that; tar, resin, and oil to fill the fireships with. We have some in the fleet but nowhere near enough."

Marty nodded. He had a good idea of what Cochrane was trying to do.

"There are boatyards up and down this stretch of coast. They will have stores of tar and oil. My men can source as much as you need."

Marty stood and picked up his knife.

"Would you join me for dinner tomorrow?" Marty asked, "I am sure Hood mentioned my cook."

"He did indeed and that you have an excellent physician." Cochrane grimaced as he stood.

"If you are in need of medical assistance, Mr. Shelby will be pleased to see you. Dinner will be at seven thirty but if you come aboard at six, you will see how we train and have time to see Shelby before we eat."

When he got back to his ship, he called his commanders to a meeting and explained what was needed. They were happy. There was nothing they liked better than stealing from the French and a good fire. They left immediately to find the fire ships and combustibles that Cochrane needed.

Marty kept the Formidiable at the blockade - the smaller ships were better suited to the work and he wanted to spend time with Cochrane whose reputation was impressive. The man had captured or sunk an enormous amount of enemy ships and was known as a firebrand. He had many critics and was branded as reckless by a number of his more 'orthodox' peers. Marty put that down to jealousy.

Afternoon weapons practice was about a half hour in when Cochrane arrived. Marty had to stop a sparring session with Matai to greet him at the entry, apologizing for not being dressed. Cochrane, elegant as ever, brushed that aside and begged Marty to carry on.

Marty decided it was time for a show and beckoned to Chin Lee to step up. As soon as the rest of the crew saw that, the training stopped. Wolfgang walked over to Cochrane and asked him to join him on the quarterdeck where he could get a better view.

Both men stripped to the waist and took up live blades.

"Is that normal?" Cochrane asked, surprised.

"With the captain, yes. He is highly skilled."

Cochrane focused on the two men who were circling each other. Marty was rotating his main blade at the wrist and held his knife wide. As he moved, Chin varied the position of his butterfly swords, made by the same blade smith who made Caroline's sword, setting up a weaving pattern.

He didn't see what triggered it, but Marty suddenly launched an attack that had Chin parrying furiously. Their blades were a blur, and sparks flew as the edges clashed. It ended as quickly as it started. Both men took a step back and started circling again.

He looked at the rest of the crew and saw bets being offered and accepted. One man dressed in a smoker's jacket was openly running a book! He glanced at Lieutenant Ackerman, who was smiling benevolently.

"You allow betting?" he asked in amusement.

"Cash bets only. No sips, tots, or tobacco," Ackerman responded.

That was a surprise, sailors usually didn't have two farthings to rub together. This was getting curiouser and curiouser.

His attention was pulled back to the contest by another clash of blades. Chin was on the offensive this time, and Marty was defending for all he was worth.

"A guinea on the Chinaman?" he asked Ackerman.

"I'll take that, sir," Ackerman grinned back at him.

Five minutes later, Cochrane dug a guinea out of his pocket and handed it over. Marty pulled off a magnificent riposte followed by a feint that led to a killing strike, which stopped short of even grazing Chin's abdomen.

Both men sluiced off in a bucket of water to get rid of the sweat, and Marty put his shirt back on. He was still doing it up when he climbed the steps to the quarterdeck.

"I will need to practice if I'm ever to live up to that standard," Cochrane smiled, genuinely impressed.

"I've been training every day since I joined the Navy when I was twelve years old," Marty informed him as they stood and watched the men resume their training.

"You do this every day?"

"Unless conditions prevent it, we do a lot of hand to hand fighting both at sea and on land and this gives us a big advantage over the average Frenchman."

"No doubt! We say your average Englishman is worth three French, but in your case, I would say at least six!"

Marty laughed and thanked him for the compliment. He looked at his watch and tapped Ackermann on the shoulder.

"That's enough playing with weapons. Bring down the topmasts," he ordered.

Orders were bellowed and weapons stacked in their tubs. The topmen raced up the masts, and the landsmen and waisters got into position. The fore topmast came down first followed quickly by the other two. The men looked practiced and efficient. No energy was wasted, and the organisation was impeccable.

"You have an efficient crew!" Cochrane complimented him.

"Thank you, Captain. We normally follow sail drills with live firing drills but as we are in the middle of the fleet, we will have to forgo that today," Marty grinned, proud of his men and ship.

"You mustn't wake up the admiral now!" laughed Cochrane, "and please call me Thomas."

"Martin."

They shook hands.

The drills finished, and Adam came and announced that dinner would be served in thirty minutes preceded by drinks served in the Captain's cabin.

"Blast, I meant to consult that physician chap of yours," Thomas exclaimed.

"He will join us for dinner. I am sure you can get a moment to talk to him in private," Marty reassured him.

Marty disappeared into his sleeping cabin to dress for dinner while Wolfgang amused Thomas with tales of their adventures. He was out in record time thanks to Adam having gotten everything ready in advance.

"… and Admiral Smith was apparently urging poor Captain Tremayne to make more speed even though they had every stitch of sail set and wetted," Wolfgang was telling Thomas, who was absently scratching Blaez's head as the dog sat beside him.

"Shelby, the captain would like a moment of your time. You can use my sleeping quarters if you need privacy," Marty said quietly to the doctor.

Shelby looked at Thomas and said,

"Bad back?"

"Ye gads, you can tell by just looking?!" Thomas exclaimed.

"Your posture, sir. If you would be so kind as to remove your coat." Thomas did as he was asked, intrigued as no other doctor had taken this approach.

Shelby stepped behind him and ran his thumbs up his spine, feeling each vertebra in turn, then asked him to turn his shoulder to the left, then right while he laid his hand on the small of his back.

"Captain, if you would be so kind as to call for Chin Lee, we can have this fixed in a minute."

Marty was intrigued and did as the doctor asked.

A knock on the door and Chin Lee walked in. He saw what Shelby was doing and stepped over beside him.

"A misalignment of the lumbar, causing his poor posture and probably pain down the right leg."

Thomas looked at Marty with a look of amazement when Chin placed his hand on his back and closed his eyes. Thomas's eyes widened as he felt heat bloom in his back. The room was silent as they all looked on. Chin asked Thomas to cross his arms in front of his chest then stood back to back with him and said,

"Please stay relaxed - this will feel a little strange," he reached behind him, held Thomas's elbows then lent forward so Thomas's feet came off the ground and his upper body was supported on his back.

"Please relax." Chin did a kind of bounce and there was a string of very audible pops. He repeated the bounce and there was another pop, then put him back on his feet.

Thomas had a look of pure amazement written clear on his face as Chin checked his back once more followed by Shelby.

"All done, sir. That should feel a lot better."

"Damn me if it doesn't!" Thomas said excitedly. "How did you do that?"

Chin looked inscrutable and said in an exaggerated Chinese accent, "Ancient Chinese medicine, big secret."

They all laughed, and despite being invited to stay, Chin let himself out.

Dinner was a triumph for Rolland; somehow, he was able to get a supply of shellfish and presented a dish he called 'un Plateau de Fruits de mer', which had muscles, oysters, clams, whelks, crab, and lobster with Mignonette sauce and preserved lemon. That was followed by grilled sole in butter with potatoes and a meat course of roasted lamb with a red currant sauce, braised cabbage, parsnips, and roast potatoes. Dessert was baked apples stuffed with dried candied fruit, cinnamon, sugar, and served with a creamy crème anglaise.

Thomas had to undo the top button of his trousers to finish the meal and as the cheese and nuts were brought to the table with the port, he sighed in satisfaction.

"I have to admit, Hood told me you set a wonderful table, but that exceeded all expectations," he told Rolland, who was summoned at his request. "I am afraid you have quite spoiled me. My cook could never live up to this." He left full, more than a little tipsy, and happy.

The next morning, Hornfleur sailed into the Roads with four chasse-marées in close company, which were full of barrels of tar and linseed oil. Angus Frasier didn't want his decks spoiled by leaking tar, so he stole the boats as well.

Just after noon, the Eagle came in with another four. The Alouette came with two and a towed barge. All were gunnel full of tar and oil. Cochrane requisitioned eight reserve store ships from the fleet and set about converting them as well. They stuffed them full of combustibles and kegs of powder and hung grapnels from the ends of the booms to tangle in their target's rigging. The boys went out again to find more tar and oil.

On the tenth of April, twelve fire ships arrived from England. They now had twenty-four fire and explosives ships.

Marty was summoned to attend a planning meeting of captains who would be involved in the assault.

There were seven frigates, including: the Formidiable and Imperieuse, Captains John Tremayne Rodd - HMS Indefatigable, Fredrick Lewis Maitand - HMS Emerald, Lucius Hardyman - HMS Unicorn, and George Seymour - HMS Pallas.   James Wooldridge was captain of HMS Mediator, a temporary position as she was a converted frigate that would be stuffed with explosives and festooned with Congreve Rockets as an explosion ship. Add to them five sloops, six brigs, two bombs, and three rocket ships and it was a crowded meeting.

There was one man there that wasn't in uniform, and he was later introduced as William Congreve, the inventor of the rockets, who had volunteered to help fix them to the fire and explosives ships. He travelled down on the bomb ship HMS Aetna.

Cochrane introduced Marty as Captain Sir Martin Stockley, HMS Formidiable, they would be joining the attack.

"Gentlemen," called Cochrane in a loud voice to get everyone's attention. "We are now ready to begin an attack on the French fleet; the fire and explosive ships are prepared. I would like to thank Captain Stockley and his Flotilla in sourcing the necessary materials," Marty nodded in acknowledgement.

"Admiral Gambier has given his permission and we will start the attack on the eleventh," he continued.

Marty knew, because Thomas confided in him, that Gambier had first refused permission on the basis that he didn't want to put his men manning the fire ships in harm's way. After a furious argument, he finally gave in to Cochrane and approved the plan.

To placate Gambier, Thomas asked Marty if some of his men would man some of the converted store ships and he asked for volunteers from the Flotilla. There was not a man who failed to step forward.

He saw an opportunity to give the younger mids some command experience. So, Eric Longstaff, Jon Williams, Archi Davidson, and Gerald Sykes all got five-man crews to take the store ships in. They were all instructed on exactly what to do and told not to put themselves or their men in unnecessary danger.

"Imperieuse, Formidiable, Unicorn, and Pallas will move up to a point North of the boom by the Boyant shoal so that they can receive the crews of the fireships after they have abandoned their charges.

The sloops, Radpole and Lara, have been equipped as light ships to guide the fireships into the channel. They will be accompanied by HMS Whiting and the cutters Nimrud and King George, which have been set up by Mr. Congreve as rocket batteries.

The Bomb ship, Aetna, and two brigs will anchor near to the battery on the Ile-d'Aix, while Emerald and five escorts will set up a diversionary attack to the east of the island.

I will command the Mediator and will lead the fireships, her greater size and weight will enable her to break the boom. The fireships will be chained together in seven ship squadrons to maximise their effect." He looked around the room. "Gentlemen you have all received your written orders, now a toast to our success," stewards were passing out glasses of port and once everyone had a glass in his hand he proposed the toast,

"To the success of our endeavours, and confusion to the French!"

"CONFUSION TO THE FRENCH!" they replied with enthusiasm and drained their glasses to heel taps.

That evening as night approached, Marty stood on his quarter deck and looked at the pennant, which snapped and streamed in a stiff breeze.

"Damn! There is too much wind! It's from the right direction but they will never be able to chain the fireships together in squadrons in this breeze," Marty commented to Ackermann.

"I think Captain Cochrane has come to the same conclusion," he pointed to the Imperieuse where a signal was flying up the yards.

Stanley Hart, who was miffed at being left out of commanding a fire ship, read the signal and reported to Marty.

"Signal commands the fireships to act independently, sir."

Marty nodded; it was what he would have done.

At eight thirty, the fire ships cut their cables and with the wind and tide behind them, started towards the boom.

Five minutes later, a number of the fireships ignited, and in their light Marty could see the crews abandoning them.

"You bloody fools!" Marty shouted at the ships. "The damned cowards have abandoned their ships far too early," he continued to Ackermann and silently wondered if Gambier had anything to do with it.

He counted the fires and of the twenty-four ships, fourteen fire ships had gone too soon. Out of control, most of them ran up on the shoals and grounded while one veered around and started heading straight for the Imperieuse!

"Get the ships boats manned!" he commanded, seeing the danger. The boats were pulled alongside in readiness to assist any fireship crews that might need help, and their crews fairly leapt over the side. Marty took charge of the barge, Ackermann, the cutter, Andrew Stamp, the gig, and Stanley Hart, the whaler.

The four boats raced across the sea towards the oncoming fireship the flames illuminating the sea for many yards around.

"Try and pull her around so she goes between the Imperieuse and Formidiable!" Marty shouted.

Bowmen stood with grapnels on stout lines ready to try and hook the bow of the burning ship and when they were within thirty feet and feeling the heat of the flames, strong arms hurled the hooks over the rail.

"Back starboard!" Marty called as his hook found a purchase, and the barge pirouetted around to reverse direction. "Give way both!"

The strain was taken. The barge and whale boat pulled side by side, straining to pull the fire ship's head around. Marty looked back and could see that the other two boats were nowhere to be seen, but then he caught a glimpse of oars on the other side of the bow and realized they were trying to push it around!

The First Lieutenant of the Imperieuse saw the danger and was busy trying to veer his anchor cable. He looked out at the approaching ship and saw the Formidiables valiant efforts end as the ropes burnt through as the bow of the ship went up in flames. The two boats that were pushing on the bow already had to back away because of the heat.

But between their efforts and the shift in position the veer gave him, the fire ship passed his stern. He could feel the heat and noted the name on the stern as she passed. Someone would pay dearly for this.

The Formidiables had just returned to their ship when there were a number of explosions. The first explosion ships went up on the boom. Marty didn't know it, but they did little damage. However, Mediator was coming in behind them and the big ship broke through the boom followed by the surviving fire ships.

Marty looked toward the French fleet and could see the burning British ships bearing down on them, rockets firing as the flames ignited them. Mediator went up, the explosion was enormous, and debris soared into the air.

The scene was like something from hell. Fireships drifted at random through the French fleet, rockets flying from the rocket ships and the fireships. The Forts and the French ships were firing their guns at anything that remotely looked like a threat. A number cut their anchors and were adrift. It was chaos.

The next morning, dawn revealed that only two of the French ships escaped the chaos relatively unscathed. The rest were aground on the mud banks.

What followed would go down in history as a disgrace. Cochrane repeatedly signalled Gambier for assistance with information that the French were all grounded. But the Admiral did nothing but call meetings and send long spelt out messages that never committed or ordered a follow up attack. Eventually, the fleet set sail only to immediately anchor again.

Cochrane cut his anchor cable and let the Imperieuse drift down on the French stern first, signalling all the while. Marty ordered the Formidiable to buoy and cut their anchor cable as well, following Cochrane.

The guns were loaded, and Marty was pleased to see the Eagle and Alouette sailing down towards him. The Admiral flew a recall signal, but they ignored him, and Cochrane signalled, "the enemy is superior to the chasing ships."

Gambier hesitated. It was becoming obvious that he did not want to engage the enemy. At a quarter to two in the afternoon, Cochrane signalled, "The ship is in distress and requires immediate assistance."

The Imperieuse and Marty's Flotilla commenced fire, bombarding the ships that were still aground. Gambier couldn't delay any more, he could not let a pair of Frigates and a couple of smaller ships take on the French fleet while he stood by and did nothing.

The frigates Indefatigable, Emerald, Unicorn, and Pallas along with the liners Valliant and Revenge were sent to support Cochrane. They formed a line of battle and started to bombard the stranded Ville de Varsouvie.

The Alouette used her carronades to great effect, manoeuvring into position to rake the Aquilon. The Eagle joined her, and they pounded the defenceless ship unmercifully.

After two hours, both ships struck, and a little after that, another French ship, that was set afire by its crew before they abandoned ship, exploded as the flames reached her magazine. The Calcutta followed suit when a boarding crew accidently set her on fire. The store ship was stacked full of powder and blew up spectacularly.

In the end, they destroyed only five of the French ships and the rest were able to retreat up the Charente when the tide lifted them off the mud banks. Gambier ordered Cochrane to return to England and summarily dismissed Marty and his Flotilla to return to Gibraltar. The battle was over.

Chapter 11: What a whitewash!

Marty received a letter from Cochrane asking him to support him at the court-martial of Gambier. He used his position as a member of parliament to publicly accuse the admiral of dereliction of duty and cowardice.

Caroline saw it as a great opportunity for the whole family to return home for a couple of months and Marty for the Formidiable to get a partial refit. They left her at Portsmouth in Wolfgang Ackermann's capable hands, and set off for Dorset.

Marty wanted to visit his family and catch up on how the Dorset estate was doing. They received regular reports from the estate managers both in Dorset and in Cheshire but for a detailed review, they had to be there. They sent messages ahead so they would be expected.

The coach trip through the New Forest was uneventful. Two coaches full of conspicuously armed people did not make an attractive target for highwaymen and covered the thirty miles to Ringwood comfortably before dark.

They rolled up in front of the White Hart where they would spend the night. Fletcher recommended it and sent a messenger ahead to reserve rooms, shamelessly using Marty's rank and titles so when they arrived, they practically had the place to themselves.

Marty and Caroline had a suite while the children, Mary, and Tabetha had another smaller suite. Tom and Amara had a room to themselves and the rest of the Shadows shared two rooms.

It took an hour to get everyone in and settled with the Innkeeper and his wife fussing over everything in their attempts to win Marty and Caroline's approval.

The Inn's kitchens had a large wood fire, in front of which was a whole young pig on a spit turned by a small boy. On another spit, turned by a spit dog on a treadmill, were a half-dozen chickens. Below the pig was a large tray that caught the fat as it dripped down onto roasting potatoes and parsnips.

Bread was baking in the ovens, and vegetables cooked in pots slung from hooks over the fire. The smell coming out of the kitchen was unbelievable and they all came down to the private dining room with mouths watering in anticipation. The landlord was surprised when earlier, Caroline told him they would all eat together. He wasn't sure whether to be amazed or to applaud.

The pork was served from large platters with the crispy crackling piled on top. Servants served everyone in order of rank and Marty soon had a pile of Pork, crackling and black pudding on his plate with crispy roast potatoes and parsnips, kale, carrots, and the best gravy he had ever tasted.

Chin found the meal novel; he had gotten used to the food served in the ship but had not yet experienced a classic British roast. He personally would have preferred a bit more spice, but the food was plentiful and delicious, so he tucked in with gusto.

Blaez and Troy were lazing by the fire having been given a bowl of raw meat mixed with cereals each, which they had wolfed down in seconds.

Ringwood wasn't a big town, so the news that a famous Navy Captain who was also a Lord was staying with his entourage, which included a black man, a china man, and a pair of wolves, soon got around and the common room was as busy as it ever got.

"My Lord," the sheepish looking landlord said as he approached Marty as he sat back after sampling the excellent cheeseboard. "I'm told you was the captain who captured the treasure fleet last year." He looked expectant and waited for an answer.

"Yes, I have to admit to that," Marty grinned.

"Well Sir, I have been asked by a large number of my customers if they could get a first-hand account. You see, we don't get much news down here except week old newspapers and hearing a tale like that will keep the village happy for weeks!"

Marty was no storyteller, especially if it involved anything he had done and he didn't quite know how to respond. He was rescued by Wilson who, prompted by the other Shadows, stood up and volunteered.

Marty and Caroline retired to their suite to spend some time with the children before they went to bed. Adam came in to turn the bed down and told them that Wilson was entertaining the packed common room with tales of many of Marty's exploits including Toulon. Marty groaned. He had been embarrassed by that tale since he was a mid.

The boys came up to their rooms in the wee hours, all were worse for drink they hadn't paid a penny for, as the locals were happy to treat them in return for tales, shanties and a weapons demonstration by Chin.

The next morning, Marty rousted them out early, hangovers and all, and they continued the journey through Ferndown and Bear Cross with a stop at an Inn to change horses and lunch. Then it was around the top of Poole and down to Wareham, another change of horses and on to Church Knowle.

The manor house was pretty much just as it was last time they were there when Marty's mother died, but the estate had grown and there were more out buildings. Only his brother, Arthur, who was the estate manager, lived at the manor. The rest of his siblings had houses in the village or over in Furzebrook.

Marty caught up on the development of the estate and the new farms they bought, which were already occupied by tenants. Arthur told him the Banks family were putting up stiff opposition to their expansion as they were now challenging them for the position as the largest landowner in the area.

Marty decided to pay a visit to the Banks to try and smooth over any potential conflicts before they started, but his letter was soundly rebuffed. The reply was couched in terms that made it clear they thought him an upstart peasant and should know his place.

So be it, he thought, *if that's the way they want to play it, then let battle commence.*

Arthur had a recent copy of the Gazette, and Marty read the account of the Battle of The Basque Roads in surprise. While it gave Cochrane some small credit for the attack, it didn't mention anything about Gambier holding back. More interestingly, neither he nor any of the Flotilla's ships were mentioned at all!

"I feel Hood's touch on this," Caroline commented when he showed her, "he can smell a storm coming and doesn't want his people caught up in it!"

Marty agreed. If he wasn't officially at the battle, he couldn't be called to give evidence at a court martial, which meant it was a single captain taking on an admiral and his supporters. This was going to get very messy.

"I think I need to talk to Hood. Will you be alright to go on to Cheshire without me?" he asked.

Caroline understood; he wanted to help his friend but needed to be sure of what he could do and what the situation was in London. She hugged him.

"Of course I will. Sam, Antton, and Chin Lee can go with you, and the rest can come with me."

"Why Antton?" he asked. He could understand Sam and Chin, but Antton rather than Wilson?

Caroline kissed him on the forehead and tidied his hair.

"Because he has a level head and will stop you from doing anything rash."

"Me? Rash? How dare you, woman!" he laughed, pulling her into his lap and planting a kiss on her lips, which turned passionate.

Two days later, the coaches carried them to Wareham where Caroline, the children, and their escorts headed towards Bere Regis and Marty toward Lychet Minster.

Marty met Hood at his house, which gave him a hint that the whole affair was a political hot potato.

"You did good work at the Roads," Hood congratulated him, "Cochrane wouldn't have been able to make his attack without you."

Marty ignored it and asked,

"is he making a mistake going after Gambier?"

Hood steepled his fingers and pondered his answer before speaking,

"Gambier has a lot of very powerful friends, which even I would think twice about taking on. They will make sure the court martial is loaded with his supporters. They are all political opponents of Cochrane to boot. Frankly, Cochrane doesn't stand a chance even if the rest of the Navy agree with him."

"Will it end his career?"

"For a time, yes, but he is hell bent on committing political suicide and there is nothing we can do to stop it."

Marty contemplated then snapped,

"It's damn unfair. He is an excellent captain and a superb commander and strategist. Whereas, Gambier is a shy, incompetent, who hides behind his piousness and has no place in the modern Navy."

"A fair assessment," Hood agreed, "but take comfort in the fact that Gambier is unlikely to get another fleet command. He upset enough of their Lordships to become a yellow admiral. He will finish his career sailing a desk."

How wrong could he be.

The court martial was held on the 26th July in Portsmouth on HMS Gladiator and went exactly as Hood predicted. Gambier's political friends included Prime Minister William Pitt, and they made sure his political ally (and Cochrane's political enemy), Sir Roger Curtis was nominated as president and William Young his deputy. The outcome was a foregone conclusion. Gambier was exonerated on doctored evidence by a panel of his friends. Cochrane was disgraced and never got another command for the duration of the war.

Marty was so upset by this that he seriously thought about resigning his commission but as Hood pointed out, he wouldn't be able to change things from the outside. So, he kept his peace but vowed that if he ever had the chance to do Gambier harm in any way, he would seek his own retribution.

Chapter 12: An explosive encounter

Marty woke up in a foul mood. The Formidiable had developed a tendency to gripe since the refit and neither he, Wolfgang, nor Arnold Grey could figure out why. They couldn't sail as close to the wind as they were used to because as soon as they got close, she tried to come up into the wind, forcing the helm to make a large correction costing them speed. The constant griping was wearing and even Blaez was not as happy as he usually was.

They tried trimming her further aft, which didn't work. They tried changing the set of the sails, which didn't work either. Marty sat down and went over the complete report from the yard on the refit. Most of the repairs were to the hull, but then he read that they replaced the foremast stays.

"Mr. Ackermann and Mr. Grey to report to my cabin," he shouted to the marine on guard duty outside his door. The marine bellowed the request in turn, and it was repeated around the ship.

"Well, what do you think? Could it be the cause?" he asked after pointing out the change to the two of them.

"If the mast were set more upright or with a slight forward rake, it might," Arnold Grey offered thoughtfully.

"They may have disturbed the balance," Wolfgang muttered, meaning the balance of the forces acting on each mast.

"Get us into a sheltered bay and anchored up so we can look into it," Marty ordered, making his mind up.

"Guernsey be the closest safe port," Arnold stated.

"Then let's get in there and get this sorted," Marty barked, impatience making him sharper than he intended.

With the prevailing conditions, Grey decided St. Sampson harbour was their best bet and set his course accordingly. However, when they got there, the fishing fleet was in and there just wasn't room for a big ship like the Formidiable.

"St. Peter Port it is then," he told Marty, who had ceased his pacing to ask what he planned now.

They entered the Port, and Marty remembered the time when he sailed the Alouette in on her maiden voyage, and he had forgotten to take down the French colours. This time, there was no doubt about what or who they were as the British flag flew proudly from the mizzen.

Once anchored, Marty went ashore to give his compliments to the Harbour Master.

"Stuart English, as I live and breathe!" Marty exclaimed as he recognised the man sat behind the desk. English looked hard at the Navy Captain stood before him and then the penny dropped.

"Martin Stockley?"

The two men shook hands. Not to be left out, Blaez butted in and demanded attention.

Marty introduced him

"This is Blaez."

English wasn't fazed by the big dog and knelt down to great him face to face.

"Hello boy, you're a big fellow. Would you like a biscuit?" Marty laughed and as English offered a biscuit, Blaez sat and raised a paw.

"Well-mannered as well, now what can I do for you?" English asked.

The two men sat, and Marty told him why they dropped in, then English asked,

"Are you still interested in the activities of our American cousins?"

Marty nodded and added,

"And anything the French are doing. I'm based out of Gibraltar now but anything they do that can affect the coming war over Spain is of interest."

"There is someone you should meet," English said and went to the door where he spoke to the secretary sitting outside.

They sipped coffee and chatted while they waited for the mystery visitor, and it was only a matter of fifteen minutes before there was a knock at the door. The secretary showed a shabby, tough-looking individual in.

"Captain Stockley, I would like to introduce Gerome Briac, an independent trader out of Brittany."

Smuggler, Marty thought.

"Bonjour Captain," Briac greeted Martin and gave him a gap-toothed smile. *"And who is this?"* he added as Blaez sniffed him.

"Blaez, my constant companion," Marty replied.

"A good Breton name, yes?" Briac responded and rubbed Blaez's head.

"Gerome, Captain Stockley is interested in the activity you told me about."

"You probably know the French are sending supplies to Soult via ship to Santander since he took it a month ago, but did you know American traders are using the

bay and now Santander to drop off their cargos, which are then taken back to France by the very same ships."

"Are they really!" Marty exclaimed, his interest piqued, *"And that is undercutting your business."*

Gerome looked a little sheepish then grinned as he realised this young man saw right through him

Marty returned to his ship to find the men had reset the rake on the foremast. He had the feeling it looked better but if he was honest, he couldn't say why.

"She was more upright than she were before, and we set her back about two degrees," Mr. Grey reported, "It's not much but could make all the difference."

"Well, let's not hang about. Get the ship ready to sail," Marty ordered.

Once out into the Atlantic, they tested the new mast setting thoroughly by sailing as close to the wind as they could. It had indeed done the trick and the gripe that plagued them since Portsmouth was gone. Happy that his ship was once more sailing like a witch, Marty set course for Santander.

They were about two days out and flying a French flag when they came upon an American flagged schooner. She was the Anne-Marie out of Charleston and was heading to Bayonne with a cargo of tobacco and whiskey. Her skipper wanted to know if the British were blockading the port. Marty answered with a very French accent that they were further North at Brest and that if he liked, they could sail in with them as that was their destination as well.

The American Captain jumped at the chance, and so it was, the two ships sailed into the Bay of Biscay almost side by side. Marty was enjoying tagging the American along but as soon as they were North of A Coroña, he sprang his surprise. The guns ran out, the colours were changed and the American was in the bag.

A prize crew was put aboard and sent to Gibraltar to return with the Eagle and Alouette. The Formidiable set out on an oval patrol pattern North of Santander.

It wasn't long before they came upon fishing boats. The August weather was fine and the Bay calm. Marty made a point of getting friendly with the fishermen, paying top price for their catches. As most of them were Basques; Antton, Matai, and Garai soon found common ground with them. Thus, they found out that they were patrolling too far West. The transports were hugging the coast to avoid any British ships and were slipping around behind them.

Marty adjusted his thinking as well as their patrol area and quickly had their first prize, a French military transport full of uniforms, boots, and hats. Worthless, so they took her out to deep water and blew her bottom out.

They didn't see anything else for a couple of days and Marty wished he had his other ships with him so he could cover more sea, but they wouldn't arrive for at least another four days.

Patience is a virtue that Marty found hard to adopt but he controlled his impulse to race around hunting prey. James and Ryan would never find him if he did that, so he kept sailing the oval shaped patrol that took him along the coast from Bilbao to Bayonne and back again.

They snagged another transport, this time loaded with powder and guns. The captain was a tough native of La Rochelle and wore his Naval uniform uncomfortably. He was, however, close mouthed and would say nothing. Marty was frustrated and sat in his cabin looking at a chart for inspiration. He was aware he was probably missing picking up incoming traders from the Atlantic, but it was more important to stop the military transports than make some money from the Americans.

A knock at the door and Garai was announced. Marty bade him enter.

"I've been chatting to the first mate of the transport, he's a Basque," Garai announced as he stood in front of Marty's desk. "He's not that happy working for the French but his family is at risk if he doesn't."

"We've heard that before," Marty commented sympathetically.

"Well, he is happy to give up what he knows," Garai continued, "as long as we keep it quiet that it came from him."

"We can do that," Marty confirmed as he sat back in his chair interested.

"That's what I told him. He says there is a convoy of around half a dozen ships coming down from Rochefort carrying a brigade of horse drawn artillery and support troops."

"That's very interesting." Marty frowned. "I thought that Gambier had that whole area bottled up?"

"That's the most interesting thing. He says the French have been making like they are going to try and break out of Brest and the majority of the blockading fleet has moved back up there, leaving only a few frigates and a liner on watch. They plan to slip out around the South end of the isle of Oleron on the full moon if it's clear. He thinks they would be escorted by at least a pair of corvettes and a couple of luggers."

Marty grabbed a chart and laid it out on the desk.

"Looks like the passage South of the island is shallow, so the Fleet will probably ignore it, but with the tide at its height, they could get flat-bottomed transports and even a corvette out."

He grabbed an almanac off his bookshelf and checked the tides.

"Spring tide is on the thirteenth of August, that's tomorrow! Damn! I wish I knew when the others will arrive."

The next morning dawned with no sign of the Alouette or the Eagle. Marty hoped they were close, but he couldn't afford to leave his patrol to find them. The spring tide came just before dawn and he was on deck, Blaez at his side. The wind was from the Northwest and he thought it might swing more to North by Northwest. Marty was trying to put himself in the mind of the leader of the convoy.

He felt Blaez nuzzle his hand and scratched his head without thinking. He called for Garai, who was down by the foremast.

"Ask your friend how well those transports sail against the wind or on a broad reach," he instructed as soon as the Basque reported.

Ten minutes later, Garai returned.

"He says they make leeway like a barge and in anything other than a quarter wind are horrible sailors."

Marty grinned.

"They can't hug the coast. If they make that kind of leeway, they will have to stay further out to ensure they don't get blown ashore." In fact, he was thinking that if he was in charge of the convoy, he would try a direct run to the port of Santander to keep the wind as much on his quarter as possible, thereby avoiding having to sail due West along a rocky lee shore.

"Mr. Ackermann, please set a course to get us more to the North of Santander."

It was a calculated risk, but he figured it had the best odds of intercepting the convoy.

They beat up towards the West and established a patrol that passed no closer than thirty mile off the coast that covered the approach to both Santander and the port of Santoña, which was better fortified than Santander and an established Navy base.

Marty calculated that if the convoy left on the spring tide, they would arrive the next morning. He was banking on them reducing sail overnight to make it easier on their passengers, both human and equine, and would only average around six knots.

Dawn broke, the sky was clear and visibility excellent. The wind had indeed swung around to the North-Northwest as he had predicted.

Two hours after sunrise at the end of their Westward leg, the mainmast lookout hailed. He'd spotted sails to the Northeast. Marty grabbed his biggest telescope, slung it over his shoulder by its strap, ran up the ratlines, around the futtock shrouds, and up to the topgallant yard where he settled himself next to the lookout. He pulled the big telescope around and adjusted the focus to the mark that had been made for his eye.

He scanned the Northern horizon from the West all the way around to the East then back to the fragment of sail to the Northeast. It was a topsail and he couldn't see any other sails set below it.

He lowered the telescope and rubbed his eye in thought. *If the transports are as slow as that first mate says they are, that could be one of the corvettes with just enough sail set to stay ahead of them,* he thought.

He waited ten minutes then raised the glass again. This time, he could see that there were indeed sails following on behind the first ones.

"Mr. Ackerman! The convoy is to the Northeast, heading Southwest, about eighteen miles distant, probably travelling at six knots. Please steer us a course that brings us to the West of them so we can engage," Marty called down. He took one last long look, slung the glass over his shoulder, and took a stay to the deck.

As they swung around in an arc to get the wind gauge, they saw the lead ship was indeed a corvette and that there was another halfway along the line of seven transport ships. The two luggers were ranging along behind and to windward ready to swoop down on any ship that attacked.

Marty would keep the French flag flying until they ran out, only showing their true colours at the last minute.

"Sir, the lead corvette is asking for a recognition signal," Midshipman Williams, who had signal duty, reported.

"Go down to my cabin and bring me the signal book we copied from that signal tower. It is in the unlocked top right drawer of my desk," Marty ordered.

Blaez and Sam appeared on deck. Blaez in his fighting collar, and Sam carrying Marty's weapons and a silk shirt. Marty changed into the shirt and slung his weapons harness. Last, he clipped his pistols into place on their underarm straps after checking their priming. Williams returned with the book, which Marty scanned then pointed to the signal that should be the recognition signal of the day.

"We will concentrate on the transports - sink, burn or capture. If the escorts take us on, we will defend ourselves. A single broadside will deal with the luggers. Get the men to quarters and load both sides with double shot, carronades with ball, but do not run out," he ordered.

Marty stepped up to the rail of the quarterdeck.

"Men, listen to me!" he shouted, and the men turned as one. It wasn't often Marty made a speech, so they were intrigued by what he was about to say. "Those ships have a brigade of artillery, guns, and enough ammunition to cause our forces in the North of Portugal a big problem. On our own, we can't take them as prizes and fend off the escorts at the same time. Aim for the waterline, send them to Davy Jones' locker," he paused, looking at the eager faces then up at the signal that soared up the yard,

"The windward corvette has changed course to intercept us," Ackermann reported, "They are running out their guns."

Marty sighed. It looked like the signal book was replaced.

"Are you ready?" he shouted to the men, who answered with a cheer, "Then let me hear your battle cry!"

Antton, Matai, and Garai moved to their traditional positions at the foremast and either side amidships, then raised their voices,

"Aye, Aye, Aye, Aye, Aye, EEEHHHHAAAAAA!" and were answered in kind by every man on deck.

The intercepting corvette increased sail and was closing fast. Marty steered as straight at him as the wind would allow, he wanted to serve him a broadside as they passed then swing around to run down the line of transports.

"Raise the colours!"

Lieutenant Henri St. Jean looked at the big Frigate sailing towards him. The out-of-date recognition signal hadn't fooled him for a minute. He recognized the ship from the Basque Roads debacle as one of the few ships the fool of a British admiral had committed to destroying their beached ships.

This was the first time he had ever approached another ship in anger and he never dreamed he would be so out gunned. He decided he would go for their rigging and try to disable him.

He looked back at the two luggers, who were hanging back as they were supposed to. Their job was to prevent the transports being boarded not get into a shooting war with a bigger enemy.

Marty looked at the approaching corvette and ordered the bow chasers to engage. He watched as, first, one, then, the other, fired. He could trace the arc of the balls as they both narrowly missed the target.

Should have made them duck, though, Marty grinned to himself. The forward carronade gunners were swinging the big guns around on their pivots to point forward over the larboard bow clear of obstructing rigging. The corvette was going to pass within two cables and they would try and serve her bows with a hail of four-pound shot.

He glanced across at the transports, they were still in line. He had expected them to scatter at the first sign of a threat.

St. Jean almost ducked as the big twelve-kilogram balls howled close by their larboard side. He focused on the ship that was now only eight hundred meters away.

The range came down rapidly, and suddenly when they were just four hundred meters apart, there were dual gouts of fire from the frigate's foredeck. His first thought was that they couldn't possibly train their cannon around that far forward but that was quickly dispelled when his bow and fore deck were raked by a hail of round shot.

Their boom was snapped off almost at the bow, and the foremast rigging was shredded. The ship shuddered as shot tore through the bow.

"My God!" he exclaimed in horror as several men were torn to pieces.

Then the two ships started to pass each other. His six-kilogram cannon spoke one after the other, aiming to take out the frigate's fore mast. The enemy didn't respond until they were abeam of each other then he watched as their side lit up in a full broadside. He was also vaguely aware of a pair of monster cannon on the fore deck that coughed as they came level with him.

Marty watched as his eighteen pounders fired as one. At this range, they couldn't miss. He didn't expect his gunners to either; he had trained them hard enough.

The corvette shuddered as she took the full force of the Formidiable's broadside and veered away. Marty saw why when he came up on their quarterdeck- or what was left of it. The wheel, binnacle, and most of the deck itself was gone. Strangely, a section stood untouched, upon which stood a young lieutenant, quite unharmed but with an expression on his face that looked like he was screaming.

Marty ignored him and the damage to his ship, they were out of the fight. He glanced at his gunners as they efficiently reloaded the guns, then looked toward the foremast where he could see men repairing the damage the French inflicted on it. Shelby's loblolly boys were attending some wounded and there were a pair of bodies laid out on the centreline. He looked across at the convoy, they were starting to scatter.

"Hard to starboard, let's take that one at the rear first!"

The ship healed as they tacked across the wind and bore down on the hapless transport.

"Christ, she wallows like a pig!" Ackermann exclaimed, his big zweihaender sword sticking up above his shoulders.

The bow chasers came into line, and Wolverton the gunner gleefully pulled the lanyard on the larboard gun as it came into line at about five hundred yards. The shot flew true and hit the transport directly amidships about midway between the waterline and deck.

Men watched in amazement as the ship seemed to expand then burst. A second later, they were deafened as the shock wave of an enormous explosion threw them to the deck and almost rolled the Formidiable over.

Pieces of timber rained down on the deck, some on fire, and the crew struggled to their feet to put them out before their ship went up in flames.

Marty was on his knees and Blaez was laid out on the floor next to him. He checked the big dog over but found no wounds and saw that he was breathing. Marty stood and shook his head to clear it. Ackermann staggered over, blood coming from one of his ears and a cut above his eye.

"A powder ship!" he exclaimed unnecessarily.

But Marty just saw his lips move. All he could hear was a ringing in his ears.

Lieutenant Trenchard grabbed his arm to get his attention and pointed over to the larboard side. The luggers were moving in on them, assuming they were disabled by the blast.

Marty looked up and saw that his sails were a mess. Any that had been set were torn to pieces and there was significant damage to their rigging. They were a sitting duck.

"GET THE GUNS MANNED!" he shouted.

His officers ran down the deck, pushing the men back to their guns. Many staggered, all were shocked.

The carronades were their best defence against being raked by the luggers with their fourteen nine-pound guns. Their ability to swivel through a broad arc would serve them well.

Marty felt a soft, cold nose nuzzle his hand. He looked down at Blaez, who stood beside him. A glance over his shoulder and there stood Sam, a bandage around his upper left arm, his broad headed short spear in his right hand.

Ackermann was organizing men to get some sails set, even if they were just courses, to get them underway.

The first lugger got in close enough to get a broadside off then veered away to get out of range. Marty knew they would try to harass them and slow down the repairs to the rigging. Chain shot shimmered and whined above the deck and more rigging crashed down.

He felt, rather than heard, the aft carronades fire and saw the second lugger shudder as she took a hit. Their commander had become overconfident and sailed in too close, fooled by the lack of return fire to the first one. He wouldn't make the same mistake again as shortly after, the side lit up as the entire battery fired a broadside.

When the smoke cleared, there was nothing left of the lugger but driftwood. The other one decided to stand back and take pot shots from a thousand yards off their larboard quarter. The carronades kept him at a respectable range, but he could still do some damage.

Ackermann tapped Marty on the arm and pointed to the South. The second corvette was beating up towards them. If he got behind them, they would be in real trouble.

Marty went down on deck to see how the repairs to the rigging were coming on. Men were swarming over the masts and splicing where they could or re-reeving tackles where they couldn't. The fore mast was having to be fished with timbers around where two shot took significant chunks out of it and the carpenter was getting ready to wrap a rope around the temporary repair to strengthen it.

He felt movement through the deck beneath his feet and looked aft. They had gotten some canvas up on the mizzen, but they needed some on the main or fore to make way in a controlled fashion.

A glance showed him the corvette would be in range in about ten minutes.

Ryan and James were pushing their ships as hard as they could and were just passing North of Suances when the sound of the explosion reached them. The lookout reported a smoke cloud to the East-Northeast but couldn't see anything on the horizon.

As far as James knew, the only reason for a smoke cloud that could be seen from beyond the horizon was a ship burning or blowing up. Given the sound of an explosion, the latter had to be the cause.

They adjusted their course, wetted down the sails, and made as much speed as they could. An hour later and they still couldn't see anything.

Marty had the stern chasers run out and the starboard aft carronades trained around as far as they would go. He had them all fire as the corvette came into extreme range just to let them know that they knew they were there and could still bite them if they got too close.

More than anything, he needed time to get his rigging repaired.

"Get a pair of the boats manned and try to swing us around so our guns bear," he ordered. Ackermann said something in reply but while he could now hear some sound, he couldn't make out the words.

"I can't hear anything, Wolfgang. Just do what you think is right."

Wolfgang gave him a thumbs up and shouted down to the deck. Men ran to pull the barge and the cutter around to the side and jumped in. Two-inch cables were dropped down and attached to their sternposts and the men rowed them to the bow. With a boat attached to either side of the bow, and the men straining, they managed to turn the ship slowly to bring guns to bear. The lugger didn't catch on to what they were doing until they turned enough to bring the stern five eighteen-pounders to bear. He got the message clearly enough when they fired, and he had balls crashing through his hull.

That prompted him to retire fully, limping away with a definite list to starboard. *One down one to go,* Marty thought and turned his attention back to the corvette. Evidently, what happened to the lugger gave its captain pause for thought as he stayed at extreme range from the twelve-pound stern chasers, which continued to bark with satisfying frequency.

James could hear gunfire now. There was the pop of nine-pounders and the cough of carronades, then there was the unmistakable roar of what sounded like half a dozen eighteen-pounders. It had to be the Formidiable.

The lookout called that there were two sails in sight and identified them soon after as French transports. James made a decision and signalled Ryan to take the Eagle and intercept them, he would carry on and investigate the shooting.

Marty saw Ackermann look up sharply to the top of the mainmast and shout something. He then listened to the reply and shouted something else.   This was infuriating!

Ackermann turned around and grinned at Marty, walked to the log, picked up the slate, and wrote one word.

ALOUETTE.

"Where?" Marty asked.

In answer, Ackermann took him by the arm, turned him to a couple of points South of West, and pointed. There, coming over the horizon, was the unmistakable shape of the Alouette's topsail.

The French corvette must have seen him as well and mistook him for another French ship. He started to edge back into range of his guns to try and serve the Formidiable with a broadside. But now Yeovilton took responsibility for laying the stern chasers. He called up a request from the transom windows for the bow to be swung two points to starboard which was passed on to the sweating boat crews.

Afterwards, Marty would swear he deliberately aimed short as the balls hit the sea about halfway to the French ship and skipped, like flat stones skimmed across a pond.

Once, twice, three times, then slammed into the corvette just above the waterline.

Marty watched through his telescope as a line of men appeared at the rail of the corvette looking down at the side. Marty became aware that the ship was turning, then the guns fired again. The balls skipped again; the starboard missing the bow of the corvette by a few feet, the larboard striking the hull.

That was enough for the corvette's captain, who turned away and sailed toward the Alouette.

James could now see the Formidiable from his perch on the top yard. He watched the stern chasers fire at the French corvette standing a mile off her stern. He could see that the frigates rigging was being repaired and knew from the fact she was dead in the water she had been badly damaged.

There was another pair of shots from the frigate's stern chasers and this time he saw a ball skip past the corvette's bow. Then to his surprise, the corvette filled her sails and turned towards him.

"GET US TO QUARTERS, RAISE A FRENCH FLAG," he bellowed down to the deck then took a stay for a fast descent.

"The Frenchman thinks we are coming to help him let's get in close and serve him with a caution." James grinned to his midshipman Archie Davidson. They loaded the carronades with grape and would go for her rigging.

The corvette kept coming and it seemed the captain was in such a hurry that he forgot to raise the recognition signal. So, he was genuinely surprised to see the British colours run up as the Alouette ran out her guns. He looked across in horror when the side lit up and the storm of grapeshot slashed through his rigging bring down yards, blocks, and his main topmast.

The Alouette spun on her heel as they passed her stern and came alongside. Swivel guns cracked and grapnels flew snagging on rigging, upper works, and even an unfortunate sailor. The two ships were tied together like lovers and the Alouette's vaulted the side howling their war cries.

It was all over in minutes; the French threw down their weapons and James had control of the ship. He took the officers onto the Alouette and installed a prize crew backed up by a squad of marines to control the prisoners.

Chapter 13: Cleaning up

James sat across the table from Marty and tucked into the excellent pie they were having for dinner.

"The second corvette will be ready to sail after a fashion tomorrow," Marty told him, "and we will be ready tonight. Do you think you will be able to escort them back to base on your own?"

"Certainly, especially with extra marines to guard the crews," James confirmed with a grin.

"You want some extra marines?" Marty laughed at his cheek.

"It would make life simpler."

"Alright, you can have them. What about the captain of the one you took?"

"It was his first voyage as senior. In fact, both of them had absolutely no experience whatsoever."

Marty shook his head. The French must be short of commanding officers if they entrusted such an important convoy to a couple of inexperienced lieutenants.

"Did you see any other transports after you left the Eagle?" Marty asked.

"No, none at all."

Marty sat back and thought about that. The last he remembered before the powder ship went up was the convoy scattering. He closed his eyes trying to picture the scene. He opened them and resumed eating.

"Well, Ryan should have picked up the two you saw and with any luck will have had the sense to maintain his patrol outside of Santander. If he has, he will pick up any that get that far."

He paused to savour a particularly tasty morsel then carried on,

"I will sweep around to the East and see if any are over that way, then circle around to rendezvous with the Eagle. I will collect up any prizes he has and escort them all back to Gibraltar where I will complete my repairs.

Get back here as soon as you have resupplied and bring supplies for the Eagle as well, as you will both stay here until I get back."

James gathered up his charges the next morning and set off for home. A pair of corvettes would net them a fair profit once the prize court got around to valuing and buying them in.

Marty got his battered ship underway and went hunting the scattered transports. The current in that part of Biscay circulated to the North in a generally anticlockwise fashion so any other ships that were caught in the blast when the powder ship went up would drift that way. Marty decided to swing up to the Northeast then make his way down the coast to Bilbao.

They didn't have to go far, just over the horizon they spotted a transport adrift with half a mast. As they approached, the rail of the ship was lined with men waving and shouting.

They hove to half a cable away and sent over the barge and cutter. The French crew was so desperate that they welcomed them on board and once they had it secured, the carpenter and doctor went over. One to tend the sick and the other to repair the ship.

"She's loaded with cannon and carriages, according to the crew she was one of two carrying the guns. There were another two, specialist transports, for the horses and two troop carriers for the soldiers. She was next in line to the powder ship and caught the worst of the blast. They managed to sail for a couple of hours then the mast broke. They've been drifting ever since," Lieutenant Stamp reported.

"Repairs?" Marty asked.

"We will have a jury-rigged mast ready by this evening and can make slow way."

"Take command of her and make your way towards Santander. You should find the Eagle down there. I will rendezvous with you at the latest in three days and then escort you and the other prizes back to base," Marty instructed.

Happy to have his own command. Andrew Stamp returned to his ship and set course for Santander.

The Bay had other ideas.

Out in the Atlantic, a storm was brewing; it was a big, low-pressure area and it was heading straight into the Bay. The winds were gusting over sixty miles an hour and the waves being pushed ahead of it were becoming monstrous.

Andrew was struggling with the ship. The wind was too much on the beam for easy sailing in this scow and he couldn't make more than four or five knots while it wallowed like a sick pig. He was making progress towards Santander but at this rate, he was looking at getting there at around the same time as Marty.

He sniffed the wind, which was swinging towards the West. It smelled of seaweed and salt. He looked suspiciously toward the horizon and saw the sunset had an angry look to it. He called the Bosun's mate,

"Check all the hatches are dogged down and get canvas over them with battens to hold it down. Seal the ship up as much as you can. Bring the French captain to me as soon as you've done that."

They continued South as the sun set and he noticed the ship was wallowing noticeably more as the sea was picking up and hitting them on the beam. The captain appeared.

"Look," Andrew said and pointed to the sky to the West.

"Oh my God, that is a storm! We have to get to shelter immediately!" cried the captain.

"With this wind, we will never make Santander," Andrew decided, *"Where should we go?"*

"Where are we?" the captain asked,

"As far as I can tell, here." Andrew indicated a point on the chart Northeast of Santander.

The Captain looked at the sky, sniffed the wind, then pointed to a point on the coast further east.

"Bilbao."

Marty also noticed the change and went to his cabin to look at the barometer. It had dropped an inch and as he watched it was creeping lower.

He laid a chart out on the desk, pulled out a magnifier from his drawer, and scanned the coast to the west of him. He stood up, puffed out his cheeks worriedly, and looked again.

His hearing was coming back and he could hear the creaking as the ship was taking the growing waves. He finally saw what he was looking for.

On the quarterdeck, the wind was picking up, and he met the master in the chart room.

"We need to head into here," he said, indicating the point on the chart. "Acheron bay, it's the only shelter East of here."

"I've never been there," Grey responded with a frown. "Looks like a river estuary."

"I don't think we have a choice. If I'm any judge, what's coming will drive us right onto the lee shore otherwise."

They set course, running before the wind. With the waves on their stern, it was a deceptively comfortable ride. The coast came into sight, and they turned South looking for the entrance to the bay. They found it, and Marty put two good men in the chains sounding the depth. They had to work hard to stay off the banks that lined the northern entrance to the bay, and they crept in under almost no sail at all.

The channel swung to the North behind a headland and Marty decided that as the light was fading, they would anchor there. The storm picked up and the wind howled through the upper rigging that was stuck up above the headland. Marty ordered the top masts taken down to reduce the force on the ship.

Ryan captured two ships full of soldiers. He was keeping them under his guns but now he had a problem- a storm was coming in from the West and there was no way he could keep them close by. His alternatives were to sink them. The thought of the wholesale drowning of so many men made him feel physically sick. Take the risk that his men would be overwhelmed, and the ships recaptured by the French in the storm as soon as he lost contact, or find shelter.

The wind and waves were picking up and he made his decision. Gunners without guns were just foot soldiers, he reasoned, so he would enter Santander bay and shelter there. If he anchored far enough out from the shore, he might even come away with his prizes.

Andrew had every man on the ship working. French sailors hauled next to English and the pump was working constantly. Even the French captain bent his back when needed.

The Ria de Bilbao was an estuary and was sheltered enough that they could anchor and sit out the storm, but they had to get there first. The transport was heavy but to jettison cargo meant opening the hatches and with the seas as high as they were it wasn't practical.

So they pumped till their hands bled and fought the bitch until they turned in and scuttled almost sideways into the shelter of the hills.

James had a different problem. The more damaged of the two corvettes was taking on water and foundering, she would never make the coast. He positioned the Alouette and the second corvette to windward of the stricken craft forming a lee so they could boat off the prize crew and prisoners. That done, they abandoned her and sailed South towards Santander. They would shelter in the bay and get out as soon as the storm allowed them.

The storm was fast moving to start with but as it entered the bay, it slowed as it was trapped by the surrounding hills and like many storms before it, all it could do was rage and spend itself there.

Rage it did for two full days before it started to run out of energy. It took another day to die down to the point anyone would want to sail in it.

Andrew sat on the shore and emptied the water out of his shoes. Most of the crew and prisoners managed to get ashore before the ship sank.

It was ironic, he thought. The ship had made it into the bay but halfway through the night had sprung a couple of planks below the waterline and sunk in a matter of minutes. Luckily, a lookout noticed the sea edging up the side and raised the alarm. He lost two men who were trapped below but the rest managed to get in the ships boat or get a hold of something that floated and gotten ashore.

His problem now was they were beached in enemy territory and to make it worse, a line of horsemen had appeared on the hill to the south of them.

Ryan was woken by a grinning Midshipman Archer.

"Excuse me, sir, but there is something you should see," he chirped excitedly.

"It had better be bloody good!" Ryan grumbled as he pulled on his boots. He had only had three hours sleep and the storm was still howling outside.

Once on deck, he looked around and his jaw dropped. There anchored in line with him was the Alouette and a

French corvette with the Union Jack flying above the French tricolour just visible through the rain. James stood at the rail and waved as he saw him.

"Rough night!" he shouted above the wind and rain. "Come over for breakfast!"

It only took a minute to boat over and he was soon down in James' cabin drinking a coffee.

"We came in around midnight and saw your ships in the lightning's light. The Eagle is easily recognizable- there aren't many Baltimore Clippers in this part of the world," James told him as his steward brought in plates of fried ham and eggs. They had indeed navigated in by the light of the lightning that had played almost constantly across the sky. "What cargo are those ships carrying?"

"A brigade of seasick soldiers," Ryan replied, "They got so ill in the storm that you could guard them with two snotty mids with buckets. What happened to the Formidiable?"

James filled him in and when he finished, they ate in silence for a while.

"All we can do is wait until this weather passes and then get back out to the patrol area," James stated and then concluded, "if they don't get here in four days one of takes the prizes back to Gibraltar and the other goes and looks for them."

That was a sobering thought- the idea that Marty and the Formidiable could be laying wrecked on the French coast somewhere made them both anxious.

James sighed,

"Whatever we will need to get out of this bay as soon as we can, the French may have a battery overlooking it and we will be sitting ducks if we stay."

At the same time, Marty sat in his cabin with Blaez's head in his lap while Shelby examined the dog carefully. Blaez had collapsed not long after Marty returned to his cabin.

Shelby sat back and frowned.

"I can't find anything physically wrong. There isn't any swelling in his abdomen, his heart rate and breathing are normal." He thought for a moment.

"Was he with you when that ship blew up?"

"Yes! We were on the quarterdeck; he was knocked out cold," Marty told him.

"Then I have an idea what is wrong. Sometimes when a person is knocked out or gets a hard blow to the head, they can carry on for quite some time as if there is nothing wrong, and then, quite suddenly, exhibit signs of concussion."

"What, like it's delayed or something?" Marty asked.

"Yes, or it comes back again after the first instance."

"Will he be alright?" Marty asked his heart in his mouth.

"With rest, he should make a complete recovery. He needs to be watched and if he tries to be sick you must prevent him choking on it."

Sam, who was listening from the door into the steward's galley, stepped forward,

"Don't you worry, boss. Sam will look after Blaez."

Marty looked up at him, concern written plain across his face and said,

"Thank you, my friend."

It was a long two days that they sat in the lee of the headland and when the weather cleared, it became obvious that to get out, they would have to go into the bay to turn the Formidiable so she could sail out. In fact, Marty was surprised they had gotten in without running aground the passage was so narrow.

Blaez slept on for another day then woke hungry and thirsty. He looked and behaved as if nothing happened and Marty spoiled him rotten.

They felt their way into the bay until they could turn the Formidiable safely around and head back out to the open sea.

Marty thought if they headed South along the coast, they might find the escaped transports and gave orders accordingly, but after about twenty nautical miles, he wished he hadn't.

They started seeing pieces of wreckage then the fins of sharks heading towards some point ahead of them. A half-eaten horse's body bumped against the hull as they slid past it, then another being feasted on by a score of sharks amid boiling water as they thrashed and spun to tear chunks off. A little further along and the sea was covered in bloated horse corpses, so many that they couldn't avoid hitting them, occasionally they burst, and clouds of fetid gas blew across the deck. Flies flew thick in the air and swarmed on the rotting meat.

Then they saw that the transport had been driven up onto the beach and pounded to pieces by the waves. The horses perished as the crew had absolutely no way to get them off the ship. Marty, hardened as he was to the sights of the consequences of war, had never seen anything like it and had to swallow the bile that came up into his throat at the sight. Other men were reduced to tears, the British sailor was sentimental concerning animals, especially horses and dogs.

They broke clear of the debris field and stood a little further out to sea in case the second horse transport had suffered the same fate.

Andrew Stamp stood and raised his hands above his head, the squad of French Lancers that had trotted down the hill now surrounded them with their lances lowered into the attack position. The French captain stepped forward and spoke to the Ensign in command,

"These men are my prisoners, they helped us to get our ship into the bay ahead of the storm where it unfortunately sunk. We should take them to Santoña or Santander where the commander of the Naval group can decide on what to do with them." The ensign looked down his nose under the peak of his hat and replied,

"No sir, you will form up and we will take you to our camp. The local military commander can decide what to do with them. If you would start in that direction," he pointed South, *"Our camp is just a couple of kilometres away."*

The trek was miserable. Some of the sailors had no shoes and it was raining hard. After the first kilometre, most were suffering - the French as well as the English. The soldiers didn't seem to care and just prodded all of them along with their lances if the lagged behind.

Their 'camp' was a fortified position that housed at least a brigade of lancers behind a palisade of logs.

Inside, it was well organized and the prisoners, as they all now thought of themselves, were handed over to the guard.

They were herded into a compound with canvas stretched out between the rails in one corner to form a shelter which they huddled under, keeping close to share body warmth.

Eventually after what felt like an age, a sergeant entered and asked for the Captain,

"Come with me. The Commandant wants to talk with you," he barked as if he was giving orders on a parade ground. The French captain, who Andrew now knew was called Cyril Dupuis, stood and followed him out, complaining loudly about the treatment of loyal French sailors and their prisoners.

A squad of soldiers came and separated the French and English into two groups. Each group was taken out of the compound, and the English were taken to a large tent and pushed inside.

Andrew looked around and saw that the tent had cots for all of them and a stove in the middle that provided some heat. There were rough blankets on the cots and the men started stripping off their wet clothes and wrapping themselves in the blankets to warm up.

The flap opened and a pair of soldiers entered with bundles of old clothes, which were unceremoniously dumped on the first cot. Andrew noticed that a further, two soldiers stood outside with lances at the ready. They left and a jolly fat man and a skinny helper came in with a cauldron of something that smelt like stew, bowls, and sticks of bread.

The bread turned out to be stale, and the stew thin with gristly chunks of unidentifiable meat and a few vegetables, but it was warm and filled them up, so they didn't care that they ate it with their fingers and mopped the bowls with a heel of bread. After they finished, an officer came in and asked who was in command. Andrew stepped forward and the officer looked at him incredulously obviously expecting an older man. Andrew was cursed, in his opinion, with looking younger than his years.

"Lieutenant Andrew Stamp, of His Majesties ship Formidiable, commanding officer of this prize crew," he introduced himself, standing as straight and tall as he could.

"You will come with me," the officer ordered and went to take his arm but stopped when with a growl the men stepped forward. He stepped back in surprise, his hand going to his sword then motioned Andrew to precede him, glaring back at the men threateningly.

"He better come back un'armed or yer will pay matey," a voice called as they left the tent.

Looking around, Andrew saw that their tent was well guarded and that the sentries were alert even if they were stood out in the rain in long-oiled capes. He was taken to a large tent in the centre of the compound and ushered inside. A moustachioed, elegant man sat behind a desk with a glass of red wine in his fist as he watched them approach.

"This is the officer?" he asked mockingly as he cast an eye over Andrew's dishevelled appearance.

"I am a lieutenant of His Majesty King George the third's Navy; an officer and I demand to be treated as such!" he snapped.

The officer looked at him in amused surprise and said,

"The puppy has teeth! Well, young man you obviously speak excellent French. I am Commandant Pierre de Lyon. Now I need to ask you to give me your version of the story the captain has told us."

Andrew took his time and tried to remember everything Captain Stockley taught them about what to do if they were captured. 'Don't tell lies; they will always catch you out. And remember, a skilled interrogator can piece together intelligence from the most innocent seeming replies.' He took a deep breath,

"We captured the Céraiste after she was damaged by the explosion of a ship in her convoy. We think it was carrying gunpowder. She was disabled and drifting when we found her and was in no position to resist. I was given the task of sailing her to Gibraltar, but we got caught by the storm and driven into Bilbao estuary. We made it in, but she had sprung some planks below the waterline and sunk. The rest you know."

The officer compared what he said to a paper he had on his desk.

"That is close enough to what the captain told me. Now, where is your ship?" he checked the paper again, *"The Formidable."*

"I have no idea. We left her before the storm and that could have driven her anywhere," Andrew replied, noticing the mispronunciation of his ship's name.

The commandant gave him a long flat look and Andrew knew his omission of the honorific in the reply was the cause, but he chose to ignore it and kept his eyes front and centre.

"How many ships did you capture?" de Lyon asked once he realised he wasn't going to get a 'Sir'.

"I do not know. We left before they captured any more." He knew he was on safe ground there as the French captain couldn't contradict him.

"What is the name of your captain?"

Andrew decided that was none of his business and didn't answer. He was asked other questions but continued to refuse to answer.

"You are lucky I am not of a mind to beat information out of you. Take him back to his tent."

When he was pushed through the tent flap, the men rushed to gather around and make sure he was alright. He was flattered they cared so much and reassured them he was fine.

A guard entered and asked who was second in command. The Bosun's Mate stepped forward and was led from the tent.

He returned after only a quarter of an hour with a big grin on his face.

"I just told 'em I don't talk French. In the end, they just gave up."

They were left alone for the rest of the night and the following day, but the third morning they were loaded into a cart. The whole camp was being packed up and the Lancers were moving out. Andrew overheard that Bilbao had resisted the French attempts to capture it and the brigade was decamping to Santoña.

The trip was wet and the road a muddy quagmire, which meant they spent about as much time pushing the cart as riding in it. In the end, it took three days to travel the forty miles.

The road followed the coast and they could see that the storm had died down and the seas quieted. The sailors looked at the sea longingly and wondered if they would ever see their shipmates again.

The Formidiable continued to follow the coast to Bayonne and Biarritz with no sign of the other horse transport.

"They either weathered the storm or made it into either the river Adour or the port down at Saint-Jen-de-Luz as they are the only places along this coast," the master told Wolfgang Ackermann.

"Well, if they made into the Ador, there was no sign when we passed. There wasn't a single ship in the estuary," Ackerman responded.

"And if they made it as far as Bayonne, it would be a miracle in that wind," Grey frowned.

"Let's have a good look into Saint-Jen then," Ackermann concluded.

Marty was called up on deck at just after six bells in the afternoon watch. He'd left the running of the ship to Wolfgang while he caught up on his reports and paperwork first with Jonathan Fletcher and later with Quinten Shelby.

"What have you found Wolfgang?" he asked as he came up on the quarterdeck.

Wolfgang pointed to the West and said,

"That is the bay of Saint-Jen-de-Luz and behind it is the port tucked into the mouth of the river La Nivelle. The lookout says there are a number of masts visible one of which could be our transport."

"And the others?" Marty asked.

"Barges and single masted coastal craft."

They were sailing very slowly past the entrance to the bay, which was about fifteen hundred yards across with a large fort on a promontory dominating it. Marty scanned it and decided that there was no way they could just sail in as the fort was fairly bristling with forty-eight-pound guns. Even as he thought it, there was a puff of smoke and a very large ball flew towards them to splash in the sea about a cable short.

"Set more sail and get us out of range before they decide that we would make a good target to practice on," Marty ordered. "Let's see what the coastline is like for the next few miles South."

The coastline turned out to be sheer cliffs, and Marty ordered them back to the North of the bay where there were beaches.

That night, boats pulled up on the sand, and twenty men got out. They looked like fishermen and spoke a mixture of Basque and French. They laughed and joked as they made the forty-five-minute walk to the Port, crossed the bridge to the South side where there were hotels and cafés in a variety of architectural styles, chose a café that overlooked the harbour, and ordered wine.

They started a party celebrating their survival of the storm, and soon other fishermen and sailors were joining in drinking cheap wine and singing along to a tambor and pipes. As these things do in a place where men lead a hard and unforgiving life, it soon took on a life of its own. Nobody noticed that the initiators slipped away in twos and threes after midnight.

On the transport, the harbour watch looked at the café enviously and cursed their captain who was probably over there in the thick of it. The ship was separated from its companions when the British had attacked the convoy and was far enough away from the powder ship to avoid being damaged, unlike the other horse transport. They scattered to the Southeast and ran ahead of the storm as it came in and made the port by complete accident.

It was as if the angels smiled on them and even though they couldn't join in the fun onshore, that didn't mean they couldn't have a celebratory wine or two. The horses had been fed and watered and the captain was planning on getting them to Santander once he was sure the British frigate was nowhere to be seen.

The glass of wine turned quickly into a bottle then two so when they heard men coming up the gangway, they assumed it was the rest of the crew returning. After that, they slept the sleep of the unconscious, courtesy of Blackjack. When the rest of the crew returned worse for wear and very happy, staggered aboard and down to their berths. They also fell into deep, unconscious sleep.

The captain fell into his bunk and was snoring without noticing that there was a figure sat in the shadows behind his desk, but in the morning, he was shaken roughly awake at dawn.

He looked down the wrong end of a double-barrelled pistol, behind which was the cheerfully smiling face of a young man who he vaguely recognised.

"Good morning," Marty greeted him cheerfully, *"How's your head?"*

Captain Delphine opened his mouth to say something, but Marty continued,

"The tide is turning you need to make sail immediately." He pulled the captain to his feet and pushed him out of the door.

On deck, there was a full complement of sailors. The only problem was he didn't know any of them. Marty had his pistol pressed to the Captain's lower back and whispered,

"Give the orders to get us under way, nice and clear now."

The captain hesitated until Marty prodded him with the barrel and he started bellowing orders. The crew worked with amazing efficiency, far better than his own, and he started to have a worrying suspicion grow in the back of his mind. If only he didn't have such a hangover, it would all become clear, he thought.

The ship drifted out of the harbour carried by the tide and as soon as they made the bay. They raised sail and worked their way out to the open sea. Once well out, they were joined by the Formidiable, and Marty gave Stanley Hart the command and a fresh set of sailors as a prize crew with Wilson as his Bosun.

Content, he set course for Santander.

Chapter 14: Rescue and Reunion

North of Santander, they spotted the Eagle, Alouette, and their prizes. Marty noticed immediately that the Transport commanded by young Stamp was missing.

"No, we haven't seen him," James confirmed at the 'all captains' meeting Marty called as soon as they were all together.

"Do you think he was lost in the storm?" Ryan asked.

"His ship was pretty beat up so he might, but he could also have made one of the estuaries along this stretch of coast," Marty replied as he looked over the map. "With the prevailing wind, I think he could have made for Bilbao."

He sat back in his chair, thought for a moment then continued,

"You two take the prizes back to base. I will take the Formidiable down to Bilbao and have a look in to see what's there. Transfer one of the army officers and ten of the other ranks, including a couple of warrants, to the Formidiable."

He noticed the puzzled look on the others faces and smiled,

"Bargaining chips in case they are in enemy hands."

The Formidiable ghosted into the Bilbao estuary flying a Spanish flag. Marty interrogated the French officer and was told, after the application of a number of glasses of brandy, that Bilbao was still in Spanish hands. It was early in the morning and there was a light mist covering the water, so they didn't see the mast of the wrecked ship until they ran into it.

Marty sent a team ashore to look for flotsam and jetsam to identify the wreck and they came back with some crates with French army markings. They told him there was body on the shore that was unidentifiable but was dressed like a British sailor.

As it had been raining incessantly for the last few days, he knew they wouldn't find any tracks that would tell them anything. As they were about to leave, after recovering the body with the intention of giving the man a proper burial at sea, Antton spotted a fisherman sculling towards them.

Marty stood back and watched as his three Basques gathered at the side and held an animated conversation with the man. Basque was a language he didn't try to learn and as far as he could tell, bore absolutely no resemblance to any other, so he had no idea what was being said.

"He says that most of the men from the ship made it ashore. They were taken by a troop of French cavalry, Lancers from their description, South to where they had a base. The word is that they moved out West a few days ago with men in a cart," Antton reported after they had made their farewells to the fisherman.

"Get that officer back up here. I want to talk to him again."

The officer looked surly and was not inclined to cooperate as he realized that Marty must have gotten some information out of him when he was drunk.

"I have men ashore that are probably in the hands of the French military and I need to know where they will have been taken so I can offer you and your men in exchange for them," Marty told him bluntly as the sight

of the dead man being brought ashore put him in a bad mood.

"Where will they have been taken?" he demanded.

"We will be exchanged if we find them?" the officer, a captain of artillery, responded.

"Yes," Marty snapped.

The officer looked as if he was about to respond to this rudeness but instead said with one eye firmly on his release,

"Santander, that is where the local headquarters is. They will be taken there for interrogation."

Marty wasted no time, and they set sail only pausing for an hour to bury the dead seaman in the depths and four hours later they hove to off the Punta el Higar.

Marty had a boat manned and the mast stepped, upon which a white flag of parley flew above the Union flag. They sailed the one and a half miles to the docks where they were met by a contingent of French Naval officers. Marty was dressed in his best to impress.

"I am here to negotiate the release of my men that I understand are being held here," Marty announced after introductions were completed. *"I have a French Army officer of artillery and other ranks to offer in exchange."*

This prompted a messenger to be sent to the army headquarters and while they waited for his return, Marty chatted with the captain of a frigate.

"We were caught in the storm and were driven to the coast where we managed to find shelter," Marty dissembled when asked, *"the prize crew were in charge of a second transport that we captured."*

"That would be one of the convoy you attacked North of here," the captain replied with a sly look.

"The captain of the transport was also brought here and told us everything."

Marty gave a mock sigh as if he had been caught out but knew that the captain in question had no idea about the Eagle and Alouette.

"That is true. We shot the wrong ship and suffered quite a lot of damage when it blew up. We captured his ship and another with troops on board." Marty knew that once they exchanged the prisoners, the truth would come out, but there was no point in just giving the French the information at this point.

An Army Major arrived with the messenger, saving him having to answer any more questions, and invited Marty to accompany him to the headquarters building. He gave his word of honour to Marty that the flag of truce would be honoured and he would be free to return once his business had been concluded.

The headquarters was in a building next to a large circular arena that the major identified as the Plaza del Toros and described in lurid detail the bullfights that were held there. Marty listened with half an ear.

Inside, they were met by a lieutenant and led to an office just off the foyer.

"Captain Stockley, may I present Marshal General Soult, Commander of the Army," the lieutenant said in almost perfect English.

The man who stood behind the desk wore a dark blue uniform coat with gold epaulettes on the shoulders and braid around the collar and cuffs, his grey hair was tied back in a cue. He had piercing dark eyes and a long face with a high forehead.

Soult gave the slightest of bows in greeting and indicated that he should sit.

"You have greatly inconvenienced me, Captain," he opened, *"I have been waiting for that artillery for a long time."*

Marty shrugged and said, "C'est la Guerre, *I only did my duty."*

Soult gave a smile in acknowledgement and waved a hand to the lieutenant, who went to a door at the back of the office and barked an order. The door opened, and Andrew Stamp walked through looking at first bemused then relieved when he saw his Captain.

"This is your officer?" Soult asked.

"Yes, this is Lieutenant Stamp," Marty replied and then to Andrew,

"Have they treated you well, Mr. Stamp?"

"Aye sir, fairly well."

"And the men?"

"Them too, although the food could be better."

Marty smiled and turned back to Soult,

"I have a Captain of Artillery and ten other ranks, including a sergeant who I propose we exchange for Mr. Stamp and his men."

Soult looked at him thoughtfully for a moment and then replied,

"You are an officer who cares for his men, a rare thing, but one I admire. We have only eight men to exchange along with Mr. Stamp."

"Well, you have fed them for a week or so, please consider the extra men compensation for your hospitality," Marty smiled.

"You know there is a substantial reward for your capture," Soult commented casually, looking down at a sheet of paper on his desk, *"it's been increased to twenty thousand Louis."* There was a sharp intake of breath from the Lieutenant who stood behind him.

"The politicos would thank me for handing you over and I would be quite wealthy."

"And break the convention of the flag of truce? I think not. You are an honourable man and wouldn't stoop so low" Marty replied softly.

Soult smiled back,

"Quite so! You must take your men and leave before they realize who you are. I will trust in your honour as a gentleman to return my men. But, be assured if we meet again, I will have you arrested and hand you to the department."

With that, Marty and Andrew were ushered into an anti-room where the men were waiting and from there back to the boat.

Marty sent the French soldiers in exchange to the port then made all sail to get to Gibraltar. He wanted to see his family all of sudden.

Chapter 15: The Doldrums

Marty was in his office at the base when there was a hail from the lookout tower that a ship was entering the bay. He gave it no thought as sometimes ships came in mistaking it as the harbour and was surprised when there was a knock on the door. Ryan stepped in with a flag lieutenant, who saluted as Marty got to his feet.

"Lieutenant Upton," he introduced himself, "I am here at the behest of Baron Mulgrave, the First Lord of the Navy."

"Welcome to Gibraltar. This must be important if they are sending flag officers with messages."

Upton smiled in agreement and Marty bade him sit.

"The French are making trouble in the Indian Ocean again; they have sent a Fleet over there to disrupt our trade and to take on the East India Company head on. They are based on Isle Bonaparte and Isle de France," Upton explained.

Marty looked puzzled.

"That is what the French have renamed the islands of Madagascar and Reunion since they recaptured them," Upton clarified

"Ahh," nodded Marty, "yes, I had some dealings with those islands some time ago."

"Admiral Hood told us you have a vested interest in helping solve this, and you have personal knowledge of Reunion."

Marty knew that was true. Caroline complained that their ships had been pursued several times in the last year or so by French country ships. His fleet was too nimble and fast to be caught by mere frigates, but they had lost other shipments that were carried on company ships that had been taken.

"What do you want me to do?" Marty asked.

"We want you to go out there, independently raid their bases with the Formidiable, gather intelligence, and build a picture of what their strength is so that we can deal them a knockout blow. Admiral Hood says that Lietenant Thompson can run operations here while you are away," Upton replied.

"Very well, I will get the Formidiable ready. When do we leave?"

"As soon as you are provisioned and ready to go."

Caroline was unexpectedly relaxed about losing her husband for several months at the least. In her heart, she knew they had been enjoying an unexpectedly long, relatively uninterrupted period together and knew it had to end. In any case, this was something that was affecting their trade and there was no one better to solve the problem than her Marty.

As he wouldn't be there, she decided she would take the household back to England. It was about time she took back personal control of some of her operations and she had some ideas for new enterprises that she thought would be profitable.

Marty sat and watched Blaez and Troy playing ball with young James and it suddenly struck him the Blaez wasn't a young dog anymore. He was a lot slower than the younger dog and had a significant amount of grey in his muzzle. James was six now and had, to Marty's astonishment, a very level-headed view on the word.

James left the two dogs to playing, went to his father, and climbed on his lap.

"Blaez is getting old," he commented.

James looked at the dogs and added very seriously,

"Daddy, I don't think you should take Blaez with you."

"Why is that?" Marty asked.

"He will want to protect you and he isn't fast enough anymore. Troy gets the ball every time," James observed.

"Oh? I think he lets him," Marty laughed but James was having none of it.

"He is getting old and it's not fair he is asked to fight anymore!" James said crossly, surprising Marty with his anger.

"Well, what do you suggest we do? He will be very upset if I don't take him with me," Marty replied, knowing in his heart he would be just as upset.

"He can stay here with me; we are friends too," James insisted.

"Well, that would be just fine! But I will miss him," Marty said quietly.

"You must take Troy. You need someone to keep you company and mommy says a dog brings you luck and is your friend."

Marty looked at his son, who was trying to be very brave as he sacrificed his dog for his father, and tears sprang to his eyes. He took a deep breath,

"Alright, we can do that, but you mustn't spoil him. He won't do well if he gets fat."

"I know daddy, and he can't play as much as Troy. I will look after him. I promise!"

Marty watched the two dogs for a while and saw his son was right.

"Alright, I will take Troy," Marty agreed, hugging James.

"That's good. I hoped you two would work it out together," Caroline said in his ear as she bent to hug them both from behind the chair where she had been listening.

Blaez made a fuss when he realised he was being left behind, but James and Beth smothered him with attention and love as they waved goodbye to the Formidiable as she left port.

Blaez settled into the role of family protector, put up with the twins pulling his ears and climbing on his back, and loved James and Beth as much as they loved him. He would stand and look out to sea, waiting for Marty when left alone but didn't pine, the kids wouldn't let him.

When the household embarked on the Eagle to move back to England, he installed himself in the children's cabin and escorted them wherever they went. Back in England, he didn't like the weather as much as Gibraltar, but he had a privileged position and could chose whichever spot he wanted to sleep, more often than not, near or in front of a fire.

Troy took to life at sea like he was born to it and exhibited all the characteristics of his father but in a calmer way. Marty missed his old friend but knew that this was for the best.

The frigate headed South and soon Marty was putting his crew through their sail evolutions and gunnery exercises, which were more to keep them busy and the standard up rather than to teach them anything new.

It was not the ideal time of year to be sailing to the Indian Ocean as the Atlantic was prone to storms, and they knew they were in for a rough time as they swung out into the Atlantic heading for St Paul's rock just North of the equator. Ironically, the area around St. Paul's rock was also known as the doldrums.

So it was that after fighting their way Southwest through howling gales, they suddenly found themselves becalmed.

Sitting motionless for two weeks played on the men's nerves and Troy was edgy and bad tempered. Minor disputes started to escalate to physical confrontations and to relieve the tension, Marty started a boxing competition for the men to blow off steam. He had the Larboard and Starboard watches each choose six champions who were divided into three weight categories.

Marty decided that the fights would be bareknuckle; fists only, no gauging, kicking, or wrestling. They would be held in a square, roped-off area fifteen feet to a side. The winner would be named when a fighter was unable to continue or yielded. The contest would be held over two days and started in the afternoon when the heat had gone out of the sun.

The first pair were in the lightest category and were a pair of topmen. They went at it with a will, but very little finesse and it came down to a lucky punch. The winner by a knockout was from the starboard watch.

The next were a pair of bruisers from the heavy class, both weighed in at over eighteen stones. This one came down to a slugging match and was stopped when the contestant from the Larboard watch's eyes were both swollen shut.

The third bout was the first pair from the middle weight class and was won by the Larboard watch, so halfway through the contest the Starboard watch was two to one up. The sun was going down fast as it does in those latitudes, and they stopped for the night as it was getting dark.

The next morning, the men were swabbing down after holystoning the decks and about to go to breakfast when a cry came from the mainmast lookout.

"Sail Ho!"

What the hell? Marty thought as he ordered Midshipman Williams up into the tops.

"Looks like an armed transport, can't see her colours."

"Armed transport or privateer perhaps?" Wolfgang asked.

Marty agreed and knew that, for some inexplicable reason, if two ships were becalmed, they tended to drift towards each other but that would take quite some time. *Well*, he thought, *it won't hurt to keep the other ship guessing.*

"Lower our colours, Wolfgang," he ordered.

The fourth bout was scheduled for mid-afternoon from the middle weight section between a gunner on the starboard watch and a waister on the larboard. These two looked to be an uneven match as the gunner, Fred Goddard, was a solid fifteen stone and five foot ten while the waister was thirteen and a half stone and only five feet two. However, looks could be deceptive, and it very soon became apparent that the waister, Brian Jones- an ex Welsh coal miner, was no novice at prize fighting.

He assumed a stance with his fists high in front of his face and his elbows tucked in at his sides and shuffled around the ring, constantly moving. He also swayed his upper body around, presenting a moving target for his opponent.

Fred was bemused by this as he was used to toeing the line and slugging it out. He could think of nothing else to do but follow Jones and try and land a decent hit. Jones just let the blows fall on his arms and waited for an opening, then one of his fists would lash out and score a solid hit. It wasn't long before Fred's nose resembled a raw steak and his eyes were almost shut. He never saw the uppercut that landed square on his chin and put his lights out.

In the twenty minutes that the fight took, the two ships had drifted enough that they could see each other from their quarterdecks. Marty was aware that they were being watched intently by the officers on the other ship's quarterdeck by the glint of light on their telescope lenses. He ordered that no one was to raise a glass to look back at them and that the other ship should be ignored by all except the lookout.

The fifth bout was the second of the heavy men. One was Wilson and the other was an equally large bruiser called Ernie Stockbridge. The two of them practically filled the ring and Marty expected another slugging match.

How wrong he was. Wilson emulated Brian Jones and adopted a defensive pose. Ernie was no fool as he had seen the result of what happened if you just bulled in against that and followed suit. The two men circled each other, looking for openings. Wilson, who was left-handed, threw occasional jabs with his right hand trying to tempt Ernie into dropping his guard. Ernie was having none of it and just waited. When Wilson eventually tried a right, left combination, Ernie drove a wicked right hand into his ribs.

Wilson stepped back and covered up, but everyone could see that the blow hurt him, including Ernie, who feinted shots at that area trying to get Wilson to move his guard. But Wilson was stubborn, held his ground, and kept his guard in place.

This carried on for almost thirty minutes and the men started to get bored, cat calls started to get mixed in with the encouragement. Then Wilson must have seen an opening and fired in four massive blows in a row, which sat Ernie on the deck.

The starboard watch cheered, and the larboard groaned, but Ernie shook his head and climbed to his feet, taking up his defence once again. Honours were even.

Marty looked out towards the other ship and was surprised that it was much closer, how could that be? He wondered, *are they towing her to close on us?* He sent a message and a glass up to the lookout, who reported that the other ship was being towed by their ship's boats and using sweeps. This was bizarre, was their captain an idiot? He couldn't have any idea who they were as they were beam on to him and he couldn't see their name.

Not only that, but it was also still hot from the noonday sun and the men in the boat had to have been exhausted.

The bout ended when Wilson put Ernie on his backside for a second time with a cut above his right eye that bled profusely. Shelby called a halt and took him below to stitch him up.

The next morning, Marty sat on the main topmast yard waiting for it to get light enough to see the other ship. It emerged out of the gloom and was a mile away. They must have rowed all night. He took a stay down to the deck and ordered,

"Wolfgang! Would you be so kind as to get the men quietly armed and ready to repel boarders. I think we can expect company before our midday meal," he ordered quietly.

The carronades were covered in canvas sheets; Marty had started doing that so enemy ships couldn't see their strength at short range. It was quite comical watching gunners squirming under the covers with charges and canister shot to load the monsters. He ordered the main battery loaded with canister as well. If it came to a fight, he wanted the other ship as undamaged as possible.

Swivel guns were brought up from below where they had been loaded and laid on the deck near their mounts. Likewise, volley guns were loaded below decks and grenades fused before being brought up and positioned quietly where they would be quickly to hand.

He wanted to give the impression of an ill-disciplined ship that was slow to wake up, so he asked Wolfgang to forego holystoning and swabbing, then kept the men out of sight apart from a few who loitered around the deck.

The other ship moved towards them under sweeps and Marty could see she was ported for ten guns to a side and by the size of the port covers, he guessed she had nine or twelve pounders. They changed course slightly and he could see they were aiming to get across his stern.

That could be a problem! If he could do that and threaten to rake them from stern to bow, they could be in real trouble.

The other ship was now about half a mile away. Marty made a decision, went down to his cabin, and opened the chest of 'dressing up' clothes he always carried for when he needed a disguise. He pulled out a suit that would be worn by a Spanish gentleman and a hat with an ostentatious feather decoration. Adam, his steward, came in, looked surprised for a moment then shrugged and helped him get dressed. He called Wolfgang in and told him to get everyone visible on deck out of uniform and for them to wander around listlessly like they were desperate.

Fully disguised as a Spanish gentleman-captain he strutted up onto deck and went to the rail.

"Hola Señor!" he hailed the other ship and was happy to see a man who could be the captain come to the rail.

"That is a very useful thing to have!" he shouted in Spanish, pointing to the sweeps.

The other man replied in Spanish with more than a hint of a French accent.

"Yes. How long have you been becalmed?"

"Almost four weeks," Marty lied, *"we are running out of water, my men have been on less than half rations for several days now!"*

The man barked an order, and the sweeps stopped.

"I have enough that I can give you some if I can come alongside," he offered.

"Please, if you can give us anything, come aboard," Marty called across, making it sound like a plea. Matai and young Williams followed his lead and hung over the rail calling pitifully in Spanish.

The sweeps started again, turning the ship so that they could run up alongside.   Wolfgang came up beside Marty and told him quietly,

"The lookout says there are a lot of men ducked down behind their gunnels. He could see their heads moving around."

Marty looked up to the tops of the approaching ship and saw they had men up there with muskets.

"Tell the marines to take those men out as soon as they can. Are the gunners ready?"

"Yes, they are well hidden under canvas near their guns and the swivels are loaded with grapnels."

Marty looked at the approaching ship.

"As soon as he is at close pistol shot, launch the grapnels and give him the benefit of our broadside through his gun ports. Carronades to target his decks, let's kill as many as we can before they get close enough to board."

As the other ship came up on them, their gun ports swung up and they ran out. Marty didn't wait any longer,

"At 'em, Formidiable! Raise the colours."

The British flag was run up and the side came alive. The ports flew up and the guns run out. Simultaneously, the swivel gunners mounted their weapons on the side and fired their grapnels. The covers on the carronades were pulled off.

Marty had a fleeting glimpse of a look of horror on the other captain's face before the guns roared and smoke obscured him. The men on the grapnel ropes were heaving the two ships together using specially prepared blocks. The marines boiled out from below, formed up, loosed a volley into the other ships tops then raced up the ratlines to get into their normal firing positions.

The smoke cleared, the ships were a scant ten feet apart and closing. Several of her gun ports were empty and others looked to have been fired. Her deck was full of men who had presumably come up from below.

"Carronades! Clear that deck for me please!" Marty bellowed in a voice that could be heard along the whole ship.

Both fore and aft carronades swivelled to rake the deck and coughed out their loads of canister. The effect on the crowded deck was spectacular, devastating, and bloody. Some men were shot to pieces, others merely perforated in multiple places, very few were unscathed, blood ran from the scuppers.

The two ships ground together, and the Formidiables leapt across to the other deck screaming their war cry. The main deck was soon secured, and a few grenades dropped down the hatches quickly persuaded any men still below to drop their weapons and come out with their hands held high.

Marty found the captain by the wheel, his arm severed above the elbow. Someone had tied a tourniquet to stop the bleeding and the man was grey with pain but in no further danger. He dropped to a knee beside him,

"Captain, I believe your ship is mine," Marty told him in French.

"British! I thought you were Spaniards," he gasped through pain.

Marty looked at the arm then checked him over. There were no other wounds, he called for Shelby.

"Our surgeon will soon have you fixed up then we can talk," Marty told him and walked away after setting a guard.

Chapter 16: The Trojan Horse

Two days later, they found some wind and were able to continue on their way to Cape Town. Shelby tidied up the captain's stump and he was able to sit with Marty in his cabin.

"How do you feel now?" Marty asked.

"I have felt better. You know, it's true what they say- I can still feel the fingers in my lost arm," Cedric Salmon replied.

"You are a privateer; I found your letter of marque. Where were you going?"

"Île de France. There are supposed to be rich pickings amongst your East Indiamen."

"I know. I was there a few years ago, in Grande Baye," Marty commented, using the French name for the port at the North of the Island.

"Yes, an excellent choice of harbour. Especially for bringing in prizes, so I am told," Cedric sighed, thinking of what could have been.

That was all Marty really needed to know. He changed the subject and chatted about where Cedric came from and his background. It turned out he was originally from Nantes and was the fourth son of a baker, had left home to make his fortune, and was a successful privateer in the Mediterranean. He spotted the Formidable and was sure she was Spanish. He guessed that with the French occupation, any Spanish ship out there had to be heading for South America.

Marty hadn't thought of that and tucked that bit of information away for future use. He let Cedric go back to his temporary quarters, sat on the bench in front of the transom windows with Troy's head on his lap, and had a long think.

They pulled into Cape Town and spent over a week working on the Bonne Marie, as their prize was called. Marty wanted her to look like she took a mauling at the hands of the Formidiable and make some modifications to the inside.

Before they left, they transferred the surviving French privateers to the military authorities ashore. Marty took command of the Marie, and Wolfgang took the Formidiable. Every French speaking sailor was transferred to the prize.

The two ships sailed on the morning tide and set course for the Isle de France, which was about fifteen hundred miles away. Marty's crew spent the time getting to know their new ship and prepare her for their arrival. Marty had two choices; to make landfall at Grande Baye or Grande Port Bourbon but as Cedric had spoken highly of it, he decided they would try Grande Baye.

Once they got within fifty miles of the island, the Bonne Marie moved ahead and raised a ragged set of sails. The deck was filthy and covered in blood stains, courtesy of a steer they bought in Cape Town. The meat fed the crew for a couple of days and the blood made the decks look like a slaughterhouse.

Anybody observing from another ship saw the Formidiable sailing like she had a filthy bottom and was struggling to keep up with her prey. They fired their bow chasers every three minutes or so, obviously looking for a lucky hit to slow their prey down.

The ship being pursued was sailing with desperate urgency. She was mauled and there were blood stains running down from her scuppers. Her sails were shot holed and the skipper was trying every trick in the book to stay away from the pursuing frigate.

The reality was what that the Formidiable had a sea anchor trailing behind that kept her speed down. It looked like she was straining to catch up and that was just the impression that Marty wanted them to give. The gunners were lobbing balls that fell short or wide with the occasional one coming just close enough to be threatening.

Wolfgang checked the cable that secured the sea anchor to the base of the mizzen mast for the umpteenth time. It quivered with the strain of holding back the thrust of the Formidiable's sails. If it broke, it could whiplash across the deck and seriously injure or kill someone, so if there was the slightest sign of any fraying, he would call off the pursuit and reel it in.

They passed several ships, none of which wanted to get involved. The sight of a British Frigate in these waters was unwelcomed but the only ones that would, or even could, take it on were the French country ships, and there were none of those in sight.

The ships closed in on Grande Baye. Dusk was approaching, and the Formidiable crept ever closer. The skipper on the Bonne Marie pushed his ragged crew, many of whom sported bloody bandages, to make the harbour before the frigate caught them.

They were all well into their roles and as they passed through the entrance and the defensive battery roared out in support of the Marie, they cheered and cavorted on the deck. Some even stood at the stern rail, making rude gestures and baring their buttocks at the British ship.

The Formidiable swung away and retreated out of range of the guns, the chase for them was over. Wolfgang hove to and made a show of observing the harbour and its defences. What they were really doing was getting in the sea anchor. It had been, in Wolfgang's opinion, a damn dangerous ploy but as usual, his captain was right - it had done exactly what he wanted. All he had to do now was stay in sight until dark then head down to Grande Porte.

As they passed into the harbour, Marty noted the location of the defensive batteries, which were on the Western point at the entrance to the bay. There were a couple of big forty-gun frigates and a seventy-five-gun liner in the bay, but far more interesting were the three East Indiamen moored in a row, sterns toward the shore.

A pilot rowed out and guided them to a point about half a cable from the British ships and almost as soon as they anchored, another boat with two senior-looking French Naval officers and a well-dressed civilian approached, demanding they be allowed to board.

"Captain Jules St. Just, Lieutenant Pierre Jardin of the French Navy, and I am Mr. Brignac, Harbour Master," the civilian introduced them as they lined up on the deck.

Harbour Master? Marty thought in surprise. The bay had no harbour as such just some wooden docks that stuck out into the sea from the many beaches. There was a town at the South end with warehouses taverns and stores and to the West of that, a pier with a solitary warehouse with an earth berm around it. The only defence was a battery on the western point, which he had to admit was probably enough.

"Cedric Salmon, Captain of the Bonne Marie," Marty introduced himself, *"how can I help you? You will appreciate I am a little busy as my first mate was killed by the British."*

"We will not take much of your time," the captain interrupted, *"we just need to see your papers and inspect your ship along with any cargo you are carrying."*

"Then please accompany me to my cabin, and we can go over my papers there," Marty made a show of reluctantly agreeing.

Down in the cabin, Marty offered them seats and a glass of wine, apologised for the draft from the broken transom stern window, and pulled out the papers he found when they took her.

"My Letter of Marque and owner's papers."

The Lieutenant made a show of examining them while the captain asked,

"Tell me, where did you meet up with the British ship and what happened?"

"We hit an area with no wind, were becalmed, and spotted him on the horizon. We have sweeps, and with the help of our boats, we managed to get close enough to see he had a Spanish flag. The ship was obviously Spanish built, so it looked legitimate.

As we got closer, we could see very few sailors on deck and those looked worn, so it seemed like we had a

chance to get ourselves a much more powerful ship. Luckily, he sprung his trap too early and we were able to pull away. When the wind came up, we got into a stern chase,"

The captain gave him a long steady look, which Marty returned with his most innocent expression, until the lieutenant interrupted,

"The papers are in order."

"A frigate should have been easily able to overhaul you," the captain stated with a challenging look.

"If she'd had a clean bottom, we wouldn't have stood a chance. But it's my belief that they have been at sea for a long time. She's worn and her bottom filthy. They were carrying full sail and barely catching us."

The captain didn't look entirely convinced but seemed to accept that for now.

"If that's settled, may we proceed to the inspection?" asked the Harbour Master.

Marty raised his eyebrows in query to the two officers and when they nodded, he led the way out. Once on deck, the Navy men were most interested in the damage,

"How any men did you lose?"

"Fully, a third. Thirty-five in total and many more wounded. The bastards blasted us with enormous guns loaded with musket balls mounted on their fore and after decks."

"Carronades," the lieutenant offered in explanation.

"Whatever, they mowed down my men and damaged my rigging. We were lucky to have sweeps to get away."

Marty and his crew had spent hours making the rigging look like a patched and spliced cat's cradle, the sails patched and ragged.

Fresh wood showed repairs where holes were torn in the transom and the fore mast had pieces of spar wrapped in rope splinting it from about five feet above the deck for about eight feet where it was supposed to have been damaged. Blood stains covered the deck.

The lieutenant stood on a gun and looked out to sea to the North, where it was still faintly lit by the setting sun.

"They are still out there!"

"We will have to do something about that," the captain snapped.

"What do you have in the holds?" the harbour master asked.

"Cases of pepper as well as silk and indigo that we took from an Indiaman," Marty answered, *"he was following the African coast well to the West of Cape Town when we found him. The ship we burnt; the cargo was worth more."*

"Let me see."

Marty ordered the hatches removed, and the four of them stood looking down in to the first hold, which was almost pitch dark. Marty called for lamps and by their light, they could just see that they were almost full of chests. The captain barked an order to the lieutenant, who reluctantly climbed down into the hold and checked the markings on the cases. Marty extolled him to be careful with the lamp as he didn't want his ship burnt down after all they had been through.

"It stinks of pepper down here!" he complained and then called up. "all looks correct, they are marked with the East India Company seal."

The Harbour master seemed satisfied and demanded the harbour fee, which Marty paid from a pouch he had in his pocket. The captain, however, wasn't finished,

"We will continue this inspection tomorrow," he snapped.

Marty just gave him a very Gaelic shrug as if to say as you please.

Once the boat returned safely to the dock, the Bonne Marie became a hive of silent industry. Crates and bundles of silk were moved in the holds to reveal a false deck. Trapdoors were prized open, and fifty men came up, deeply breathing the fresh air and stretching stiff limbs that were in the confined space for too long.

"Was getting worried when we heard you admonish that French chap to be careful with the lantern," Lieutenant Trenchard commented, "it was damn stuffy too."

"It's lucky French ships stink," Marty teased him, "you lot smell worse than a night soil man in old London."

He gathered the officers around with only a shielded lamp to illuminate him and spoke quietly. Trenchard and Midshipmen Hart and Longstaff were in attendance as was Wilson.

"That damn Navy captain senses something's not right with this ship and will be coming back for a closer look tomorrow. I will put a guinea on him bringing a team of men with him," Marty explained, "so we will go tonight. There are three East Indiamen at anchor just half a cable off our starboard bow, which look like they are still fully laden."

He paused to look at each man in turn then continued,

"You will take one each. Mr. Longstaff, you will take the closest. Mr. Hart, you will take the middle one. Mr. Trenchard, you will take the furthest as you have most experience. I will take a team ashore, neutralize any lookouts and provide a diversion, which you will know as soon as you see it as it should light your way out."

He looked up at his big Bosun Wilson.

"When the diversion starts, you will get this tub under way and wait for the shore party two cables off the Point aux Cannoniers. Burn a red lantern on your stern to guide us in." He turned back to the others,

"Here are the compass bearings the quartermaster took on the three ships while I was entertaining the French in my cabin. They have soldiers aboard and we saw men exercising under guard who are probably the crews. You should endeavour to be as silent as possible. Your men have crossbows to take out sentries, use knives and clubs where you can. You all know the drill."

He held up a finger to test the breeze.

"The wind is from the Northwest, so you shouldn't have too much trouble getting out of the bay. Once out, head East around the island, Wolfgang will be waiting for us around twenty miles off of Grande Porte Bourbon, where there is supposed to be a blockading British fleet. If we all get there, we should have made our escape."

The Marie had three ship's boats, and Marty had the gig from the Formidiable stored under the upturned cutter the French kept on deck.

The men quickly got into their teams and armed themselves. They were all dressed in dark clothes and were busy blacking their faces with a mixture of burnt cork and the sludge from boiled salt beef.   The individual weapons were down to personal choice, some preferred blackjacks and knives, others, clubs or tomahawks. Several men had small but powerful crossbows; a couple had slings in their belts, and one was carefully coiling a garrotte wire.   The common factor was they were all silent, there was not a single pistol on show anywhere.

Marty was armed, more or less, as usual; stilettoes on his forearms, throwing knives in sheaths clipped to his weapons harness instead of pistols, his hanger and fighting knife.

The Shadows were going with him and were all dressed like Marty in loose black trousers and jackets buttoned up to the neck with an attached hood that covered the whole head except the eyes. Their shoes had soft chamois leather soles and all wore black gloves. They left thirty minutes before the others to give them time to deal with the sentries.

The boat pulled up at a wooden dock extended out from the beach, the shore team disembarked and melted into the darkness. All but two, headed straight for the isolated warehouse, the others followed the beach around to the town.

Marty and Sam came upon the first sentry walking up the beach. He didn't see them crouched with their heads down as they looked just like any other part of the beach. He walked straight past them, and Marty rose up silently, slipped a garrotte over his neck, choked him, and as he dropped to his knees, placed a knee in the small of his back and a with jerk of the chord, broke his neck.

The second sentry stood on a dock and was outlined against the stars. He walked up and down the dock to stay awake and suddenly stiffened as he heard a noise. He brought his musket around from his shoulder and moved to the edge of the dock with the bayonet advanced. He stopped and peered into the dark, then suddenly his feet flew out in front of him and he landed with a thump, back first on the deck with a squeak of surprise. He was even more surprised as he was hauled out into thin air, but his surprise ended as a leather bag of lead shot smashed into his temple, crushing his skull.

Two dark patches of night slipped from moon shadow to shadow along the front of the shops until they came to one that sold general goods, including lamp oil. The locked door opened after a few seconds of manipulation and the two moved into the interior. Carboys of oil were opened and spilled over the counters and floor, a small pile of priming powder was poured, and a brass timer/igniter set on top of it.

Their next stop was a ship's chandlers, and they were halfway through gathering inflammables when the door opened, the shape of a French soldier silhouetted against the starry sky. Sam was behind the counter, but Marty was exposed in the centre of the room as he piled up some cloth and hemp.

"Who are you? What are you doing?" he advanced his musket, pointing it straight at Marty.

Marty stood slowly, raising his hands above his head as he turned around. He knew that all the soldier would see was a dark shape, so he stepped forward into the scant light from the stars that shone through the window.

The soldier stepped forward.

"I'm just doing some cleaning up," Marty told him.

"At this time of . ." he started to say when Sam stepped out behind him and broke his neck with a vicious twist of his arms.

"Get the timer set and let's get out of here," Marty instructed him and went to the door to check for any other unexpected visitors.

The rest of the Shadows moved up the beach to the North, eliminating any sentries that they found on the way to the warehouse. They found two more stationed at the gap in the berm, who were efficiently disposed of. The doors to the warehouse were secured with a large padlock but that only held them up for a moment and as it opened, the unmistakable smell of gunpowder wafted out.

They had a shuttered lantern with a reflector that shone a faint beam of light in through the door. It was just enough for one of them to be able to see to stove in the top of one of the casks and set one of their brass timing devices on top of the powder. As insurance, a second cask was broached, and a slow fuse was set.

"Is that long enough?" Matai asked.

"I tested this fuse and it burns at a foot a minute. There be twenty foot of it here," John Smith answered. "You want to set it?"

Matai didn't answer the irascible quartermaster, just led the team out and along the shoreline towards the battery.

Eric Longstaff was nervous. Not only was this his first night cutting out mission, it was the first time he had been out in sole charge of a team. Captain Stockley had trained him well enough and he knew exactly what he and his men had to do, but his stomach was knotted, and his bowels rumbled.

They left the Bonne Marie some thirty minutes after the captain and his team and with muffled oars, made the short trip across to the closest East Indiaman. His job was to secure the ship. A second group of men would join them when the boat returned after dropping them off. That would give him enough men to sail the ship out. If the captain and crew were still aboard, he would enlist them to move the ship out.

Before he knew it, they were alongside, and the lead men were shinning up the bow chains, a soft twang and a grunt as a guard was brought down with a crossbow. He leapt from the gunnel and pulled himself up the side, dropped quietly over the rail, and made his way aft, almost tripping over the body of the guard on his way.

The men spread out across the deck and soon he was told that it was secure. Now, he had to take care of business below. He led five men down the stairs and once below, they un-shuttered a lantern that they had brought with them. By its dim light, they worked their way to the captain's cabin where they found a sleeping guard propped against the door. A thrust through the heart ended his vigil, and Eric quietly opened the door after the body was moved out of the way.

Snoring came from a compartment off to the larboard side. Eric pulled the curtain that closed it off from the main cabin aside and shone the lantern on the face of the man lying in the bed.

"Can't you let a man sleep in peace, you whore son," he cursed. "It's not as if I can go anywhere!"

"Captain, I'm Midshipman Eric Longstaff, Royal Navy. We are here to rescue you," Eric announced and smiled at the look of surprise on his face.

"Navy? You have recaptured my ship?" the captain asked, then added as he realised he was being rude, "Stenson, Alan Stenson at your service."

"Almost. Can you tell me how many guards are on board and where they sleep?"

"Ten in all and the cheeky bastards have taken the state rooms," he replied and when Eric asked, he added, "Down the corridor the first four cabins either side."

"We took three out up top and one outside the door, so we have six to deal with. Please take care of it, Crabtree," he ordered to the senior hand and then asked the captain,

"Did you have passengers?"

"Yes, the men are being held with the crew. The women are in the next cabin on the larboard side after the French."

"If you would kindly get dressed, we can go and tell them they are free, and you can get your ship ready to make sail."

"What? It's the middle of the night!"

"Exactly, you wouldn't want to be trying to sail out in broad daylight with those French country ships in attendance and the barrage at the entrance, would you." Eric stated flatly just the way his captain would have done. He looked at his watch.

"We have about fifteen minutes, so I think we should get a move on."

The captain dragged on a pair of trousers and shoved his feet into a pair of shoes. In the background, they heard a number of screams and several thuds. He didn't look into the cabins, which were now lit by lamps, after seeing the Formidiables carrying out bodies.

Minutes later, his crew were freed and racing up the ratlines to make sail. Eric had a couple of his men with axes ready to cut the anchor cable after the captain bemoaned the loss and wanted to raise it with the capstan.

Some damn people get their priorities all wrong! Eric cursed silently.

"How do you know when to move?" Captain Stenson asked.

Eric pointed East along the bay where the first signs of the fires Marty and Sam had set were showing.

"Set the fore courses and topsails!" Stenson bellowed and as the sails started to fill, the sound of chopping came from the bow.

The East Indiamen were all moored stern to shore, so they swung in turn to catch the wind as the anchor cables parted. Eric's moved first and as she moved away, so Stanley Hart got his moving, and lastly, Phillip Trenchard.

The bells were ringing in the church in the town to sound the alarm that there were buildings on fire and seemed to Eric to bid them farewell.

Marty and Sam ran along the beach past the powder store and on up towards the battery. They passed several shapes they knew would be dead sentries and ignored them. They had a deadline to meet.

Marty expected to rendezvous with the rest of the shadows at the battery then to meet up with their boat, which would be pulled up on the beach as planned. A whistle like a corncrake call sounded, Marty slowed to a walk, and responded in kind. A shape separated from the shadows and beckoned them forward.

"The battery gunners are berthed in a barracks set back from the battery and the magazine is in an underground store well away from both the guns and the barracks," Antton reported in a whisper.

"Can we blow the magazine?" Marty asked.

"That's no problem. We have several pipe bombs left. What do you want to do with the rest?"

"Put a couple at the door of the barracks and scatter the rest through the battery around the guns."

Antton grinned at him,

"That should cause some mayhem."

They joined the rest of the team and John and Garai were sent off to mine the magazine. Chin Lee and Matai went to the battery, which left Marty, Sam, and Antton to set the bombs at the barracks.

Hoods up, the three of them slunk down the path to the barracks. They planned to place the two bombs just outside the door set to go off after the magazine went up.

They were placing the first bomb when the door opened, and a sleepy soldier looked out in surprise. To give him his due, he didn't hesitate,

"ALARM, ALARM!" he shouted at the top of his voice before one of Marty's throwing knives took him in the throat, but it was too late! The gunners were awake,

and the alarm was being shouted as they grabbed their weapons.

Marty had a primed bomb in his hand and threw it through the door, hoping the wheel-lock would trigger when it hit something, but it just clattered across the floor and did nothing.

"Run!" he yelled and matched the order with action. Shots rang out and Sam, who was right behind him, grunted and stumbled. Marty looked around to see him fall to the ground and slowed to turn around and help him. Bullets fizzed past his ears as the gunners flooded out of the doors. Antton grabbed his arm and pulled him away into the dark. The last he saw in the light spilling from the barracks door was Sam surrounded by the French, who had their bayonets pressed to his body.

They ran for the beach where they should meet up with the rest of the team. There was an explosion behind them, which they thought must have been the pipe bomb in the barracks. Across the bay, they could see that the shops were on fire and by the light of the flames, he could just make out the three East Indiamen sailing out of the bay.

They almost stumbled into the rest of the team in their headlong flight. The shouts of officers getting the gunners organised echoed behind them.

That was when the next problem came up- the boat wasn't at the rendezvous. Marty's first thought was they were in the wrong place, but then the powder store exploded, and the bay lit up. He could see the East Indiamen and the Bonne Marie, but no boat.

The blast wave from the powder store reached them, and a wave of hot air washed over them. A second huge, much closer explosion deafened them as the battery magazine went up.

"We need to get out of here. The boat is nowhere to be seen and this beach will be awash with soldiers soon."

There was only one thing to do- head inland then try and get to Grande Porte and the blockading force, after they rescued Sam, that is.

Chapter 17: Run Rabbits Run

The Shadows melted into the countryside as the bombs around the battery started going off. They needed to get off the point as the number of soldiers prowling around and shooting at anything that moved made it an especially unhealthy place. They also knew that as soon as the sun came up, the military would sweep the area.

The land behind the bay was a coastal plain that stretched back some ten miles to the central mountains. There were areas of forest and streams, so they had cover to hide in and water to drink.

Marty had no doubts about their ability to hide but he was very worried about Sam. He must have been wounded, but where? Would he get any care from the French or would they just torture him for any information they could get out of him? Where would they hold him?

Whatever the answers were, they would have to wait for later. They needed to get away first and figure out what they could do about Sam after.

He steered them South across farmland, hoping to run into a wooded area where they could hide but as false dawn came. They were still in open country.

They kept going, using whatever cover they could find and eventually spotted a column of smoke, which looked like it might come from a farm. They made their way to it and were lucky; it was a farmhouse and there were outbuildings.

They chose one that looked less used than the others and slipped inside. It was a cowshed, and it was occupied by a solitary heifer and her muscular bull calf. They needed something to drink and took it in turns, squirting a few mouthfuls of milk from her full udder while the others kept the calf at bay. The warm milk reminded Marty that they needed to sleep. There were several stalls in the bier and only one was occupied, so they took the furthest one, which was being used to store hay, burrowed into the pile, and settled down for the day.

Come dawn, the farmer led the cow and calf out to pasture then mucked out the stall. They all held their breath as none of them wanted to have to kill a man who was just going innocently about his daily business. Much to their relief, he took some fresh bedding from another stall, spread it around, and left the barn.

Marty slept, their standard practice was to run two-hour watches so everyone could get as much rest as possible, and John Smith woke him after around six hours when it was his turn. He felt refreshed but hungry and decided he needed to do something about that.

He removed his black jacket to reveal a simple cotton shirt underneath and slipped out of the briar. A quick look showed that there was a track that ran past the farm, and he made his way to it, staying out of sight of the farmhouse.

Acting the innocent traveller, he sauntered along the track into view of the house as if he had just been passing by. Then, as if on a whim, he walked up to the farmhouse and knocked on the door.

A middle-aged woman with a sharp face opened the door and greeted him,

"What do you want?"

Marty wasn't bothered by her sharp tone and smiled his best smile.

"I am a traveller and I was hoping that I could buy some food from you as your farm looks to be well kept and prosperous."

She looked at him through narrowed eyes.

"You can pay?"

Marty feigned surprise and said,

"Oh, of course." He pulled out a pouch and tipped a few silver coins into his hand. She took one and bit it. Satisfied it was real, she invited him in.

"You just walked up to the door and bought it?" John asked incredulously as he tucked into his portion of bread cheese and some ham. It wasn't much as Marty had only been able to buy food for one, but he had gotten the old girl to give him generous portions.

"Why not? They are looking for a number of men dressed in black and I was just a wanderer on my own. Besides, it didn't seem that the farmer or his wife heard anything from the military and were asking me if I knew anything about the explosions."

"Well, thanks for the grub. What do we do now?" John asked.

"Find out where they are holding Sam and establish whether we can get him back before we leave the island. We will stay hidden for a couple of days then, when they give up searching for us, we head back to Grande Baye and see if we can find him."

Because Marty was the only one the French captain and his lieutenant saw close up, and John Smith and

Chin Lee didn't speak French, it fell on the Basques to go into the town and find out what they could.

"He is being held on the Fore. She's a forty-four. According to one of their crew who likes to gossip, he was shot in the thigh and the ball passed clean through. Their doctor was going to take his leg off, but Sam threatened to bite out his throat if he so much as touched him. He asked for some herbs, garlic, and ginger, made a poultice, and is treating himself," Garai reported.

"Did he say what they plan to do with him?" Marty asked.

"Yes, as he doesn't speak French and no one in Grande Baye speaks English, they are planning to move him to Île Bonaparte where there is an office of the Department of Internal Affairs," Antton added.

"Why not Grande Porte?" Marty wondered out loud.

"That's simple. They don't want to run the blockade," Garai clarified. "Oh, and the captain of the Fore is the one who came aboard the Marie."

"Did you get a look at that ship?"

"Oh yes, pretty as a picture and shines like a new pin. I would put money on her captain being more interested in her looks than her fighting ability," Matai chipped in.

"Is he really," Marty replied thoughtfully. "Any mention of them looking for us?"

"They assume we were picked up by the Marie, they don't have anyone who can read tracks by the sound of what we heard and think we left by the beach." Garai replied with a grin.

The boys went shopping while they were in the town. Prices were extortionate due to them having burned down half the shops, but they managed to get some clothes, food, bags to carry it in, and most important, a basic map of the island.

They headed to the Pointe de Flac, a fishing village about ten miles to the East of where they were hidden and where they hoped to be able to acquire a boat of some type. The other advantage of heading there was they wouldn't have to make their way through the mountains that covered the centre of the island.

Traveling overnight took longer but was safer, and they arrived at the village just as dawn broke the next day. As luck would have it, the fishing fleet was out and there wasn't a boat to be had anywhere. All they could do was wait. The people in the village were all natives and had as little contact with the occupying French as they could. Most spoke Creole and Marty thought he could make himself understood.

As all the men were out fishing, he cautiously approached an old woman who was mending a net by gripping it with her toes to keep it taut, then using what looked like a kind of bobbin with the twine wrapped around it, tied new mesh into the tear. Her hands moved so fast he couldn't really see what she was doing. She had a burning pipe clenched between her teeth.

"Hello mother, can I ask where a man can buy or hire a boat?" Marty asked in his worst French accent.

She didn't stop what she was doing or take the pipe out of her mouth but replied in barely understandable Creole,

"That depends on where you want to go, now doesn't it?"

Marty decided on a hunch to take a risk.

"I want to get me and my men to the British ships."

She stopped knotting, took the pipe from her mouth, and pointed at him with the stem.

"And why would you want to go there?"

"The French are looking for us. We did something to upset them a lot and they have one of my men captive. I want to get him back and to do that, I need to get to the British."

She cackled a laugh, showing more gums than teeth.

"Boom!"

Marty smiled and shrugged modestly.

"My son has a boat big enough for all of you, and he trades fish with the British ships. They pay well for it, not like the damn French," she hawked and spat, hitting a seagull on the back of the head. It flew off squawking. *"He will be back in the morning and I will talk to him. What will you pay?"*

"Thank you, mother. I will pay whatever he asks," Marty promised.

"He will take you for free, but you must do something for me in return," she said, suddenly getting serious.

Oh, oh. What's coming? Marty thought, but nodded anyway.

"My son's wife is very pretty and when he is away, there is a French officer who keeps coming to the village and pestering her to have sex with him. She has resisted so far, but it won't be long before he loses patience and just takes her, and that would break my poor Jean's heart. He will come again today on his fine horse. You must make him stop. I don't care how as long as it cannot be linked to my Jean."

Marty agreed, relieved that all he had to do was kill a French officer and make it look like an accident. The old lady, he refused to think of her as a crone, invited them to the house she shared with her son and daughter in law for a morning meal.

Her son's wife was as pretty as she said, a dusky beauty with large brown eyes and luxuriant hair that hung almost to her very pert backside. Her name was Gabrielle.

"Where does the Frenchman come from?" Marty asked

"Laventure, it's about five kilometres from here," Gabrielle answered in quite good French and pointed to the Northwest. *"There is a track that leads here, which he rides down. He found me when I visited the market."*

"What would Jean do if he knew this man was forcing himself on you?"

Her eyes filled with tears and she bit her lip before she answered,

"He would challenge him and would be killed; he is not a fighter."

"Don't worry, we will take care of it," Marty assured her. They left as soon as they finished the meal.

There were only two dirt roads leading into the village, and they made their way up the one that headed Northwest until they found a place where it passed through a copse of trees. There was ample cover to hide, and John climbed a tree to watch for the over amorous Frenchman.

It was around eleven o'clock in the morning when he dropped out of the tree.

"There's a horseman coming. Looks like he's a grenadier from his uniform. He ain't payin' much attention to what's goin' on."

"You all know what to do. Chin, are you ready?"

The Chinaman nodded and rolled his shoulders.

"Let's do it."

They hid behind trees and waited. The Grenadier came into view around the corner thirty yards before the trees. He was whistling a merry tune and his horse was at the trot.

As he got to the middle of the copse, the shadows leapt out from cover and surrounded the horse, yelling and waving their arms. The horse reared, and the rider tried simultaneously to control it and draw his sabre, but Chin leapt up behind him, grabbed him by the shoulders, and pulled him out of the saddle. He landed flat on his back and had the wind knocked out of him. As he struggled to sit up, Chin knelt behind him, and using a similar technique that Marty saw Sam use, broke his neck. One of the boys managed to grab the horse's reins, and Matai was doing his thing and calming it.

Grabbing the dead man's left foot, Marty tried to push it through the left stirrup so the iron was around his ankle. It was a struggle but with Chin's help, he managed it. Then they turned the horse back toward the way from which it came and slapped it on the rump.

The horse started out with the rider dragging beside it, which spooked it into a gallop.

"It probably won't stop until it gets back to his barracks," Antton observed wryly as he got some brush and swept out their tracks, leaving just the horses. "Do you think his foot will stay attached all the way or break off?"

"He had good boots, so I bet it makes it back to the barracks with what's left of him still attached," John quipped.

Marty chuckled, the dark humour of his men lightening the moment.

They returned to the village and told the old lady that Gabrielle wouldn't be bothered anymore. They didn't tell her what had happened as what she didn't know couldn't hurt her. She told Gabrielle, who embraced each of them and when she kissed Marty on the cheek, she told him that now Jean's unborn child would be safe.

Jean returned from his trip and talked to his mother as he unloaded his catch.

"I would be pleased to take you," he told them, and after grabbing a meal and some provisions for the trip, they set out to find the fleet. He was a good boy and always did what his mamma told him. The smell of the boat, a mixture of fish and rotting seaweed, evoked memories of the early days of the Flotilla when they smuggled spies in and out of France.

They sailed down the coast, staying out beyond the reefs for around four hours before they saw sails on the horizon. As they got closer, they saw that they were frigates. As they closed even more, Marty recognized the Formidiable and directed Jean to take them to her.

Before he climbed the side back onto his ship, he gave Jean some silver coins, which he tried to refuse saying that his mother told him they had already paid her. Marty pressed the coins into his hand and told him it was a present for his first child, which, with a nudge and a wink, he was sure wouldn't be long in coming.

"Please join me in my cabin, Wolfgang, and bring me up to date," Marty instructed as he gave Troy a head rub and a, "who's a good boy, then!" in greeting.

He stripped off and sponged down to clean himself as Wolfgang gave his report.

"The boat that was supposed to pick you up was accidentally run down by one of the East Indiamen. Two crew were lost, but the rest were picked up. It was partly their own fault as they were resting in the middle of the bay instead of closer to the shore."

"That nearly cost us our lives. Have you talked to the man in charge of it?"

"Oh yes, and so have some of the others, I believe," Wolfgang smiled grimly.

"Then I don't need to. Carry on," Marty commented as he sponged his armpits.

"We had gotten all the ships away and were admiring the fireworks displays when we realized what happened. I recalled the Bonne Marie and went to Grande Porte as planned. Wilson wanted to wait for you, but I thought you would try and get to the blockading force once you realized the boat wasn't coming. Once we got here, I sent the prizes on to Cape Town escorted by the Marie with Mr. Fletcher on board to make sure we don't get swindled out of our money."

Marty had moved on to shaving and looked at Wolfgang in the mirror.

"Very wise, the salvage money will be substantial." He wiped his face down and reached for the fresh shirt that Adam, his steward, laid out for him,

"Sam was shot and captured. They will be taking him to Île Bonaparte to be interrogated by the Department," he explained using their shortened title for the Département de la Sécurité Intérieure, the French version of British Military Intelligence.

"He is being held on a forty-four, and to all accounts, treating his wound himself."

"A forty-four? One of the new ones? The commodore told me there were a couple of those out here. They are supposed to have a couple of carronades mounted by all accounts as well as eighteen pounders," Wolfgang exclaimed.

"Well this one is new, very pretty and shiny, and her captain is an arse. I have met him; he likes to throw his weight around with those who can't hit back." Marty gazed out of the stern windows for a moment as he shrugged into a uniform jacket.

"I wonder if he has the balls to take Sam himself?"

Marty had to pay his respects to Commodore Rowley, who was in charge of the blockade and as usual, had to show him that he had independent orders from the Admiralty and, no, he couldn't be absorbed into the blockade squadron.

That out of the way, he ordered the Formidiable to set course for Grande Baye to see if all the French ships were still there. His guess would be that they would move Sam in their own good time, probably during a scheduled visit to the other island. He wasn't senior enough to warrant special treatment. His other worry was because of his colour, they would just sell him into slavery.

Grande Baye emerged from the morning gloom and their appearance caused a rush of activity around the battery on the point. The lookouts got a good view into the bay before the French gunners got their act together and let of a ragged salvo, which was also informative as it looked like they were missing some guns.

"Looks like our bombs did some damage. The boys planted them in the carriages so when they went off, there was a chance that we could disable a gun or two," Marty told Wolfgang as the two stood watching the puffs of smoke.

"They must have brought powder from the ships as we blew up all they had on shore," he concluded as he watched the shots fall short and wide.

"What do you see?" Wolfgang called up to the masthead.

"A seventy-five and a forty!" the lookout called back.

"Damn, they've left already!" Marty cursed; things just got more complicated.

"Get us under way, Wolfgang. We need to go to La Possession."

Chapter 18: Deception

The Formidiable was sailing as close to the wind as she could and was making excellent time, but they were having to tack to make progress against the prevailing wind, so the one-hundred-and-sixty-mile trip became a two-hundred-and-sixty-mile trip. It would take them almost a complete day to make the crossing, but the good thing was that in the winter, the chances of a monsoon storm were slight.

It was shear and utter chance that they tacked just at the right time to spot the Fore heading back to Île de France.

"He has the wind gauge," John Smith observed from his position at the wheel.

Marty was tempted to make a sarcastic comment but something in the way the French ship was behaving caught his eye.

"Bugger me!" he exclaimed. "He is running away."

"But he's bigger than us and has the advantage of the wind," second Lieutenant Phillip Trenchard, who had the watch, confusedly commented.

"He's shy, probably worried we might scratch his paint," John replied with a smirk.

Marty was silent and deep in thought.

"Set a course to intercept. I want that ship," he ordered, coming to a decision.

"But what about Sam?" John Smith blurted out in surprise.

"They will let him stew for a couple of days before they start working on him, now set the course," he snapped.

It wasn't often that Marty showed his temper and it was an indication of the strain he was under and the conflict between what he knew he had to do and what his emotions were screaming at him to do. He took a deep breath and focused the energy into doing what was needed now as it was the best way to help Sam in the long run.

The Fore swung more to the North, putting the wind on her quarter, her best sailing position. Marty was hoping the captain believed the Formidiable had a filthy bottom when in reality, it wasn't that bad. In any case, the next hour would tell him if they stood a chance of catching them or not.

The Fore was heading Northeast and was Northwest of the Formidiable, which was tacking to the Northwest when they saw her. They steered in an arc to bring them on the same heading as the Fore about two miles behind and slightly south of his track.

Marty thought that at some point, his prey, as he thought of him, would try and break for the Île de France and safety as the further he went on this heading, the harder it would be to get back to Grande Baye. He edged a little further South to narrow the intercept angle for when he did.

They had closed to a mile and he was contemplating letting the fore chasers have a go when the lookout cried, "THEY'S GETTING READY TO TACK."

Marty was pleased. He spent many hours teaching his lookouts to watch for indications that ships were getting ready to change course. Early knowledge of what they were intending was enough to give him the edge a lot of the time.

"Get the ship to quarters, Phillip, if you please," he ordered. Wolfgang came on deck, looking around to check all was in order. Satisfied, he left Trenchard in command for the moment while he went to talk to Marty.

"Chasers?" he asked after glancing at the closing angle between the two ships as the Fore turned towards the Southeast.

"I think so. We will cut the corner and be within four or five cables soon," Marty replied.

"Mr. Trenchard, I have the deck. Please attend the chasers and give our friend over there our best greetings," Wolfgang ordered calmly.

Phillip called for the chasers to be readied as he walked the length of the deck, and by the time he got there, they were loaded and ready. He was excited. He had been studying gunnery under Wolverton, their misshapen master gunner, and this was his first chance to put his knowledge into practice in anger.

Marty watched from the quarterdeck. The Fore was about to cross their bow, and he started to turn so he would come astern of her and bring his starboard fore chaser in line.

The guns had notches filed in the barrels to aid sighting, and Phillip bent to the starboard gun and lined his eye along the barrel. He had judged the distance to be around eight-hundred yards and ordered the barrel elevated accordingly. Fine adjustments were made with jack staves to the direction and he was ready.

He stepped back until the lanyard was taut, and as the ship started its up roll, jerked it to fire the gun. Through the cloud of smoke, he watched the ball arc through the air dead in line with the Fore's stern.

"Got him!" he yelled and urged the crew to reload while he ran to the larboard gun. They closed another fifty to sixty yards, and he set the elevation to be the same as the other gun as the last ball had hit quite low on the Fore's stern.

BOOM! The second gun fired and again, the ball arced away and for a moment, he thought it would pass over the deck. But it hit the stern rail, sending a shower of splinters across the quarterdeck.

"He's a natural," Marty smiled to Wolfgang as they watched their protégée move back to the starboard gun. They were expecting him to be able to fire at least a couple more shots before the Frenchman struck when the Fore started to reduce sail to a fighting configuration.

"What the hell! He wants to make a fight of it," Marty barked in surprise as he saw them take in their mainsails. "Larboard battery double shot, carronades grape," he ordered.

Wolfgang was already bellowing orders to reduce sail, and the marines were rushing up to their positions in the tops.

Marty did not want to get into a long pounding match. He didn't have the time to spend days on repairs. He planned to get in close and board after a couple of broadsides. What he didn't understand was how he underestimated the Flore's captain; he was sure he was the type to fire one broadside for honour then strike.

They came up abeam, and both ships fired almost at the same time. Chain howled through their rigging as the French sought to dismast them. Marty found himself bowled to the deck when Wolfgang knocked him down as the French carronade sent a hail of shot across the quarterdeck. He picked himself up and saw Troy crawl out from behind the quarter deck starboard carronade where he had been lying in the shade. He didn't look happy and his hackles were up.

The Formidiable's gunners aimed at the Fore's gun ports, and the big eighteen-pound balls smashed star shaped holes in her hull, sending deadly splinters spinning across her gun deck. Blood ran from her scuppers.

The Formidiable's well-drilled gunners had their second broadside ready in a little less than half the time the French were taking, and it roared out in almost perfect unison.

"Bring us alongside, John. Wolfgang, prepare to board," Marty ordered.

"Grapnels ready!" Wolfgang shouted and men manned the swivels pre-loaded with hooks and lines.

"Carronades, clear their deck!" Marty shouted as he took his place at the rail. It felt strange having Troy beside him and not Blaez. He was also missing Sam but Matthew, one of Sam's brothers, appeared and stood at his shoulder armed with one of their short, broad-headed spears.

The ships were just thirty feet apart and Wolfgang, who had his zwiehaender out and ready, gave the order to fire the grapnels as soon as the carronades had sown their deadly seeds. The marines in the tops were keeping up a steady rate of fire and as the hulls ground together, Marty called,

"AT THEM BOYS!" and launched himself over the side where he was immediately faced with several angry Frenchmen. He engaged the closest, and Troy launched himself at the same man, dragging him to the floor. Marty skewered him through the throat and moved on to the next, who was thrusting a boarding pike at him. He knocked it aside and shot him with the pistol in his left hand.

Troy was ready. He sensed the tension and wasn't fazed by the gunfire at all. They had put a different collar on him, which smelled of Blaez. He kept close to the boss, instinctively knowing he had to work with his Alpha.

They leapt the rail almost together, and he focused on the man directly in front of Marty. He leapt grabbed his arm and pulled him down. The Alpha killed him, and they moved on to the next. The boss took care of him but there was another moving in from the side.

He leapt, going for the man's face and felt a blow on the collar, which he ignored. Something stung his thigh, but now he had his teeth around the man's throat. He bit down and shook his head at the same time. Ripping flesh, he tasted blood, bit harder, and shook again, causing even more blood to gush.

He heard the Alpha telling him to let go. He obeyed and looked around. There was no more fighting.

Marty accepted the surrender from a lieutenant. The ship was theirs and the French crew was throwing their weapons to the deck. Some looked in horror at the blood-soaked dog at the officer's side. Others were too shocked to react.

"Where are your captain and first lieutenant?" Marty asked.

"Killed when a ball hit the rail at the stern. A piece of rail hit the lieutenant and pierced him through the stomach, and the ball cut the captain in half," replied the young lieutenant.

"You took command?" Marty asked, not unkindly.

"Yes, the coward was about to strike. You killed him just in time. We have lost with honour not as craven dogs as he would have made us."

Marty looked around at the dead and wondered at the cost of 'honour'. He didn't need to give any orders. His lieutenants knew what to do, and soon the ship was secure in their hands. The dead of both ships were buried at sea with all due ceremony. The Formidiable had only lost two. The rest were all French. Marty saw no reason not to respect men who fought and died bravely.

Troy had a cut on his thigh which Shelby treated once the men were taken care of, he was now a blooded warrior and seemed to walk a little prouder.

Because the Formidiable was overmanned as usual, they had no problems in crewing both ships. Marty's problem was that if his plan was to come off, he needed to get rid of the French sailors. Marty, Arnold Grey, and Wolfgang examined a chart of Île de France with a magnifying glass, concentrating on the coast. What they needed was a beach or inlet with enough depth of water to get in close enough to boat the French ashore. It also needed to be far enough away from any of the ports to give them time before the French found out that the Fore had been taken.

"There," Arnold said, pointing to a spot on the West coast. "Tamarin has a beach and enough depth."

"Looks ideal, set a course," Marty ordered.

The offloading of the French went smoothly. The presence of the marines ensured there were no last-minute heroics. Then life got entertaining for many of the crew.

"I want the Fore's stores gone through and every spare item of Navy issue clothing brought up on deck. Paul, I would be obliged if you would take my steward and go through their wardroom and cockpit and find any spare officer's uniforms."

A thorough search produced a pile of clothes, cloth, shoes and uniforms. It also turned up three men hiding in the hold. They all looked like Indians.

"Who are you and why were you hiding?" Marty asked after they were dragged up on deck.

They looked at him blankly, so he tried again in the Hindi he learned in India. That triggered a torrent of Indian from all three men, and once he got them to speak slowly and one at a time, he found that they were lascars who were captured by the French when their ship was taken. They were given the option of being thrown to the sharks or joining the ship.

"Sign them up, Wolfgang. They look fit enough but get Shelby to check them over just in case."

"Now I want the majority of the crew transferred to the Fore and dressed as French sailors. I will command her as a lieutenant, and you will command the Formidiable as a prize. Make her look as if she lost a fight." He looked at his officers, who were all beginning to grin as they understood what he was going to do,

"Mr. Trenchard, you will come with me along with Mr. Hart. Mr. Longstaff, you stay here with Mr. Ackermann."

He was missing his third lieutenant and youngest mid as they were on the Belle with a prize crew. He could have made use of the extra hands, but he would manage with what he had.

"The Fore was in a fight and was victorious. The Formidiable is her prize. The Marines will act the part of English prisoners."

"Not many of us to do that," Marine Captain Paul la Pierre commented.

"Oh, I'm sure you can run around and look like a crowd," Marty smiled.

"We will sail into La Possession victorious! Our Captain is dead but I, a humble third lieutenant, have led our brave men to an unusual victory and captured the Roast beef frigate."

Now he was looking at a crowd of grinning faces and could hear the crew passing on what they overheard like a wave along the ship. Laughter and banter rippled down the deck as men teased each other over how they would look in French clothes.

The services of one of the men, who was a former tailor, were needed to get Marty into a third lieutenant's uniform and Trenchard into a fourth's. Stanley Hart was dressed as a mid along with one of the larger ship's boys. The crew sorted out their own disguises.

Bandages would be applied to make them look as if they had taken wounds.

The next morning, the two ships set sail. The tricolour streamed from the Fore, and the Formidiable had the tricolour flying over the British flag.

They approached La Possession, and Marty studied the signal books the 'brave lieutenant' forgot to throw overboard. Marty hoped his men wouldn't ever be that foolish. He found the recognition signal for the day and took it up to the quarterdeck so Stanley could raise it in answer to the inevitable challenge.

They were met by a pilot who guided them to anchor not far from where they had burnt the frigates a few years before. There was only one other ship in port and that was a twenty-eight-gun corvette.

Marty had a boat pulled around and, along with Matai and Antton, went to visit the port authority. He was directed to a building further down the port when he asked the pilot where he should report to.

The building was the only one that stood out as being 'official'. It hadn't been there, as far as Marty could remember, last time he had been there. It was stone built and had two stories where most of the other buildings were single- or two-story wooden structures. It was clearly built to impress.

He entered the portico, which had Doric columns on either side as well as elaborate carving around the frieze. *Why build something as fancy as this,* he wondered. *The cost of shipping the stone alone must be enormous.*

There was a pair of blue uniformed guards on the door, who snapped to attention as they passed through. Inside, it was noticeably cooler and dimmer. Once their eyes became accustomed to the light, they saw that they were in a large reception room with several doors leading off and a man sat at a desk in the middle.

"Lieutenant Bouvier of the Fore," he introduced himself.

"Where is your captain," the official asked, managing to look down his nose at him even though seated.

"Dead as are the first and second lieutenants. Killed early in the fight with the British frigate," Marty told him and added with a show of pride, *"I assumed command and completed the victory."*

"So you say. Do you have a report?" the official asked, completely unimpressed.

"Certainly," Marty said, but didn't hand anything over.

The official looked at him, and Marty looked back. He was used to dealing with officialdom. The official cracked first,

"The Port Director's office is the second door from the left."

"Thank you," Marty said with a smile as he walked over to the door and knocked.

"Enter," came a brusque voice.

Marty looked at the boys.

"You had better stay here. Keep an eye out for any signs of Sam."

He opened the door and stepped inside a well-appointed office with a large, dark wood desk in the centre. Sitting behind it was a portly man dressed in a lightweight suit studying some papers. Marty scanned the walls as he walked forward and saw a door to the right in the rear wall and another that presumably led to another office to the left.

He stopped in front of the desk and waited. After a minute, the man grunted, closed the folder, and placed it in a tray to his left.

"Lieutenant?" he asked.

"Bouvier of the Fore, acting commander," Marty barked in his best military manner.

"And what of Captain St. Just?" the director asked.

"Killed in the line of duty, sir." Marty held out a packet that contained a written report (he had carefully copied the style of a report he had found in the captain's cabin), making sure his hand shook ever so slightly.

The director took it and his look softened as he took the shaking as strain.

"Forgive me. I have had a bad day. Please take a seat. My name is Director Livarot."

Marty sat and pasted a grateful look on his face.

"Your former captain dropped a problem in my lap."

Marty looked surprised.

"That British black man he brought here for the Department of Internal Security is refusing to tell us anything except that someone called," he checked a note. *"'Troy is coming and will bite our balls off,'* whatever that means."

Marty had to cough to cover a laugh.

"The captain of the ship we captured had a dog called Troy. Maybe that is what he means," he offered.

"Well, he will now face interrogation by Dupreeh from Internal Security,"

There was a knock on the door to the rear of the office. Livarot sighed and looked tired before calling out,

"Enter."

A man dressed in a black suit standing at about five feet, six stepped into the room. He had long, lank hair that surrounded a completely bald pate, which made him look like a monk. The bland face and dead eyes of the professional intelligence officer are what stood out the most.

"Aah Dupreeh, I was just telling the good lieutenant about you," Livarot stated.

"Really," Dupreeh responded in a flat voice then turned his attention to Marty. *"And you are responsible for bringing that English ship in as a prize?"*

"Yes sir, I had that honour," Marty replied.

"The heroic Captain St. Just didn't survive the exchange then," Dupreeh commented without a hint of sarcasm in his voice, and before Marty could say another word,

"Did you capture the British captain alive?"

"I am afraid not. He died when our carronade targeted his quarterdeck," Marty lied.

"That is a shame. Do you still have the body?" Dupreeh asked.

"We buried him at sea as is the usual practice," Marty answered, sounding confused.

"Well, never mind. I am sure you will still be able to claim the twenty thousand Louis reward for his head."

"My God! How much?" Livarot squawked.

"That ship was captained by non-other than the infamous Sir Martin Stockley. My department has been

at odds with him since the end of the revolution. He has been a thorn in the Emperor's side since before he came to power."

Marty and Livarot made amazed/surprised noises.

"If you have, indeed, eliminated him, then you have done Napoleon himself a great service."

"Then the captive was one of his crew?" Livarot asked.

"I would believe so. The attack on Grande Baye is typical of the way the man works," Dupreeh replied. *"We think he was behind an attack here several years ago when he was active in India."*

"Well, thank God he is finished," Livarot shuddered.

"I would like you to come with me to see the captive, Lieutenant. The news that his captain is dead may persuade him to be more cooperative."

Oh shit, Marty thought, *if Sam reacts in the wrong way, we could all be up shit creek.* But he followed the two men and surreptitiously loosened his stilettoes in their forearm sheaths.

Chapter 19: Extraction

"I have to give Sam his due. He never batted an eyelid when I walked into the room, and when I told him I was dead, he reacted just as you would expect. Dupreeh was completely fooled," Marty told the gathered Shadows and officers.

"No chance of getting him out then?" Wolfgang asked.

"Not on my own. There were too many guards and they have him in a slave collar, which has been riveted shut and chained to a ringbolt in the wall that has also been forge closed. Dupreeh knows how we work and assumed that Sam could pick locks."

"Well how do we get him out? Guards, we can deal with, locks are no problem, but breaking a chain is going to make a lot of noise," Wilson commented.

"That is where our friends over there in the Corvette come in," Marty grinned.

"He's 'ad one of 'is ideas," John Smith whispered into Chin's ear and sat back.

"We can't wait to get Sam out because the longer we stay here, the more chance there will be that someone from either the corvette or the ministry building will want to come and see where the famous Captain Stockley and his evil minions met their doom," That caused a ripple of laughter.

"So, my idea is that we pay a visit to the corvette. We have captured a fine prize and want to boast a bit and share some of our joy with our fellow warriors of the sea."

The room waited. They knew there was much more to come and there would be plenty of time for questions and suggestions later.

"There will be a shore team who will go get Sam, a second team that will neutralise the battery, and a third, mine by the way, that will go party on the corvette." That caused a round of banter and some good-natured accusations that he was getting too old to do the real work.

"Alright, alright, that's enough," Marty called and restored order.

The corvette team needs to be all French speaking, so it will be me, Antton, and Matai. Garai, Chin, John, and Wilson will get Sam. Paul and Phillip will lead the third team made up of marines to spike the guns in the batteries."

"Can I suggest they take marine Rigglesworth with them to get Sam? He was a smith's apprentice before he joined the marines and will be useful to get him free," Paul offered.

"Perfect, are you alright with that Garai?" Marty asked and got a thumbs up in reply.

"Right, then let's work out the timing," Marty said, and they all gathered around a large sheet of paper spread out on the dining table.

Marty sent a note to the corvette's captain telling him that they would be visiting and bringing some loot from the Formidiable that they would like to share. At 8 PM, they loaded up a boat and were rowed over.

They had a couple of cases of wine from Marty's private stock and a very large keg of rum, which were hoisted aboard after Marty, Antton, and Matai had climbed the side and introduced themselves.

The captain, a young lieutenant, was delighted by the excellent Bordeaux and insisted on sampling the rum. He took one sip and almost collapsed in a fit of coughing,

"Holy mother of Christ!" he exclaimed, *"The British sailors really drink that stuff?"*

"A pint a day," Marty laughed, *"but they dilute it four to one with water and lime juice. Keeps away the scurvy apparently."*

The lieutenant insisted they join him in his cabin with his officers where they broached a few bottles and ate some reasonably good food. It was a slightly worse for wear trio that returned to the Fore.

Marty was drinking his eighth coffee when the watchman rang eight bells. He put down his cup and waited. There was a loud explosion, he got up to go on deck.

Matai and Antton met him at the entry port, all three were armed to the teeth. They led Marty down into the waiting boat and were rowed to the dock. As soon as they were ashore, they slipped away into the darkness heading towards the ministry building. The corvette was burning and there were a number of secondary explosions as barrels of oil or brandy detonated.

A pair of soldiers were running towards the Ministry building and suddenly fell to the ground, bolts embedded in the middle of their backs. No one would be able to say for sure the next day, but the evidence was that they had been shot in the back by something like a crossbow.

A group of men left the ministry building. One was helped by two of his mates who acted as human crutches. They made their way towards the dock, the burning corvette lighting their way like day. Anybody who approached them died, cut down before they got within twenty feet, most killed from behind, knives or bolts protruding from back or neck. The trail of corpses would be used the next day to work out the route they had taken.

At the dock, there was a boat waiting for them and they were helping their wounded mate into it when a man dressed in a black suit came out of the shadows by a warehouse and pointed a pair of pistols at them.

"Zat is far enough. You will return to ze dock," Dupreeh said with a thick French accent.

The men stopped and just looked at him. They appeared to be waiting for something or, it suddenly occurred to him, somebody. The thought had just registered when he felt a sharp blade against the side of his neck,

"Now you never told me you spoke English. That was very rude," a soft but familiar voice said from behind him. "I would be obliged if you would lower the pistols and hand them to my friend here."

A figure appeared beside him and held out his hands, the blade dug a little deeper, and he felt a trickle of blood, he handed over the pistols. The blade was removed from his neck and moved around in front of his eyes. He was fascinated by it; it was about thirty centimetres long, eight wide, with a wicked double edged clip point. The steel had a pattern in it that seemed to shift in the flickering light of the burning ship. It looked beautiful and as sharp as it had felt.

He followed the blade back to a hand, then an arm to a face he knew,

"I think I can conclude you are not Lieutenant Bouvier,"

"Bravo, you are quite right."

"Captain Stockley?"

"Bravo again. You are one of the few members of your department to have seen my face and still be alive."

"Let me guess, the ones who have seen you do not know it was you."

"You are doing very well, but that is not true. They know me well enough to put a price on my head. Why didn't you torture Sam?" Marty asked suddenly, curious.

"Is that his name? Torture only gets you what you want to hear. There are more sophisticated ways of getting the information that you need," Dupreeh replied. Marty agreed although he had found that a little 'persuasion' was handy to start people talking and save time.

"They should promote you; you are wasted on this rock," Marty told him.

"I am going to die." It was a statement not a question.

"I'm afraid so. I thought about bringing my dog, Troy, to do it since Sam promised you he would bite off your balls, but we don't have time for that."

"Get on with it then," he said, suddenly angry at Marty's urbane manner.

It was the last time he saw Marty or the team as sharp tap from a blackjack knocked him out.

"Get this ship underway. That corvette is likely to blow up at any minute," Marty ordered as soon as they were back on board the Fore. The Formidiable was already on its way out of the harbour, pausing only to pick up the marines who had been spiking the guns in the battery.

The crew was ready, the anchor straight up and down. It took just a single command to get the ship under way. They were just in time because as they passed through the harbour mouth, the corvette's magazine went up with an enormous explosion, the shock wave pushing them out into the night.

Marty had a moment's regret as he thought of the fine wine that went up with it but shrugged as he figured Sam was worth it. He asked himself why he didn't kill Dupreeh and concluded that the world needed more men inclined to use their minds rather than force then he chuckled at the irony of that particular thought.

Chapter 19: Recall

They returned to Grande Porte, and Marty reported to Commodore Rowley,

"Well, Sir Martin, you seem to have been busy," he commented as he finished reading Marty's report. "Your man is recovering well, I hope?"

"He is, Sir. He will be up and around in no time now our physician is caring for him," Marty replied.

"Tell me, in your opinion can Reunion be taken?" Rowley asked, looking at him intently.

"They will beef up the defences and probably bring in extra troops at La Possession, but they are still making the same mistakes they made last time I was here. They only have a minimal guard on the fishing port to the west. It's got no depth of water for a large ship to get in but with ships boats full of soldiers you could make a landing there and take La Possession from behind," Marty replied.

"And Grande Baye?"

"The fortifications and defensive battery are strong enough to hold off any kind of attempt from the sea. As you know, they have a large number of troops concentrated on the coastal plain behind Grande Baye, including infantry, cavalry, and artillery. So, any invasion will need a significant number of troops. You could land them at Poste de Flac."

Rowley called his steward,

"May I offer you some refreshment?   I have an excellent Madera or a Bordeaux I acquired in Madras."

Imported by Candor shipping, Marty chuckled to himself and accepted a glass of Madera.

"I have mail for you that came in on the packet yesterday. I believe there is something from the Admiralty in there. Would you like my clerk to bring it in?"

Curious, are you? Marty thought but replied,

"If that would be no trouble, thank you."

The clerk, a small man with round glasses perched on his nose, thin wispy hair, and a rounded back caused by the hours spent pouring over documents, came in with a bag and a separate packet of oiled paper sealed with the fouled anchor of the Admiralty.

Marty thanked him, propped the bag by his chair, took out his knife, and slit open the packet.

"My God, do you carry that around with you everywhere?" Rowley exclaimed.

Marty treated the question as rhetorical and opened the letter he extracted from the wrapping. A glance showed it was from Hood and he quickly read the important parts, then folded it back into the wrapper. He sipped his Madera in thought.

Rowley was watching him and asked,

"Orders?"

Marty started out of his reverie,

"Oh sorry, yes. I am being recalled to Gibraltar. My services have been requested by Lieutenant General Wellesley."

"The chap that was governor in India?"

"The very same. We became acquainted when I was here last time."

Rowley, a politically aware landowner in his own right, realized that the young man in front of him had some politically powerful allies and decided that it wouldn't hurt to cultivate him a little.

"Would you join me for dinner before you leave?" he asked. "Seven thirty this evening?"

"I would be honoured," Marty answered, knowing exactly what was going in.

Dinner was a formal affair; Rowley invited all the captains in his squadron. Marty was the third most senior Post Captain present, so he was sat two seats below the Commodore. Opposite him was Corbett of the Nereide, and closest to the Admiral; Lewis of the Argon and Standish of the Leopard. Below them were two captains who hadn't made flag yet; Stimpson and Yale.

Marty took an instant dislike to Corbett. The man was brash and talked of his men as if they were just objects. To Marty, he came across as insecure and spent most of his time trying to make Marty aware of his superiority. That was until Stimpson asked with a sly glance at Corbett,

"Sir Martin, how is your wife, the good Lady Candor? My family lands border yours in Cheshire you know."

Corbett, who hadn't a clue who Marty really was, sat with a stunned look on his face when Marty answered,

"Very well, thank you. She is back in England now but whether she is in our Cheshire, Dorset, or London homes, I have no idea."

Rowley, who also didn't like Corbett because of his attitude and lack of social grace, chipped in when he saw his discomfort,

"I heard that the Prince Regent deigned to be godfather to your youngest; must be a great honour."

"Indeed, it was. And he takes his duties to the twins seriously, contrary to his reputation." Marty smiled proudly.

"Did you know Nelson," Yale asked.

"I met him a couple of times and had the honour of being of service to him on occasion," Marty answered modestly. "He was a great man and it was with great regret that I missed his funeral."

"Did his zeal really shine through like the stories would have us believe?" Yale followed up.

"It did, indeed. The man was a fount of energy and had absolute belief in everything he did. He had the rare ability to inspire those around him and I valued his respect above all else."

The conversation then became a series of tales of personal encounters with the great man which Corbett found himself only on the periphery of and in an attempt to win back some ground, he interjected,

"Of course, Admiral Smith was a better frigate captain."

"Well now," Marty said, looking the man in the eye, "Nelson would be the first to admit that there were many that exceeded him in the collection of prize money, Thomas Cochrane, Sidney Smith,"

"And yourself," the slightly drunk Lewis added.

"I have been lucky," Marty replied.

"Pha! You just added another frigate to your tally. I expect you have made more than either of those two."

"Do you know either of them?" Yale asked.

Marty just smiled and started telling the story of the blockade of Lisbon, leaving out the several cartloads of treasure he picked up.

By the end of the evening, he made friends with his brother captains with the exception of Corbett, who became moodier as the others told stories of their exploits.

Marty didn't miss the glare he got as he bid a fond farewell to Rowley and smiled his wolf smile as he said goodbye to Corbett.

The next morning at dawn saw Marty and his two frigates heading around the Southern tip of the island, making their way to Cape Town, and a rendezvous with the Belle.

Marty wanted both ships to be able to fight and, as he habitually had enough crew to fight both sides, he decided to divide the crew between the two ships. That left them both undermanned as they only had so many sail handlers, but with two broadsides available he thought it was justified.

He discussed this with Rowley, and he offered his Sixth lieutenant and a midshipman to help with the shortage of officers Marty had. Marty thanked him, and Lieutenant David Clark and Midshipman Augustus Mayhew joined his ranks. They both wanted to return home, Clark because his father died and Mayhew because he wanted to leave the Navy and join his father's company. Marty got the impression that Rowley was glad to be rid of him.

"Maybe we can pick up a few more crew when we get to Cape Town," Wolfgang suggested before he left to take command of the Fore.

Marty rearranged his crew with Trenchard as first, Midshipman Longstaff made acting Lieutenant and was second with Mayhew his temporary third.

Midshipman Williams went over to the Fore as acting second lieutenant under Clark, who was Wolfgang's first. To cover the divisions, the Shadows were divided between the two ships and became temporary officers.

This worked well with both Marty and Wolfgang running their crews through drills to bed them in and soon both ships were operating acceptably.

They were passing the southern tip of Madagascar when they spotted a strange sail. Knowing that a bit of a chase would do more to pull the crew together than any amount of drills Marty signalled the pursuit.

The two frigates looked magnificent as they sped along under almost full sail, bearing down on the hapless merchantman. It was a Dutchman, and at that time, there wasn't a treaty between Britain and the Kingdom of Holland as Marty knew only too well, so it was fair game.

The captain knew he didn't stand a chance and hove to well before the two frigates caught up with him.

"Van der Poll," he introduced himself.

He was transporting ivory and timber from Mozambique and not wanting to have to dilute his crews anymore. Marty ordered the ivory and exotic woods transferred to his ships, pressed all the lascars in his crew, and sent him on his way. A disgruntled Van der Pol turned around and went back to Mozambique as

Marty had been deliberately lax in searching his ship and not found the bullion chest he had hidden under a deck plank in his cabin. He would get another cargo and some more lascars there.

Marty was happy. The crews worked well together and were pleased with the loot they had acquired.

At Cape Town, they rendezvoused with the Bonne Marie and the East Indiamen. Re-provisioned and re-watered, Marty signed on a dozen new hands who were loitering around the docks looking for a berth and 'borrowed' a few from the East Indiamen. Before they knew it, their convoy was heading back out into the Atlantic following the trades to the coast of Brazil.

They had no problem with the doldrums this time because a storm caught them just North of the equator and blew them all the way up to Trinidad. It was September and the middle of the Hurricane season.

Wolfgang and Marty discussed what to do as the merchant captains were reluctant to risk travelling until the season was over.

"If we travel up past the Dutch Antilles, we will be well out of the Hurricane belt," Wolfgang argued.

"I agree but can we persuade the other captains? They are all undermanned, like we are, even if we pick up a few extra men here," Marty added and sighed, "I think we can only talk to them and see if they will go with it."

He called an all captains meeting in a tavern in Port of Spain.

"Gentlemen, we need to come to an agreement on how to proceed. So far, we have been escorting you as a convoy and if that is to continue, we may have to all compromise a little." He paused and assessed the room. At least they were listening.

"I am under orders to get my ships back to Gibraltar to support General Wellesley in his mission to purge the peninsula of the French, and as such, must make all haste." He looked around the room and saw that some were looking alarmed at the thought of losing their escort, the Caribbean was still not the safest of places.

"I would normally head from here straight up to Jamaica and then up to the Carolinas and home." There were murmurs, and he nodded to the senior captain to speak.

"You might get away with that with those greyhounds you sail and your big crews, but we could never do it," McTravers of the Indian Queen told him.

Marty nodded in understanding then offered his compromise,

"The hurricane belt goes up through to the Eastern side of the windward islands, correct?" he paused and waited for them all to agree. "I propose we go West and take the longer route past the Dutch Antilles to the coast of Colombia where we swing North to Jamaica. Then if the conditions are right head up to the Carolinas and pick up the trades, we head East and home."

"I've never sailed those waters, so I can't comment," McTravers stated, looking stubborn.

"I have," Captain Freeman of the North Star chipped in. "The Caribbean current runs along that stretch of coast and will push us along nicely. The problem comes if the Dutch are feeling belligerent."

"Oh, we don't need to worry about them, I have what you might call a special relationship with the Antilles Island governments," Marty smiled at them.

"You have your own private treaty with them I suppose," McTravers commented sarcastically.

"Well yes, I suppose I do," Marty grinned back at him.

The discussion went on for a couple of bottles of wine and ended up with the captains voting two to one to go with Marty's plan, McTravers being the dissenter. Marty had a chat with the port admiral and managed to get a few more hands from the local gaol. Muscle was all he needed, and thieves and murderers would fit right in.

They set sail, circling the island to the south and continuing around it anticlockwise to enter the Caribbean to its North, picking up the current and the North-easterly trade wind. They steered a scant point North of West to follow the Venezuelan coast to pass Bonaire on its leeward side, then Curacao on its windward side, followed by Aruba.

They saw a few sails, but no one wanted to take on three warships, even if they were escorting three fat merchantmen. As they came up on Barranquilla, Marty altered course to the North-Northeast towards Jamaica and Kingston, and they noticed the sea was getting up. It was strange, the waves were getting bigger and coming in from the Northeast, but the wind hadn't increased.

"Mr. Grey, what do you think of this sea?" Marty asked the Master.

"There is probably a hurricane over to the Northeast of us if these waves are anything to go by. What we are feeling is like the ripples on a pond when you throw a stone in. The waves are moving out from where the storm is," Arnold Grey replied.

"The storm's somewhere over Puerto Rico? That's six hundred odd miles away!" Marty gasped and wondered at the power of something that could send twenty-foot-high waves that far.

It was making for a really uncomfortable ride as the waves were coming in on their beam and were growing bigger by the minute. They had no choice but to change course to take them on the stern and ride them out, which pushed them towards the coast of Costa Rica. They would now have to swing around the North end of Cuba following the gulf stream current and pick up the Westerly trade wind and have no chance to re-water or provision at Jamaica. They would have to try the Bahamas.

The weather got worse, and the Merchant captains dug in their heels by doggedly running head of it forcing Marty to follow. There was no way they were taking their ships across the hurricane belt given the present conditions until the middle of November at the earliest. The Bahamas had been regularly savaged by hurricanes in the past years and September was the height of the season.

Marty considered stopping at George Town in the Caymans but the risk of getting hit there was too great. So, they slid into the Gulf of Honduras and headed to Tela, which was under British protection, where they could re-provision and water. The town was rough and offered little in the way of entertainment but at the least the men could go ashore and stretch their legs.

Shelby, however, was in his element and soon disappeared into the town to study the local people and their diseases. He would pop up unexpectedly and deposit bags of herbs, all carefully labelled, in his quarters, deal with any sick then disappear for another few days.

The Formidiable still had a large amount of the citronella oil they had utilized the last time they were in the Caribbean. Marty made sure that all the ships were burning it while they were in port in the belief that it drove away the bad vapours. The merchant captains were sceptical, but Shelby persuaded them to try it, the mosquitos were thick in the wet season and the oil kept them away too.

There was one incident of note. The first mate of the North Star went missing, and his captain asked Marty to help find him. Marty detailed the Shadows with the task as he figured they could do with the exercise. It took them two days to track him down to a hut in a forest clearing about a mile outside of town. He was with a young native girl of around seventeen years old, and they were making house together.

"He is totally besotted with her," Antton told him when they got back, "and her with him. A real pair of star struck lovers. He doesn't want to go back to his ship, says he's had enough of being at sea and wants to stay here and have a family."

"Have you told his captain yet?" Marty asked.

"No, we thought we would leave him lost. He is happy where he is."

"You old romantic," Marty teased him. "Alright, I will tell him we can't find him."

October passed tediously with innumerable dinners with the passengers of the merchantmen. Marty found himself pursued by the widow of an Army colonel who succumbed to the fever in Calcutta. Mrs. Hall, a woman of early middle years, was relentless in her efforts to ensnare him in a dalliance. Marty took to travelling with Sam at his side if there was a chance that she would be around. The Shadows thought this was great entertainment.

In the end, the problem sorted itself out when the dear lady was out with some of her fellow travellers exploring some ruins on the edge of the rain forest. She was, apparently, an amateur herpetologist and was convinced she had found a new species of tree frog. It was bright blue with red eyes and she picked it up without checking with their native guide. She became sick and died in agony a day later.

Marty discovered that that particular frog was well known to the natives as they used the mucus excreted from its skin to coat the darts they fired from their blowguns.

"We need to get some of those darts and a few blowguns," he told his men. "It killed her in a day when she just got it on her hands and ate a sandwich. If it's on the end of a dart, it apparently kills in seconds."

November arrived with crystal clear skies and soaring temperatures. Marty decided it was time to move on. He pulled his trump cards out and slapped them on the table.

"Well, I am sorry if you object gentlemen," he said as the captains refused yet again, "but as a shareholder of the company and the owner of the cargo on two of your ships, I think I am going to insist. Not only that a delegation from your passengers has also approached me, urging we get underway. The loss of Mrs. Hall has upset many of them."

The Captains put their heads together and had a whispered conversation. Troy, who had been laying on his bed, sat up and cocked his head from one side to the other as he listened.

"Captain Stockley," McTravers started, but Marty interrupted,

"You can address me as Sir Martin or Baron Candor for the purposes of this discussion."

All three looked even more surprised and another whispered exchange took place.

"Sir Martin," McTravers corrected, "We will comply with your 'request' but want our objections duly noted. We can be ready to sail in three days' time."

"You will be ready tomorrow. You are all fully provisioned and watered, and we will sail on the tide," Marty insisted, fully out of patience.

He held up his hand as McTravers opened his mouth to complain again.

"You can take it up with the commissioners once we are back in England. I take full responsibility." The meeting was over.

They sailed in the morning.

They looped around the North of Cuba, bypassed the Bahamas, and followed the American coast until they picked up the Westerly trades. From there, it was a tedious three week crossing to the Canary Islands and another week to get them of the straits of Heracles where the Formidiable and Fore left them to go to Gibraltar leaving the Bonne Marie to escort them to India dock in London.

Marty sent a sealed letter to the commissioners of the Honourable Company making it clear that even though he owned part of the cargo, he expected to get a full salvage payment from Lloyds. He didn't want to see his men done out of their just reward because of him.

Chapter 20: Viscount Wellington

They put the Fore in to be purchased by the Navy and would have to wait for the prize court to condemn her. Marty estimated she was worth in the region of one-hundred and seventy thousand pounds. The amount of salvage on the three East Indiamen was unknown, but Fletcher would bring that news with him when he returned. The Bonne Marie would be sold off privately along with the Ivory and timber they had in their holds.

"All in all, a quite profitable little jaunt." He wrote at the end of his long sea letter, which he sent on the Marie to Caroline. He had also written to Hood, telling him they were back and enclosing his report. He had fulfilled his mission. Now, he was looking forward to renewing his acquaintance with Arthur.

Back in his office, he had a mound of correspondence to get through. He was just getting stuck in when there was a knock at the door and Ridgley, the local head of intelligence came in.

"The intrepid captain has returned, laden with prizes as usual, and hot for his next mission," he crowed.

"You are very chirpy if not more than a little annoying for this time of day," Marty snapped.

"Oh, come now. You are just grumpy because of all that paperwork," Ridgley grinned.

"You have me there, my friend. It's one of the perils of command." Marty sighed as he looked at the pile again.

"Then you will thank me when I tell you of your next mission."

Marty's ears pricked up at that.

"Is that coffee in the pot over there?" Ridgley asked and went to the sideboard where Will had placed a fresh pot of coffee not ten minutes earlier. "Can I get you one?" he asked as he poured himself a cup, added milk, and half a spoon of sugar.

Marty resigned himself to the fact that Ridgley would tell him in his own time and nodded, "Black, no sugar or milk."

Ridgley handed him his cup then made himself comfortable in one of the comfy chairs by the fire.

"Will you join me?"

Marty moved to the fire, sat, and gave Ridgley a flat look that said, 'talk or you won't like the consequences.'

"You know that Arthur, now Viscount, Wellesley has taken command of the Army of the peninsula from that dolt Dalrymple?"

Marty nodded and sipped his coffee, be damned if he would show impatience.

"Well, he is busy consolidating the defences of Lisbon by building lines of fortifications- in total secrecy, I may add. The main aim is to protect his retreat and evacuation, should it become necessary as he is seriously outnumbered by the French and needs time to build, train, and otherwise prepare his army," Ridgley explained.

"Well, I am a sailor not an architect, so I'm not sure why he has asked for me to be recalled from Mauritius," Marty stated, somewhat puzzled.

"Ah now, but it's not your sailing ability he's interested in, but your sneaky, murdering, thieving, spying alter ego."

"Now, I wonder where he got that impression of me," Marty smirked.

"India, I imagine," Ridgley responded, missing the sarcasm. "But whatever. The good General wants, no, demands, your services as his chief of intelligence."

"HIS WHAT?" Marty sputtered, snorting coffee out of his nose in shock.

Ridgley grinned. He didn't get one over his friend very often and this time he had done it in spades!

Epilogue

Hood walked into Canning's office and pulled up a chair without waiting to be asked. He had an air that gave away the annoyance he was feeling and trying to hide.

"Good afternoon Admiral, to what do I owe this unexpected visit?"

"You heard that Prince George has been at it again?"

Canning raised his eyebrows in question and asked,

"Precisely at what?"

"Trying to get young Stockley a Viscountcy,"

"Is that a problem? I thought you would be pleased your protégée was honoured so,"

"The timing is all wrong and will attract too much attention, it should wait until he makes admiral," Hood grumbled.

"Yes, I can see that, he is about to take on the job for Wellesley isn't he, does the Prince know about that?"

"No, it's not something we publicise."

Canning bit back a comment at the implied sarcasm in that comment and thought for a while then said,

"I have a meeting with the Prince tomorrow, let me talk to him, I might be able to persuade him that he will be doing his friend no favour by pushing this at this time."

Hood nodded and said,

"Thank you. It's not that Martin lacks support, his wife has made sure of that, but we don't need to hand his enemies any ammunition."

"He is largely above all the politics, I understand," Canning commented.

"Yes, he frankly doesn't give a damn about it. His wife, however, is acutely politically aware and has taken steps to protect him," Hood replied his frown easing at the thought.

"Just how many members of parliament does she 'own' now?" Canning asked.

"A round half dozen at the last count, either because she has loaned them money or controls their business interests." Hood answered. "She has Pitt worried as a couple of them control the votes of several rotten boroughs."

"That tallies with what I know," Canning confirmed, "but she hasn't exercised her power yet has she."

"The mere threat is enough," Hood replied, "added to the fact that she controls several markets that could be used to make life very uncomfortable for the Government."

"And you have a very cautious Prime Minister when he is dealing with her," Canning finished for him.

"I think she is more frightening than Martin, truth be told." Hood pondered.

"Ah well that comes from her ancestry you know," Canning grinned knowing he knew something Hood didn't.

Hood looked up intrigued.

"Her great times four grandmother was Scarlett Browning."

"What the pirate?" hood exclaimed.

"The very same," Canning grinned, "that is where her family got the money that took them from being Yorkshire smugglers to legitimate merchants."

"Now there's a story that I'd like to hear," Hood grinned.

"At another time, my friend. For now, let's just see how Martin gets on in Portugal." Canning concluded then asked, "can I tempt you with a Brandy?"

The Dorset Boy – Book 7: The Trojan Horse

Authors Note:

Research, research, research. This book took as long to research as it did to write and that is all part of the fun! I achieved two goals and that was getting Marty together with Smith again and introducing him to Thomas Cochrane. Many of the influential authors that I have read have based their characters on Cochrane but there was one aspect of his career that none had covered as far as I could tell, and that was his fight with Admiral Gambier. The whole affair was brought about just as I have written it and the outcome too. Cochrane then went on to be further disgraced when he was found guilty of swindling the stock market, although whether he did or not is still open for debate.

The attempts by the French to capture Marty are obviously total fiction but again a lot of research went into the locations. George Canning taking over from William Wickham is factual.

If you are wondering about the epilogue and the reference to Caroline's ancestor Scarlett, I must admit to slipping in a teaser. Her story is going to be told, just watch out for it next year.

I love it when people send me emails and I always try and reply so feel free to send ideas or suggestions. And now I must thank my Beta readers who spend their time helping get as many of the errors out of the books as we can. Angela and Gary thank you!

And now. . . .

An excerpt from book 8

Chapter 1: A New Role

The Formidiable slipped into the mouth of the Tagus quietly and without fanfare, she fired no salute just dipped her flag to Admiral Smith's flagship as she passed.

Smith, who was on deck getting some exercise at the time, watched the frigate ghost by and smiled. He had talked extensively with Wellesley and agreed wholeheartedly with him on the appointment of their talented friend as his Head of Intelligence. The war that would be fought on the Peninsula would be as much about intelligence as the armies that would fight it.

The world is changing, he thought as he raised a hand to the figure on the Formidiable's quarterdeck, *we need quick minds and to play the game better than the French.* That not only meant having better intelligence gathering than them, but effective counterintelligence as well as demonstrated in Malta and London.

It helps that Martin is the luckiest man I have ever met, he chortled, causing his flag lieutenant to ask,

"Milord? Do you need something?"

"No, nothing thank you, just thinking out loud." He smiled as the Formidiable faded into the mist.

A week before in his office. Marty had been nervous, everyone seemed to be gleefully dropping him in deep water and waiting to see if he floated or sank. Ridgley had followed up the revelation of his next mission with a packet of double sealed orders that had, "Not to be opened until at sea," written on them. That was bad enough but there was a second written order to report to Admiral Collingwood 'at his earliest convenience'.

"Captain Stockley Sah!" Announced the marine guarding the Admiral's door.

"Enter!" ordered the Admiral.

Marty stepped through and presented himself in front of the desk at which the Admiral sat going through a paper.

Collingwood waved a hand at him,

"sit down Captain if you please, I won't be a minute."

Marty perched himself on the edge of one of the padded armchairs that faced the desk and waited.

Collingwood scratched his signature on the paper with one of the new steel tipped pens, placed the paper in a tray to his right, after blotting it, and wiped the pens nib with a cloth before replacing it on a stand.

"Sir Martin, it's very good to see you again," he smiled.

"It's good to see you as well sir, may I ask if your health has improved since last we spoke?" Marty replied politely.

"It is at least not getting worse thanks to your Mr. Shelby," Collingwood confirmed.

More pleasantries were exchanged about wives and children until Collingwood cut to the chase,

"You should have received some sealed orders by now," it was a statement not a question, "and I have been asked to set you on your way, so to speak."

Marty nodded and waited; the old boy would get to it in his own time.

"Your successes against the French intelligence service have not gone unnoticed and you have supporters, and enemies, at almost all levels of the government. Even Pitt cannot gainsay you, even though you are known to be contemptuous of his ally Admiral Gambier. A view held by the majority of the service I may add."

Marty smiled quietly at that, he frankly didn't give a shit what people thought of him and was gloriously ambivalent to politics.

"I am told that your good lady wife has been dabbling in politics and seems to have established somewhat of a power base in your support," Collingwood said with a grin.

"Has she? I wasn't aware," Marty replied genuinely surprised, he knew Caroline had pocketed a couple of MPs but had no idea what she had been up to recently.

"Yes, she does it quietly, but she uses your wealth wisely and has established strong ties with some very influential people. Be that as it may you need to get yourself to Lisbon as soon as you can, your orders will explain what you will be doing, I have been asked to make sure that you keep your Flotilla intact and to provide any assistance I can if you need it.

I believe that your new role will give you significant powers, I have been asked to provide you with advice and council should you need it as a favour to Admiral Hood."

"I am honoured and grateful Sir," Marty said with genuine gratitude and affection.

"I would have done it even if he hadn't asked." Collingwood smiled, "Now, let us have a glass to the future and the defeat of Napoleon." Collingwood concluded and called his steward.

Marty sat at his desk in his cabin and opened the double sealed packet; one seal was the Admiralty's fouled anchor the other was the portcullis of the Government.

Inside were two letters; the first was from the Admiralty signed by the First Lord himself and after the usual preamble said,

You are hereby commissioned to take the position of Head of Intelligence on the staff of Viscount Wellington, Lieutenant General Wellesley, and take responsibility for both Intelligence and counterintelligence operations. You will maintain command of the Special Operations Flotilla and at all times conduct yourself in the best traditions of the Navy.

That was the meat of it, there were other minor details but that one paragraph gave him an open remit answerable only to Arthur.

The second was a letter commanding whoever read it to lend all assistance to the holder by the command of Mr Pitt the Prime Minister himself.

"Ppff," he said to Troy who was sat at his usual place beside his desk, "this is more than a bit of a challenge."

"Adam!" he called and a second later his steward appeared from the pantry.

"Sir?" he enquired.

"Pass the word for Mr Ridgley to attend me please and get some coffee prepared I think this will be a long meeting."

Now as he stood on the quarterdeck and returned Sir Sidney's wave, he braced himself for the meeting that would launch this next phase of his career. It would make him or break him; of that he was sure.

He had discussed with Ridgley the existing spy network that he had established and where it needed strengthening and how much it could be trusted. Likewise, they had gone over everything they knew about the French intelligence network and the military hierarchy in Spain.

What he had was an embryonic mainly amateur spy network with a good foundation that needed expansion, and on the other side a professional French intelligence network that he needed to frustrate.

Now he needed to know what Arthur expected, only then could he plan ahead and see how he could help make this as short a war as possible.

Printed in Great Britain
by Amazon